DEADLY
Will

DEADLY

A DEADLY PAST MYSTERY

MARION MOORE HILL

PEMBERLEY PRESS

PEMBERLEY PRESS
P O Box 1027
Corona del Mar, CA 92625
www.pemberleypress.com
A member of The Authors Studio
www.theauthorsstudio.org

Cover design: Kat & Dog Studios
Cover illustration: Aletha St. Romain

Library of Congress Cataloging-in-Publication Data

Hill, Marion Moore, 1937-
Deadly will / Marion Moore Hill.
p. cm. — (A deadly past mystery)
ISBN-13: 978-0-9771913-1-4 ((pbk.) : alk. paper)
ISBN-10: 0-9771913-1-1 ((pbk.) : alk. paper)
I. Title.
PS3608.I4348D43 2006
813'.6—dc22
2005030753

This book is dedicated to the memory of
my friend Howard Starks,
whose encyclopedic knowledge and generous guidance
helped inspire me as a writer,
and to that of other deceased loved ones,
especially my parents, Glenn and Flossie Moore,
and my cousin Leota Cook Smith.

★ *Prologue, 1789*

"That's my scheme, Dr. Franklin." Nathan Henry inhaled snuff from the back of a ruffled wrist, eyes watching his host for signs of approval. "Is it not a worthy refinement on your own remarkable legacy?"

"Interesting, Henry." Benjamin Franklin actually thought the plan overly complex, possibly even foolhardy. "But have you considered what changes may occur over two centuries? In the way banking and legal business are conducted, for instance."

Henry stiffened. "Detailed instructions shall guide my executors, sir. They must adapt them to practices then current."

"Your personal belongings will certainly deteriorate. In any event, why leave such items as a map, a quilt, and a rifle to these unknown descendants?"

Henry patted the waistcoat snugging his girth. "The keepsakes are symbolic of my various selves: merchant, domestic man, revolutionary. And my heirs are bound to prize any memento of such an illustrious forebear, in whatever condition. My favorite, of course, is that letter you wrote me from Paris."

Franklin winced as a kidney stone stabbed him. He had nearly forgotten writing that polite but distant reply to Henry's fawning missive. Snowflakes wafted through the window he kept ajar winter and summer, yet the room felt close, laden with the scents of snuff and hickory burning in the fireplace.

"You can hardly leave a token for each, Henry, even if you could know how many will then be living."

"I flatter myself I have anticipated all difficulties."

Franklin frowned. "The money troubles me most. It should grow to a great sum in two centuries' time. Have you considered what conflict it may cause among your descendants? Remember what Poor Richard says about man's character with regard to greed: 'He's a fool that makes his doctor his heir.'"

Henry waved away the warning. "Please don't distress yourself, sir. We may trust *my* progeny to behave properly."

Strength spent, Franklin lay back, his thinning locks gray against the creamy pillow. At least he wouldn't be around to see the consequences of Henry's folly.

★ *Chapter One ~ 2001*

Humming a popular tune, Millie entered the drab lobby at her apartment complex and worked the combination lock on her mailbox. She flipped through the mail: a utility bill, a sweepstakes offer, and a yellow slip of paper indicating that a registered letter awaited her at the post office.

Registered? Anxiety prickled her spine, halted her humming. If Danny's father was in trouble again, asking for money . . .

Worse, he might be renewing his bid for custody of Danny. Her mouth went dry. Even if she won again, the fight would be emotionally exhausting, the financial cost devastating—

The lobby door jerked open, and a small figure dashed through.

"Come quick, Mrs. Kirchner! Danny's hurt!" Her son's friend Jeff flung the heavy door behind him, banging the outside wall.

The mail slid from her grasp. "Where? Show me!"

She grabbed his small shoulder and pushed him from the modest brick building. He led her towards a tiny park across the street.

God, Millie thought with a hammering heart, Danny's fallen on his head and killed himself.

They reached the jungle gym sheltered by a showy, deep-rose crepe myrtle. Below the parallel bars lay her son's motionless form, one tennis-shoed foot curled under his other knee. His eyes were closed. The whole side of his face, forehead to chin, was a moist red.

Her throat closed. Memories of another scene slashed through her brain—*blood, blood . . . wet, sticky human life spilling . . . .*

She knelt beside Danny and touched his narrow wrist with a trembling hand. Thank God, she felt a pulse!

He raised his head, his snaggle-toothed grin impish.

"Surprise! Foolja, didn't we, Mom?" He wiped blood—catsup, she now realized—off his cheek.

Relief, then fury, coursed through Millie. A minute ago, she had thought him dead, or seriously hurt. She would have given her own life to spare his. And he'd been teasing, not giving a thought to the awful fear and pain he was causing his mother. She swallowed a taste of bile welling up in her esophagus and managed to quell the urge to paddle both boys till their fannies glowed red. Yanking her son erect, she glared from him to his partner in crime.

"Daniel John Kirchner, just for that, you can't play with Jeff for a whole week."

Rolling his eyes at Danny, Jeff sidled away towards his house down the street.

"Aw, Mom, it was just a joke," Danny whined.

"Scaring the poop out of your mother isn't funny." Millie took a deep breath and felt the remnants of panic ebb away, leaving only anger. "Come on, I'll be late."

Her thin shoulders rigid with ill temper, Millie stomped home through a humid Texas morning. Danny plodded after her, toes scuffing the pavement. They entered the apartment-house lobby, where she scooped up her fallen mail and shoved it into her uniform pocket.

Minutes later, she sat next to her sullen son on a Dallas Area

Rapid Transit bus as it sped along Greenville Avenue in Richardson. He slumped away from her, lower lip out, toe tapping the seat ahead.

Had she overreacted? A week was forever at Danny's age. It was hard to get it right, the balance between teaching him proper behavior and letting him be a kid.

The bus passed a strip mall containing an Asian food store, a Vietnamese restaurant, and other ethnic businesses serving immigrant families who, like her, had been drawn by the area's relatively low-cost rent. She and Danny often walked to the grocery, shopped a little, and browsed a lot. She was learning what to call the unfamiliar foods, and the friendly owner had taught her some simple recipes. Millie loved the shop's aromas, hinting of distant lands. She had scanned the restaurant's menu, longing to try the exotic-sounding spring rolls, lemon-grass chicken, and stuffed squid. Yet even its moderate prices exceeded her budget.

At eight, Danny was rooted in the here-and-now, or in the fantasy worlds of TV and video games. But Millie tried to encourage his lively curiosity in the direction of other places and times, her own passions. She was determined that once she finished her degree and got a better job—if ever—they would travel, especially to historical sites

Mingled odors of perfume and sweat from a passenger behind them made Millie faintly nauseous. She twiddled her finger at the back of Danny's neck, but he twisted away.

The only travel on her schedule today was a series of short hops complicated by a teachers-meeting holiday. Usually, Jeff's mom chauffeured both boys to and from school and kept Danny till Millie returned in late afternoon. But today Mrs. Thompson was taking Jeff clothes-shopping. Millie would have to drop Danny at the sitter's, get another bus to work, bum a ride with a co-worker to do errands at lunchtime, reverse the two-bus process after her shift, bolt a quick supper at home, and catch a third bus to the University of Texas at Dallas. At least a friend in their building would baby-sit while she was in class.

Life would be so much simpler with an automobile, she thought for the thousandth time. But even a second-hand car and its upkeep lay beyond her reach.

"Sorry, Mom," Danny mumbled, so low she barely heard him. "We didn't mean to scare you."

"I know, Danny, but you did." She stroked his slim arm.

"Can I play with Jeff tonight? Ple-e-ease. We'll be good, I promise. His mom's going to let us plant beans behind their house." Tears glistened in the beautiful hazel eyes, so like Jack's, part of the reason she had made that disastrous early marriage.

She was tempted. Her son loved anything to do with plants, digging in dirt, watering, and watching their window-box flowers grow and change.

But she couldn't retract the announced penalty. Could she?

"Both of you need time apart, to think about what a mean trick that was, and about how you'd feel if Jeff's mom or I did it to you."

"Aw-w-w, Mom."

Millie hesitated. "After tonight, though, you're off the hook." She tousled his hair, got a scowl in return. But when she pulled him close, she felt him snuggle against her.

Later, in the afternoon, she sank into her favorite chair on the nursing home patio, grateful for the breeze stirring her ponytail. Propping an elbow on a wrought-iron table, she grimaced at the frail-looking woman in the wheelchair beside her.

"Sylva, you always give me good advice. Was I too hard on Danny? He's still just a kid."

Sylva Jaeckel shrugged her withered shoulders. "A week away

from his best friend sounds a bit much, hon, but you have to do what seems best at the time. If there's a parenting rulebook, I never found it."

"Or was I wishy-washy, reducing his punishment that way?"

"Don't beat yourself up. You're not your mother."

"How do you always know what I'm thinking, Sylva? She tried to be a good mom, I know, but when I was a kid I could never be sure where the boundaries were. Mother'd go ballistic about something one day, then let it slide the next."

The faded eyes lit in a sympathetic smile. "From what you've said, she was unstable. You're far from that."

"I haven't told Danny much about her. He's not old enough to hear it all. But I'm afraid I sometimes make him suffer for what she did."

"You can't help the way she died."

"It terrified me this morning, seeing him like that. But the boys meant it as a prank." Millie rubbed a chigger bite on her wrist, and heard paper crackle under her forearm. "Oh—the mail. I've been running all day, had to deposit my check and go by the post office at lunchtime—" She removed the pocket's contents, dropped a stamped bank slip on the table, and fanned out three envelopes beside it.

"You can forget about that sweepstakes," Sylva said. "I've already won. Me and eighty million others."

Millie picked up the fat, official-looking envelope she had signed for at the post office. Of creamy expensive-looking paper, it had black engraved lettering in the upper left corner that said "Pope, Emerson and Caudill, Attorneys at Law."

"I haven't even opened this one yet. Can't be good news. I swear, if Jack's trying again to get custody of Danny— Philadelphia? What's he doing up there? Jack always said he'd never go north of the Red River except in chains or a pine box."

"It's a radical idea, but you could open the letter and see."

"Anybody ever tell you what an old nuisance you are?" Millie slid a fingertip under the flap and took out several sheets of stationery.

"That's how they wake me for breakfast: 'Yo, Old Nuisance!'"

Millie smiled then, drawing a resigned breath, ran her eye over the first paragraph. She stopped, read it again.

"Oh! Oh, wow!"

A sobering thought struck. This had to be a mistake. Still, the letter was addressed to her . . . .

She re-read the opening and continued through the other pages, her breath quickening as one amazing sentence followed another. She reached the signature, shut her eyes, and clutched the sheaf of stationery to her forehead.

Sylva fidgeted with the loose gold band on her finger. "So what's the bad news from your ex?"

A jumble of conflicting emotions made Millie feel her head was spinning. She mustn't let herself believe the letter's tidings—if there later proved to be a Catch 22, the disappointment would be crushing—but oh, if they should be true! She fought to stay calm.

"It's the . . . strangest thing I've ever heard of, Sylva," she said through quivering lips.

"Strange how?"

"Just plain weird."

"I don't have many years left, Kirchner."

"Well, it's—"

A memory of Danny's triumphant grin this morning brought Millie up short. This could be someone's idea of a prank, another cruel one. But who disliked her that much? And why such an elaborate scheme?

Maybe it wasn't a joke. Just maybe.

"This lawyer . . . Arthur Pope . . . says there's a . . . legacy.

Danny and I are heirs of someone named Nathan Henry." Spoken aloud, the words seemed even less believable.

"A rich relative!" Sylva cried. "Congratulations, hon! I gather you two weren't close."

Millie smiled ruefully. In the elderly woman's privileged sphere, inheriting wealth was probably a real possibility, perhaps even expected. The thought steadied Millie, restoring something of her usual protective cynicism.

"I'd never even heard of him till now," she said. "But get this part, Sylva: the letter says Henry died two *hundred* years ago."

"What?"

"Read these." Millie laid the pages in front of Sylva. If their promises weren't on the level, as she suspected, this canny old woman would spot the flaw.

Sylva skimmed the sheets, then studied each. "I've never heard of anything like this. But a legacy—how wonderful! What a shame the lawyer doesn't say how much you'll get."

Encouraged by her friend's favorable reaction, Millie linked her fingers behind her head, looked up at a spreading liveoak branch, and imagined herself doing the things mentioned in the letter: taking a magnificent journey with Danny, receiving wealth, meeting new, possibly exotic people—

Just inheriting money could change life as she knew it. "Wouldn't it be super if I'd get enough to pay my debts and next semester's tuition?"

"I hope it buys you a car. You sure need one."

"Amen to that. Or we might be able to move closer to my school or to work. Even rent a little house with some yard for Danny . . . ."

A cloud of gloom settled over Millie. What was she thinking? The whole pattern of her hardscrabble life argued against any of that coming true. And such dreams would only make her more discontented with reality.

Things weren't so bad. She and Danny got by, never ate lavishly, but didn't starve.

"If only the part about having living relatives could be true, at least," she said wistfully. "I've often wished Danny had family besides me."

"Better not celebrate that part till you've met them. Something I'm wondering about is those 'keepsakes.' Henry's personal items. What do you s'pose they are?"

"Rusty razors and threadbare tea cozies. Anything two centuries old would be falling apart by now."

"I'm not sure the tea cozy was used that early, hon. But anything from those days could be valuable."

Millie shook her head. "This'll turn out to be a big disappointment, you'll see. It's a law of the universe: The Millie Kirchners of this world don't inherit wealth. Or travel to exciting places. Or have ancestors who knew famous people."

"You're too young to be so pessimistic."

"Just realistic."

"Tell you what, hon. I'll have my lawyer son check this Pope guy out, make sure he's on the level."

"Oh, that's a great idea, Sylva! Thanks."

"Even if the inheritance doesn't prove to be much, at least you and Danny will enjoy that trip."

"I would love to see Philadelphia with Danny." For a moment, Millie envisioned the two of them retracing Washington's and Jefferson's steps.

She shook herself. "But there's no way we could go."

"They have 'kids fly free' deals."

Millie grinned sadly. "Unless I'd go gratis too, it's impossible. I juggle bills as it is to get from paycheck to paycheck." She shrugged, trying to resign herself to actualities.

Sylva stretched a shriveled hand towards her. "My treat, hon.

Even with the quacks pushing drugs at me, I have plenty. What's left'll just discourage my kids' initiative. You need and deserve this trip, hard as you work."

Millie laid her young hand over the old one. "I appreciate the offer, Sylva, I do. But staff can't accept money from residents. I could get fired."

"A loan, then. Pay me back a buck a month."

"Can't do that either. But you're a dear to suggest it."

They sat in silence for a time, Sylva gazing thoughtfully down at Millie's papers spread out on the table. Millie looked out across the shady lawn, towards traffic sounds a block away on North Central Expressway, the artery linking Richardson with Plano to the north and Dallas to the south. North Texas was home, but Philadelphia offered Independence Hall, the Liberty Bell . . . . She glanced at her watch.

"Speaking of getting fired, my break's over."

"Hon, would you run get me some juice? I'm parched."

Millie eyed the dark fluid in the catheter hooked to the wheelchair. "Gladly, sweets. You don't drink enough liquids." She left, returning shortly with a tumbler of cranberry juice.

"Thanks," Sylva said, lifting her delicate hand from the table. "This is fantastic news, Kirchner. Aren't you just over the moon about it?"

"Ye-e-es, sometimes. But it seems too much like that prize we're both supposed to have won. What'll be in the fine print?"

"Make that Philly trip, Kirchner. The way you feel about history, you mustn't miss it."

"If only I could," Millie said.

"You've a legacy coming, remember. Borrow from a bank on the strength of that."

For a moment, it seemed possible. Then Millie sighed. "Sure. I've no clue how much money there is or how many people will split it. I could inherit a nickel after spending hundreds of dollars to get there. Any banker would leap at that deal."

"Do it, Kirchner. Or I'll never speak to you again."

"Even more incentive to stay home." Millie gave Sylva's knee an affectionate tap. "Anyway, the letter says Danny and I would get our shares even if we don't go. So whatever money there is—if any—we can sit tight and wait for it."

"Then do it for me, hon. When you get back, you'll take me out of my fee-ee-ble old self, telling me about the people you've met and showing me great caricatures you've drawn of them."

"Sylva—"

"I'll go along in spirit. This place may hold my body, but not *me*."

"Why don't *you* pretend you're Millie Kirchner? *You* make the trip, and tell *me* all about it when you return."

"Deal, Kirchner. Let's go pack my evening gowns and eye shadow."

★ Chapter Two

The taxi that had brought Millie from the Philadelphia airport wheeled away, coughing exhaust back at her. Three weeks after getting the attorney's letter, she stood on a sidewalk in the old part of the city, Society Hill, admiring an eighteenth-century house. White shutters and dormers dotted the gray-brick exterior, and stone steps led from sidewalk to columned entry. Afternoon sun glinted off a stone lintel over the door, while ancient oaks threw the third story into shadow. A metal-rail fence surrounded the property.

Ritzy place. Glad you came now, Kirchner?

Sylva's voice. Since leaving home that morning, Millie had heard it in her mind, supplying tart comments the elderly woman might have made about everything from an obnoxious fellow plane passenger to traffic in the City of Brotherly Love. By some finagling of time-space laws—or more likely by power of suggestion—Sylva had indeed managed to come along.

"It's gorgeous," Millie murmured, her stomach queasy with apprehension. "But I'm out of my depth here, Sylva. This place screams Old Philadelphia and old money. My grungy apartment doesn't belong on the same planet."

Texans walk tall, Kirchner. And you've faced worse challenges.

Like that awful foster home you told me about.

Stalling, Millie looked around at the neighboring structures, similar in style to the Henry house but more modest in size. A ripple of excitement went through her as she imagined men in knee breeches and buckled shoes tramping along the narrow, tree-lined street.

Her eyes fell on a green Oldsmobile parked some twenty yards away across the street. A man sat in it, looking at her. It gave her an odd feeling, finding herself watched in a city where she knew no one.

Deciding he must be waiting for someone in another residence, she picked up her battered suitcase and started up the steps. Behind her, a car door opened, then slammed.

"Pardon me, miss."

Millie turned. The man from the Olds, rangily built with a slight stoop, was striding across the road towards her. She set down her bag, ready to explain she could be no help if he needed directions. He reached her, straightened a sedate navy tie, smiled ingratiatingly and handed her an engraved card.

"Allow me to introduce myself, miss. I am Winston Akers, a dealer in antiques."

His eyes shifted from her to the Henry manor and back. His bottom-heavy face—anvil chin, narrow forehead, and skimpy brows—made her wish for her sketch pad. She glanced at the card, then questioningly at him.

"You *are* a descendant of the late Nathan Henry?"

The query raised her guard. How would someone outside the family know of the legacy?

"Suppose I were?"

"Please pardon this informal approach, miss. Ordinarily I— well, no matter. You will contact me should you have anything to sell?"

"I'm afraid I don't follow."

"I understand Henry's heirs will participate in a lottery for personal effects of his, called 'keepsakes' in his will. Is that not correct?"

Millie hesitated. "You seem to know a lot, Mr.—" she checked the card— "Akers. What's your interest in this?"

"Well, naturally, the mementoes are all antiques." Akers's affable smile faded, and he flicked invisible lint from a sleeve. "Such trivial household things aren't terribly valuable, naturally, but each would fetch something. And I pay top prices. Better than you could get at auction."

"These keepsakes—what are they? You seem to know."

"You weren't told? Another of Henry's eccentricities, I suppose. Well, there's a decorated bowl, a candlestand, a few samplers—household bric-a-brac, you know."

"What would be 'top prices'?"

"Naturally, I couldn't be specific without seeing them."

"A ballpark figure, then. Hundreds? Thousands? Millions?"

"Millions—that's a good one." Akers took a handkerchief from his breast pocket and dabbed at his perspiring forehead. His eyes resumed their restless movements. "Hundreds, almost certainly. For the most desirable ones, *perhaps* tens of thousands."

Despite the June heat gluing her blouse to her shoulders, Millie shivered. Tens of thousands sounded like a fortune. Still, it was all speculation at this point. Besides, there was something about Akers she didn't quite like. Wishing Sylva really were here to advise her, she pocketed the card and picked up her case.

"I'll keep your offer in mind, Mr. Akers. Excuse me."

He reached out a hand as if to detain her. She stared at it until he retracted it.

"Naturally, you could choose not to sell whatever you draw," he said. "But caring for antiques can be a bother—protecting from breakage, controlling temperature and moisture—"

"Goodbye, Mr. Akers." Millie started up the steps.

"Don't forget," he called. "You won't be sorry."

She reached the entry, put down her suitcase, and looked back. Akers was opening the door of the Olds. He got in, but instead of starting the motor he sat looking down as if reading or writing.

Shrugging off the strange interview, Millie took a deep breath, lifted the knocker, and rapped. Moments later the door opened, framing a gaunt, balding man in a conservative dark suit. His discreet gaze moved from her limp hair to the worn flats she had polished to presentability.

"Mr. Pope?" she ventured.

"I'm Fansler, the butler," he said with a thin smile.

A butler. Tony touch.

And intimidating, Millie thought. Determinedly, she lifted her chin.

"Millie Kirchner. I believe you're expecting me?"

"Please come in," Fansler said tonelessly. "Mr. Pope is in the library." He stood aside for her to enter, then brought in her bag.

Cool air chilled her moist temples. "Feels good in here."

"Electricity, air-conditioning, and indoor plumbing have been installed." A note of pride crept into the butler's proper tones as he added, "But generally it remains authentic to its period."

She gazed approvingly around the wide entrance hall with its high ceiling, carved woodwork, and paintings of men and women in Colonial finery. She was wondering if any was Nathan Henry himself when a stocky man entered through an archway at one side of the hall and offered a hand.

"Good afternoon," he said. "I'm Arthur Pope, co-executor of Mr. Henry's will. You must be Sharmilla Kristalynn Johnson

Kirchner. Welcome to your ancestral home."

Millie had pictured the attorney as a stuffy sort, but his beaming cherubic face, cropped ginger hair, and tan silk suit suggested a nattily dressed teddy bear. And despite his mannered speech and use of her disliked full name, he seemed friendly.

She returned his smile and shook hands. "Thank you. Just Millie, please. How'd you know—?"

He chuckled, jiggling fleshy jowls. "We're expecting only ten heirs, and you're the ninth to arrive. The other's a gentleman."

"Ten descendants, after all that time? I thought there'd be hordes."

"I'm afraid Mr. Henry's line nearly died out a few times over the years."

Millie eyed him more closely. His opening words had sounded rehearsed, his heartiness a trifle forced, but his voice now seemed to contain real interest in the Henry clan.

Lawyers fake sincerity well.

"Also," he added more briskly, "there are six other living heirs who didn't come. Your son, for instance."

"Sorry Danny didn't make it. His Cub Scout troop had a camping trip planned, and he really wanted to go to that."

"The innocence of youth, eh? I'm afraid you find us having very hot weather—"

Over his commentary on the Philadelphia climate, Millie heard rhythmic noises coming from beyond the arch. *Pop-pop. Pop-pop.* The cadence sounded like a Ping-Pong game, incongruous in the elegant residence.

"—promised cool front materializes." The weather topic exhausted, Pope smiled awkwardly like an actor forgetting his next line. He recovered, cleared his throat, and said, "Right, then. Fansler will show you to your room, Mrs. Kirchner. My co-executor, Soames Endicott, was sorry not to be here to greet all the heirs on their arrival, but he's president of a large bank and couldn't get away. He'll be joining us this evening, however. We'll gather in the parlor at six-thirty for pre-dinner drinks. You may just relax until then." Bowing politely, he scurried down the long hallway.

Millie followed the butler through the arch into a smaller hall dominated by a handsome staircase. Here the regular sounds were louder. POP-POP. POP-POP.

"No-o-oh!"

"Yes!"

"That's the game room, originally a second parlor." Fansler motioned to an open door on the left from which the staccato beat and the two deep voices had come. "And over there is the library." He indicated a closed door facing the game room.

Millie would have liked to see the rooms mentioned and meet the players, but the butler was climbing the stairs. On the second floor, midway down a lengthy hall, he showed her a bathroom she would share with other women heirs. Reaching the end of the hallway, he stopped at an open door and tapped on the facing.

"Miss Bennett? It's Fansler, and your roommate."

A shapely dark-haired woman of about Millie's age, wearing a stylish top and slacks that matched her violet eyes, floated towards them. A beauty.

Probably stuck-up, Millie thought with a sinking feeling. She searched for a resemblance to herself in the exquisite face but saw none.

"Letitia Bennett," said the roommate in a musical voice, waving away Fansler's attempted introduction. "Mr. Pope told me your name earlier, but it's a mouthful. What do I call you?"

"Millie's fine."

The butler crossed the large room to an alcove, where he set Millie's tattered lone suitcase beside a mound of expensive luggage. Then ascertaining that neither woman needed anything, he made an aloof farewell.

Millie glanced around at dusky-rose walls and furniture glowing with the patina of age: a four-poster bed with sprigged counterpane, two chests, a drop-leaf table, an easy chair, and a tall cabinet. These pieces must all be from Nathan Henry's day, she thought, elated to realize she'd be living in such grandeur for a whole week.

Letitia opened the cupboard doors.

"There's no closet and only this one wardrobe," she said. "It's a big one, but with my things in it already. . . ."

Millie eyed the collection with distaste. She had been in dress shops that contained fewer garments. Letitia must be as wealthy as she was gorgeous.

Don't let a world-class clotheshorse wreck the trip for you, Kirchner.

"No problem," Millie said airily. "I brought mostly shorts and jeans."

Shutting the cabinet doors, Letitia perched cross-legged on the bed. Millie drew up the chair.

"So," Letitia said, "let's compare notes. I'm an interior decorator from Seattle. If this legacy's large enough, I plan to open my own business. Or I may not work at all. Wish I knew how much money there is."

"Probably so little nobody'd have come if we'd known."

Letitia laughed. "Aren't you the optimist? I suppose old Henry specified we not be told for some reason. He must've been a real oddball. Where you from, Pollyanna? And *what* are you?"

"Dallas—actually, Richardson, a northern suburb. I'm a single mom, college student, aide at a nursing home."

"Good life?"

"Not bad." Millie had been disposed to dislike this

dauntingly gorgeous, acquisitive creature, but found herself warming to Letitia's cheery friendliness. "I was glad to know Danny and I have relatives. We hadn't any before, that I knew of."

"No kidding. I at least have a mom, a brother, and a paternal granddad."

"You been here long?"

"Couple hours. I just adore this mansion. And the furniture, couldn't you kill for it? I know people who'd pay beaucoup bucks for this bed."

"Worth a lot?"

"I've seen similar ones go for five figures. The place is full of neat stuff. Brad and I arrived first—Mom broke her leg last week and couldn't come—and Mr. Pope gave us a personal tour. Some furnishings came from England, he said, but most were made by cabinet-makers here. Seems old Nathan liked to support other local businesses." Letitia's voice lowered conspiratorially. "That chest over there isn't what it looks like— no drawers. Has a bed inside, called a 'deception bed.' Isn't that a scream? I intend to sleep there at least one night."

When her roommate paused for breath, Millie said, "It's a beautiful place, only now I know what the bed's worth, I'm almost afraid to sleep in it. Is Brad your brother?"

"Yes." Letitia jumped up and clapped her hands. "You have to meet him. You'll both fall in love, I predict."

Millie smiled. "Could we delay the nuptials till after I've unpacked and changed?"

"See you downstairs, then. Don't be long."

After Letitia left, Millie wedged her two dresses into the wardrobe, stacked other clothes in drawers and put toiletries and drawing supplies in a washstand in the alcove. Carrying a robe and fresh underwear, she strolled up the hall to the bathroom.

The house must be well built, she thought. No sounds of movement came from behind the closed doors to indicate which rooms were inhabited.

Finding the bath untenanted and furnished with fluffy towels and up-to-date fixtures, she took a leisurely shower. As hot spray pricked travel dust and tension from her shoulders, she realized with a twinge of self-pity that she already missed Danny terribly. *He'll be okay, hon. You need some travel and fun in your life. Wasn't that antiques dealer too much?*

· Now Millie had time to ponder the encounter, questions came to her mind. She had no experience of the antiques trade, but assumed it to be formal and dignified as a rule. Couldn't Akers have called for appointments with the heirs and met them either here or at his office? And why had he seemed jumpy? Did accosting people in the street violate some law or code of conduct governing antiques dealers?

One thing seemed certain. Lying in wait for her outside had cost Akers time and effort, so the "trivial household things" must be worth more than he had let on.

"Odd situation," she mused, as she toweled off. "Lots of unknowns, including the people."

Letitia turned out nicer than you expected. Besides, remember all the history here.

"You're right, Sylva. I'll try."

Millie returned to her room, donned T-shirt and shorts, brushed her long chestnut hair into a ponytail, and studied herself in a wall mirror.

"I'm certainly no Letitia. Skinny and sallow-complexioned— that's me."

Nonsense. You could add a few pounds, but you're well-proportioned. You've got a cute nose, and those big gray eyes are pretty, if a mite wary-looking.

"I almost believed you were here just then, Sylva. Thanks."

Feeling better, Millie descended a back set of stairs she had noticed earlier, steeper and less grand than the front ones. An aroma of baking rose from below, making her nostrils flare. On the ground floor, she gazed through French doors at a shady, shrubbery-dappled lawn. Sunlight filtering through a hickory tree shimmered on the fur of a squirrel gazing marble-eyed at her. Amused at his boldness, she tapped gently on the glass.

"Okay, honey," a female voice whined behind her. "But you know, he wasn't happy when you quit that last job." A pause. "I know, honey—"

The squirrel's twin dashed down the trunk, and the two set off in a game of tag around the tree.

Millie turned to look for the speaker. A floorboard creaked under her.

"Got to go, honey," the voice said hastily. "'Bye."

Millie strolled up the hall to the first room on her left, the apparent source of the one-sided conversation, and peered inside at an aggressively modern kitchen. Its navy tiled floor, chef's range, and gleaming stainless-steel appliances looked a far cry from early-American cooking arrangements. As she took it in, a short pear-shaped woman in blue uniform and apron appeared in the doorway, her dark eyes narrowed in a pronounced squint.

"Can I help you?"

Millie smiled and introduced herself. "I just arrived and was looking around. This is a wonderful house."

"I'm Mrs. Fansler, the cook." She hesitated. "My kitchen wouldn't interest you—it's been re-done several times—but I'll show you the other rooms."

She brushed past Millie, wafting a scent of fresh cake with her, and pointed out what had been Mrs. Henry's sitting room across the hall from the kitchen. Millie glanced in, then followed her swift guide up the hall. On the sitting-room side they saw— briefly—an office, a music room, and a parlor, on the kitchen side an ample dining room, a sizeable storage closet, and the arch into the staircase hall.

"I know where I am now, thanks," Millie said when they reached the archway. "Hope I didn't take you away from anything important."

"I wasn't far into dinner preparations, but it's a busy kitchen. You'll probably want to avoid it in the future." The cook wheeled and headed back towards her domain, wide hips waggling.

Millie entered the stairway hall, thinking that neither of the Fanslers seemed overjoyed at her presence. This heirs' gathering must mean lots of extra work for them.

Not a great start, Kirchner. If there's anyone you don't want mad at you, it's the people preparing and serving your food.

★ *Chapter Three*

Millie found her roommate seated at a wet bar at one end of the game room, watching two perspiring young males who appeared locked in a competition of some kind. The dark-haired one, so handsome he had to be Letitia's brother, hauled away at a rowing machine, his muscles undulating under a Tommy Hilfiger T-shirt. His classic features, broad shoulders, and assured way of moving stirred Millie's interest.

Bring that hunky rower back with you, Kirchner, she imagined saucy Sylva urging.

No way, Millie thought. He's even better-looking than Jack, and we know how great that turned out.

The other man, slim, sandy-haired, and nondescript in ratty shorts and a frayed shirt, furiously pedaled a stationary bike. Teeth gritted, he appeared exhausted.

The two saw her at about the same time, stopped their machines, and climbed off. The biker leaned on his handlebars, catching his breath. The rower panted over to the women.

"Millie Kirchner, Brad Bennett," Letitia said and winked at her roommate.

Brad flashed a grin, showing teeth as bright and even as his sister's. He gripped Millie's hand firmly.

"Great to—meet you, Millie," he gasped.

"Hi. Likewise."

The other man came over, and Letitia made introductions. "Millie Kirchner from Texas, Scott Wyrick from Colorado. Scott's a grad student in English, Millie." Letitia smiled at him and touched his shoulder.

"'Lo, Scott. It's nice to meet another student."

"Hi, Millie." His tentative handshake and the quick glance from his dark brown eyes suggested she wasn't the only one feeling awkward here. She smiled, and the nervous grin he returned brightened his lean face.

"Drink, guys?" Brad offered. They all gave their preferences, and he served colas from a refrigerator under the bar, then took a stool beside Millie's.

She gazed around at the long room, wondering what it had looked like in Henry's day. The twelve-over-twelve windows must be original, she decided. But probably the cabinet running under them, its glass doors revealing stacks of puzzles, games, towels, and first-aid supplies, was not. Two modern tables sat at the other end, one equipped for table tennis, the other surrounded by captain's chairs.

"Mr. Pope said this was originally a schoolroom for Nathan Henry's children," Letitia said. "He evidently had a troop of them. It became a game room when the Fanslers' boy was growing up here. They must be valuable old retainers, to get a room done over for their son. He's left home now, though. I got the impression Pope thinks the boy's spoiled."

Millie wondered if young Fansler was the "honey" of that overheard phone conversation. "Were you guys competing just now to see who could have the first heart attack?" she asked Brad.

He shoved a wavy lock off his forehead. "Wyrick refuses to admit I'm in much better shape than he is. I challenged him to see who could hold out longer. Due to your arrival—a welcome one, incidentally—the question's still unresolved." He gave Millie a look of admiration that made her heart skip.

Easy. Remember Jack, Sylva's voice warned.

"Were you two playing Ping-Pong earlier?"

"The record's clear there," Brad chortled. "I beat Wyrick three games out of four."

"Pity losses on my part," Scott muttered, seated on Millie's other side. He perched stiffly on his stool, eyes on the bar, one calloused hand clutching his drink can.

"Face it, Wyrick, you're outclassed. I'm champion of my law firm at racquetball, tennis, whatever."

"What kind of law do you practice?" Millie asked.

"Litigation. I'm not long out of law school, but I'm already working on interesting cases. My firm won a huge product-liability suit last month, and two of our partners are very big in Washington state politics."

Amused by his little-boy boasting, Millie turned to Scott. "You're studying English? I'd like to do a double major in English and history, but that would give my adviser apoplexy. He's pushing me towards a computer major—guarantee of a good job, he says."

"Advisers have been known to screw up students."

"Whatever I settle on, it'll take me forever to finish, studying nights and working days at the nursing home. How about you? You always carry full loads?"

"Yeah, but I've had to work my way, too, so I know how that goes."

His sympathetic smile made Millie feel they were somehow allies here.

Letitia turned from checking her image in a cabinet door. "What kind of work have you done, Scott?"

"Harvesting wheat, hauling sod, laying pipe." He shrugged.

"All hard, hot jobs."

"Emptying bedpans and wiping up puke ain't fun either."

At Millie's teasing tone, Scott's shoulders relaxed. "That's inside work, at least," he said, grinning.

"We've all done menial jobs," Brad put in petulantly. "I've caddied and tended bar at the country club."

"I've sold dresses and cosmetics." Letitia returned to her reflected self.

"You three only have yourselves to support?" Millie scoffed. "Piece of cake."

Scott drew himself up. His eyes held a teasing challenge as he faced off against her. "I'll have you know that after paying tuition I sometimes exist a couple days on stale doughnuts."

"Try a week on canned green beans when the rent's due."

Brad sighed theatrically. "One-downmanship's boring, guys."

"Yeah, get over it, both of you." Letitia arranged a curl in her improvised mirror.

"A wino gave me a pair of shoes once." As he boasted, Scott leaned easily onto the bar. "I wore 'em, too. They were better than what I had."

"You made that one up," Millie said.

"Okay," he conceded with a laugh. "But I always buy used textbooks, and that's the truth."

"Lame. I've gotten by whole semesters without a text."

"Change of subject." Brad cut in. "What's your son like, Millie?"

She smiled. "Bright. Cute. A budding con artist. Heavily into Cub Scouts, dinosaurs, and baseball. Wish he had come with me."

"If you want to call and check on him," Brad said, "Pope says we can phone home whenever we want. Telephone's in his office. Where's *Mr.* Kirchner?"

"Jack the Rat beat it when Danny was a month old. He

pops back into our lives periodically, but never does anything to make me miss him."

"Foolish man." Brad grinned.

"At least you're not bitter," Scott observed dryly. But he gave Millie a look of respect.

"How'd you get here, roomie, if you're so poverty-stricken?" Letitia paused in her grooming to ask.

"Money suddenly appeared in my checking account. Enough for round-trip air fare to Philadelphia."

"Get out!" Letitia said. "Where from?"

"I thought at first the bank had credited someone else's money to me by mistake. But it turned out my name and account number were on the deposit slip."

Letitia stared. "Ever find your secret Santa?"

"I'm pretty sure it was an elderly friend at the nursing home where I work—Sylva Jaeckel—though she denies it. She must've gotten my account number somehow. I hope the legacy's enough to let me reimburse her."

"Neat story. How'd you come, Scott?" Letitia fluttered long lashes at him.

"Hitchhiked. A rainstorm in Chicago nearly drowned me. And riding with a drunk almost did me in too."

Palms up, Millie mimed the movements of scales. "Turbulence and bad food versus drowning or a head-on collision. You win the harrowing-travel sweepstakes."

"Promise me you won't hitchhike any more, Scott," Letitia said, laying a hand on his. "It's too dangerous."

"Depends on how much the legacy is. Otherwise. . ." He moved his hand, waggling his thumb in the recognized "need a ride" signal.

Letitia asked about his family. He said he had none except the aunt who had raised him, adding sadly, "She's in a care facility for Alzheimer's patients, in Boulder."

Letitia smiled sympathetically. "We're an odd group, aren't we? Other people seem to have flocks of relatives. You like your roommate, Scott? Brad says Wes Koontz is a neat freak."

"I left a hairbrush on the dresser," Brad growled, "and you'd have thought I'd murdered his mom."

"I doubt bunking with Gilbert Johns will be much fun," Scott said. "He misplaced some pills and implied I'd stolen them. Like I'd want someone else's meds."

Millie tossed her empty can into a trash basket. "Think I will call Danny. Let him know I got here okay."

She entered the stairway hall just as two short blond men came through the arch.

"Hell, Gilbert," one snarled, "age hasn't improved you a lick. —Well, hello!" He thrust a hand at Millie, and she took it. "Wes Koontz, from Wilmington, Delaware."

"Millie Kirchner, from Dallas."

"My cousin, Gilbert Johns." Koontz jerked his head at the other man.

Hands behind his back, Johns inclined his head slightly.

The two men looked remarkably similar, she noticed, both about forty, slight of stature, with prominent ears. But Koontz's face was fuller, his eyes greener, his hair parted rigidly on one side, while Johns's lank strands drifted across his forehead.

"I'm a salesman," Koontz said, straightening a perfectly straight tie. "Boss didn't want to let me off for this, so I quit."

"You gave up a job to come here?"

"I can sell anything, always find something else." He braced narrow shoulders. "May not have to if the haul's good here. Excuse me, got to look up an old pal. She'll be *very* happy to see me again."

Johns lifted an eyebrow. "Wes imagines himself a ladies' man."

"You just wish you had a tenth of my sex appeal."

"Girls in high school laughed at you behind your back."

The fair skin on Koontz's neck reddened. "At least I'm not a sociopath like you. What possessed you to come, anyway? And don't say you wanted to meet new people."

"To make sure I get all the money coming to me, of course."

Uncomfortable at the cousins' sniping, Millie tried a diversion. "Is the friend you're meeting someone you knew in Delaware?"

Koontz puffed out his chest. "Met Terri on a sales trip here. We spent some very enjoyable hours together."

"What do you do, Gilbert?"

"Pharmacist."

"Where?"

"Ohio. Cincinnati."

"A pill-pusher who hates taking medicine," Koontz said. "Ever hear of that, Millie?"

"My pills!" Johns cried. "*You* swiped that bottle. That's like your warped sense of humor."

"Bull. You just forgot to bring it. Besides, if that was your antidepressant, you don't take it half the time anyway."

"I—did not—forget—to pack—my medication."

His cousin eyed him coldly. "Pitiful. Just pitiful."

"Watch yourself, Wes," Johns said, his voice ominously quiet. "I mean it."

"Some threat, Gilbert. If you had any guts, I wouldn't have lived to grow up. Remember how I broke your toys? You knew it was intentional but could never convince your ma."

"We're grown now, Wes."

"I'm shivering with fear. Later, darlin'."

Blowing Millie a kiss, Koontz started for the archway. Johns stuck a foot out and tripped him. Koontz fell, his head thumping the wall. He righted himself, rubbing his crown, then drew back a fist and threw a punch at Johns. His cousin stepped aside, letting Koontz's momentum carry him into the plaster again. This time his hand hit it, hard.

"Jeez, Gilbert, not *too* childish. Look how you've wrinkled my coat!" Koontz shook his injured fingers. "Just for that, expect some adult-type revenge. When you're least prepared."

Koontz strode on through the arch. His cousin watched him depart, then began to climb the stairs.

Nice relatives you've got, Kirchner. Neither of those boys plays well with others.

★ Chapter Four

"I'd kill for that quilt."

The quiet intensity of the words startled Millie, and she looked more closely at the speaker. With her thinning salt-and-pepper hair and crêpey neck, Vera Peeples appeared grandmotherly from the shoulders up. But her gray wool-blend dress outlined a stocky, muscular frame, and powerful arms bulged under sleeves worn thin at the elbows. Face and form seemed at odds, like seeing King Lear's head on the Incredible Hulk's body.

The heirs had gathered in the parlor and were getting their first look at Nathan Henry's keepsakes. Arthur Pope, flushed with self-importance, had displayed and commented on the items, while his co-executor, Soames Endicott, looked on with an air of amused tolerance.

Millie felt in awe of the quilt herself. To think it had been owned by her ancestor, that it might even become hers! When Pope had first produced it, she had exclaimed at its beauty. After he'd told its history, it had taken on the aura of a priceless masterpiece.

She warned herself not to want it too much. In her twenty-six years, sky-high hopes had often crashed into canyons of disappointment.

Pope, too, had seemed impressed by the keepsake. "This first item is very special," he had said in an unsteady voice while spreading the coverlet reverently over a sofa in the Henry parlor. "Note the woodblock print in the middle done by John Hewson at his Print Works in Philadelphia. Hewson quilt centers are unparalleled in eighteenth-century American textile printing. Most examples of them are in museums."

Millie and her fellow heirs had moved in for a closer look. An exquisite urn of flowers and fluttering birds and butterflies centered the bed cover, amid rows of patchwork set together with delicate hand stitches. The colors were lovely, though somewhat muted and mustardy.

"It looks faded," Wes Koontz complained.

"In the eighteenth century," Pope explained, "dyes were primarily natural—madder used for red and indigo for blue, for instance—and hues weren't as bright as the ones available today. These have also dimmed somewhat with age."

He pointed a trembling finger at a corner. "Note the quilt-maker's name and the year and number of manufacture. That's the way Quaker ladies typically labeled quilts they sewed." He lowered his voice respectfully. "See? Elizabeth Griscom Ross, better known to us by her nickname."

As his meaning had become clear, Millie had gasped. Now, moments later, she was still struggling to take in the astonishing news.

Peeples seemed to have no such problem. "Betsy Ross," she murmured adoringly. "*The* Betsy Ross. Our nation's first flag-maker."

Her worshipful tone was too much even for Millie.

"Imagine wrapping that around you on a chilly evening," she teased, trying to inject a light note into the solemnity.

"You wouldn't *use* it!" Peeples cried, whirling towards Millie.

"I make quilts myself, and I always frame my best ones. But they're not nearly as fine as this."

The brawny woman was a quilter? She seemed to be a bundle of contradictions.

Peeples's horrified exclamation drew a loud snicker from Wes Koontz.

So much for gay banter, Sylva's voice commented in Millie's head.

"The idea that Mrs. Ross made the first American flag has been pretty well discredited now," Pope was saying, "but there's no doubt she was an accomplished seamstress. Her sewing shop was close by, and she often made linens for the Henrys. This quilt was special-ordered by Mrs. Henry."

Though Millie's knowledge of antiques was sketchy, even she could tell this piece was no mere "household bric-a-brac" as Winston Akers had claimed. To distract herself from her longing to own it, she focused on memorizing details of the parlor's décor to tell Sylva. The carved mahogany furniture, marble tabletops, and figured carpet of yellow, salmon and deep blue seemed to epitomize eighteenth-century luxury. The canary-colored silk damask drapes, Pope had said, were not original but were authentic copies.

Only the heavy steel cabinet from which he had taken the quilt appeared out of place. Dual-locked metal outer doors and glass inner ones had required two sets of keys to open, one produced by the executor, the other by a stolid, blond young man in security-guard uniform. Clearly, the possibility of theft had been considered.

The heirs had met each other during a social hour with canapés and drinks, and their attire presented a wide interpretation of evening dress. The cousins' identical white jackets emphasized their similarity in appearance. Their attitudes did not. Gilbert Johns stood disdainfully apart, while Wes

Koontz circulated, alternating between making caustic comments on the proceedings and trying to catch Letitia's eye. A vision in a white beaded gown, she ignored him.

"Wouldn't you love to have that, Scott?" she murmured, brushing a well-turned arm against his chest.

"Only one of us can," he said. "So I yield to you."

"Aren't you the gallant one." She patted his arm and gazed into his eyes.

He flushed and looked at the floor.

Sylva's likely reaction flashed in Millie's head: *In my day, we'd have called that brazen. Now I suppose it's considered mere friendliness.*

Brad sported an impeccably tailored dinner jacket. Earlier, he had been attentive to Millie, complimenting her and making witty asides about other heirs, but now he seemed focused on the keepsakes. Millie had decided she enjoyed his charming manners and sense of fun. Even his bragging might cover an inferiority complex, she told herself.

Can't imagine why someone with his looks would have one, though.

Eileen Goggins, a woman a few years older than Millie, in a red strapless dress that clung to her voluptuous figure, giggled at a muttered remark from Ed Cunningham. Heavy black mascara and magenta lipstick overwhelmed Eileen's pale eyes and skin, at once aging her and giving her a child-playing-dress-up look. Cunningham appeared twenty or more years older than she with his bulbous nose, florid cheeks and implausibly dark hair. A green-plaid jacket strained across his middle like an overstuffed sausage casing.

"Old goat," Peeples grumbled as she watched, stony-faced. "Could be her father."

Millie recalled that the older woman was Eileen's roommate here. Overly protective, she thought.

Pope removed a long-barreled weapon from the cabinet. "This is the Pennsylvania rifle used by a son of Nathan Henry in the Revolutionary War, specially made by William Henry of Lancaster, a kinsman and skilled gunsmith."

As he held the gun for the heirs to see, Millie noticed that his fingers shook.

A lawyer, used to public speaking, nervous?

"May I?" Brad asked.

Pope hesitated, then gravely handed over the firearm. Brad whistled as he caressed it.

"Silver inlaid stock. Pretty fancy for a soldier to carry."

"Young Henry was a very wealthy soldier," the executor said with a smile. "Part of Philadelphia's famed Silk Stocking Company."

Reluctantly, Brad gave the rifle back. Pope laid it on a nearby table.

"Prob'ly got them fancy socks muddy a time or two in the war." Cunningham dug Eileen in the ribs. She tittered.

"You look really nice," Scott murmured diffidently, as he moved nearer Millie.

"Thanks." She touched the multicolored scarf topping her sand-colored sheath. "A friend lent me these clothes."

His mouth twitched. "Right."

"It's true."

"Wish I'd had someone to borrow from," he said ruefully. "All my grad-school buddies are as broke as me." He plucked at the lapel of his rusty brown suit.

"Pity."

"You don't seem heartbroken over my misery."

"I—" She broke off as Pope took out a footed tray of gleaming silver. On it were two small lidded boxes, flanking a taller cup that held several quill pens.

"This is by Philip Syng, Jr.," he said, as if expecting his hearers to be impressed.

They all looked blank.

Cunningham reached for the dish. "Say, let's see that."

The attorney resisted, and the two briefly played tug o' war. After a moment, Pope surrendered.

"Do be careful, please!"

Cunningham rubbed the inkstand's glowing surface, tilting it and setting the quills twirling. Then he shrugged and passed it to Eileen. She took it gingerly and handed it back to Pope.

"Philip Syng, Jr., was one of the eighteenth century's foremost silversmiths." The condescending voice of Soames Endicott broke in. "That ink standish closely resembles the one used at the signing of the Declaration of Independence, which was also by Syng. You'll see that one tomorrow when we tour Independence Historical Park."

A slim man with fine-boned features and a patrician manner, Endicott seemed more at ease in his formal dress than Pope in his equally well-cut tuxedo. Millie had noticed that the attorney often glanced at his co-executor as if seeking approval for his conducting of the proceedings.

"How much is that ink thing worth?" Cunningham asked.

The lawyer's eyes widened. "You mean if it were *sold?*"

"Yeah. If that ain't too crass, deary." Cunningham pinched Eileen's bare arm and grinned.

She gave him a coquettish smile, provoking a glare from Peeples.

"Great question," Brad said. "How much?"

"Arthur," Endicott said with an indulgent smile, "you and I love these things for their own sake, but we mustn't expect everyone to."

"Well . . . the signers' stand would be extremely valuable," the attorney admitted. "Perhaps a million and a half or more. Of course, it would never be offered for sale."

"How about this one?" Letitia prompted.

"Yeah, let's have an estimate." Koontz winked broadly at her, but she appeared not to notice.

Pope glanced at the banker, who nodded slightly.

"Oh, much less," the lawyer hedged.

"But easily a hundred twenty thousand, wouldn't you say?" came a new voice, deep and sure.

All eyes turned towards a man who had entered unnoticed and now stood beside Endicott. Powerfully built, the new arrival had cropped ebony hair, an air of confident reserve, and skin as dark as the mahogany tables.

"Good evening," he said amiably. "I'm Hamilton Ross. Sorry to be late. My flight was delayed."

"Delighted to see you, Mr. Ross. You're the last heir to arrive." Pope extended a hand and made introductions.

A black relative, huh? Gets more interesting all the time.

Millie, the Bennetts, Scott, Eileen, and Endicott returned the newcomer's smile and shook hands. The cousins and Peeples nodded hello. Cunningham pointedly stuck his hands behind him, but Ross didn't seem to notice.

"What do you say to my estimate, Mr. Pope? Fair?"

"A hundred twenty thousand? Ye-e-es, I suppose so."

"Definitely," Endicott said. "You know your antiques, Mr. Ross. Are you a collector yourself?"

"In a modest way, as far as a high-school principal's budget allows. But I'm an avid student. These are wonderful pieces."

"We all gonna get one?" Cunningham asked.

Pope shook his head. "There are nine keepsakes and sixteen of you, including the six not present."

"It's not fair for them to get a share," Peeples grumbled. "I spent what little savings I had on my train ticket."

The attorney's cheeks reddened. "That wasn't necessary, Miss Peeples. Mr. Henry insisted that each of you pay his or her own way, 'to show a spirit of adventure,' but he did realize that some might be too old or ill to make the trip."

"Can we take whatever we win home with us?" Koontz asked, his slight form tense with eagerness.

"Yes, and if an absent heir gets a keepsake, it's to be sent via 'overland coach or sea.' Mr. Endicott and I interpret that to include rail, truck, or air in today's terms."

"If Mother wins something, may Brad and I take it to her?" Letitia asked.

"I'm afraid each item must go directly to its owner, Miss Bennett. Mr. Henry was quite specific about that."

"He must've been . . . unusual, even by another century's standards," Endicott said. "Shall we see the rest, Arthur?"

Pope showed a black Wedgwood bowl with red figures, six embroidered samplers, an ivory miniature bearing a woman's likeness, a walnut candlestand, and a map of early Pennsylvania.

"Scull and Heap, 1752," he said proudly, spreading the map on the table. Taking a deep breath, he exchanged a look with Endicott, who again nodded. "There is one additional item," Pope announced and paused again.

The puzzled heirs looked at each other.

The attorney pivoted to the cabinet and lifted out a wooden glass-fronted case, placing it with ceremony on the table. Moving in close, Millie saw that it contained a yellowed paper covered in an inky scrawl.

"In my view, this is the prize of Mr. Henry's collection." Pope's voice vibrated with emotion. "It's from the man who gave him the idea for his unusual will."

His watchers strained to read the signature. Ross found his voice first.

"Benja—my God! It's a letter from Benjamin Franklin."

★ *Chapter Five*

Millie gasped. She had managed to maintain her composure even when seeing that quilt, but now she felt herself quiver with excitement. Here was an actual letter penned by an inventor, diplomat, statesman, and philosopher she had long admired. And she had a chance of owning it!

Not so blasé now, are you, Kirchner?

"Awesome," Scott breathed.

Koontz left Letitia's side to get a better view, and even his cousin edged forward. Cunningham elbowed Johns back, jostling him into a tea table.

"Watch it!" the smaller man cried. "Big rhinoceros!"

"Shut your face, twerp," Cunningham growled. "Or I'll squash you like the ant you are."

"Gentlemen, gentlemen," Pope said, his tone belying the fitness of the word. "Let's preserve our courtesy, please. And do be careful of this valuable furniture."

The butler, Fansler, had served refreshments and cleared away the dishes before the keepsakes were brought out. Black-suited and spindly-framed, he had hovered since then like an emaciated bird of prey. He now whisked the little table out of the traffic area.

Millie bent to squint at the faded writing. One phrase stood out as if written with a quill fresh-dipped in ink: " . . . continued to work till late in the Day . . . ."

If only—

Forget it, she thought. One in sixteen is not a strong chance. Still . . . .

It's a far better chance than none at all.

"Mr. Pope," Millie said, "I've read biographies of Franklin, but I don't recall any mention of a Nathan Henry. Were they really good friends?"

He grinned. "I'm glad you asked, Mrs. Kirchner. Mr. Endicott and I have pondered that question over the years. We've found no other examples of correspondence between them, but clearly they knew each other. Tell her what we've concluded, Soames."

Something about the executors' demeanor towards each other stirred a memory in Millie's mind, a mere wisp of thought, indefinite and elusive. Some literary parallel, she thought. Try as she would to recall it, however, the specific reference wouldn't materialize.

"Henry's notes hint that they were close," the banker was saying, "but he may well have exaggerated. No independent authority mentions such a tie, and the formal tone of this letter suggests a lack of intimacy. I personally suspect that Franklin only tolerated Henry because his wealth helped support the Revolution."

A spark of something—discomfort? anger?—flashed in Pope's eyes. "That's a bit strong, Soames. Let's just say they were friends, but maybe not as close as Mr. Henry believed."

Pope's pretty defensive about this Nathan Henry.

"Can you tell us about the two men's wills?" Millie asked. "How did they differ?"

Again, he seemed happy to be asked. "Franklin's will—a

codicil to it, actually—left money to the cities of Boston and Philadelphia, stipulating that it be lent at low interest to young apprentices just starting out in business. After a hundred years passed following his death, the cities were allowed to use part of the proceeds. A century later, at the final distribution in 1990, the cities each received millions."

"Hear that, babe?" said Cunningham, elbowing Eileen. "We're gonna be rich."

Pope frowned at the interruption, then went on. "Mr. Henry, being more conservative—or less philanthropic than Franklin, depending on your view—put his money in a bank account and made his own descendants the beneficiaries. He was much younger than Franklin and died several years later, in the early nineteenth century."

Ross's long supple fingers patted the letter's case. "Franklin must've gotten a kick out of influencing events from the grave, long after his death."

"That probably also appealed to Henry's ego, which was evidently substantial," Endicott said.

Pope shot his colleague an offended look.

"We're gonna get millions, too. Right?" Cunningham said.

Pope glanced at Endicott, who shook his head almost imperceptibly.

"Patience, Mr. Cunningham," the attorney replied, turning back to the heirs. "The agenda we're following was partly prescribed in Mr. Henry's notes, then fleshed out by Mr. Endicott and me. The savings account is to be discussed after dinner."

Cunningham gave him a contemptuous look.

"Henry may have been a copycat," Scott offered tentatively. "But he put some interesting spins on Franklin's scheme."

"That's perceptive, Mr. Wyrick," said Pope, beaming. "For that matter, Franklin's plan wasn't entirely original. He got the idea from a French correspondent, Mathon de la Cour."

"How much would this letter sell for?" Koontz demanded.

"Why, I can't say, Mr. Koontz," Pope said. "If I owned it, I wouldn't part with it for any amount of money."

Koontz raised his eyebrows at Letitia. She turned away. He winked at Millie, but she, too, ignored him. From the corner of an eye, she saw Johns grin.

"How much?" Cunningham insisted.

Pope cleared his throat and looked at Endicott. The banker nodded. Again, Millie felt the teasing in her brain. A literary reference, she felt sure, perhaps a speech by a Charles Dickens character. But whatever the executors' behavior suggested to her still wouldn't come clear.

"Perhaps forty thousand," Endicott said. "Mr. Ross, what do you think?

"I'd need to study the content fully," the principal's deep voice said. "If it's of historic significance, the value could be much higher. A letter by Thomas Jefferson sold at auction years ago for three hundred thousand."

"True," the banker said. "You're well informed."

"But the letter's worth less than this?" Koontz straightened the inkstand, now sitting beside the rifle. "Then this is what I'm shooting for. When do we find out what we get?"

"Later this evening," the attorney said shortly.

"Speaking of the keepsakes' value," Brad said, "what was that fellow doing prowling around the mansion earlier? Akers, his name was. Said he was an antiques dealer. Offered to buy what I win in the lottery."

"Akers?" Pope's eyebrows shot up. "Sounds like the name of the man who called several times asking to make appointments with you heirs. I said we had a full program and I didn't want you bothered. He was actually waiting outside when you arrived, Mr. Bennett?"

"Me, too," Millie said. Others chorused agreement.

"What gall!" Pope's rosy complexion reddened further.

"I, for one, plan to deal with Akers," Koontz said, smoothing the too-crisp part in his hair. "Antiques leave me cold. Give me new stuff every time."

Pope's smile looked forced. "That's up to you, of course. There'll be buyers enough if you wish to sell. But consider what you'd be giving up, Mr. Koontz—a part of history preserved two whole centuries just for you."

Millie privately agreed, thinking that she and Danny would have to be destitute before she would sell Ben Franklin's letter, should she be fortunate enough to get it.

"Mr. Ross—Hamilton, if I may," Endicott said, "your fellow heirs want estimates, but Arthur can't bear to think of the keepsakes that way. As for me, I defer to your judgment. You've noticed, of course, that the quilt's by a certain seamstress with your last name."

"Indeed," Ross said. "That's a marvelous piece. Even if she weren't involved, one seldom sees quilts that old. I'm not an appraiser, understand,"—His eager face belied the modest words— "but I suppose I could suggest some figures."

He moved from one displayed article to another, gently lifting and replacing them, then struck a pensive pose. "It's only a rough guess, but I'd say the inkstand and quilt would each fetch around one hundred twenty thousand."

"I knew it," exulted Peeples, brawny arms crossed on chest. "But if I draw that quilt, I'll keep it myself."

"The letter could be worth forty thousand, as Mr. Endicott suggested," Ross went on, "or more. The map, probably eighty-five hundred."

"Oo-oo-ooh, I hope my daddy gets that," Eileen Goggins crooned. "He's wild about old maps."

"The candlestand's lovely," Ross said, his brow knit in

concentration as he stared at the little walnut table. "The claw-and-ball feet make it especially desirable. I'd put it conservatively at thirty-five thousand. Might command as much as sixty."

Check the cash-register tapes in people's eyes, Kirchner.

"Eighteenth-century samplers." Ross mused, caressing a length of cross-stitched linen. "When you can find them, they're worth a lot. Five to six thousand apiece, at least."

The educator moved to the Wedgwood bowl. "Classic red figures on black basalt, signed by Josiah Wedgwood himself." He paused as if uncertain for the first time. "Mr. Endicott, help me. Six thousand?"

"I would've said sixty-five hundred to seven thousand."

"Probably right." Ross stroked the rifle. "Quite nice, with the silver stock and the maker's initials. Eleven to twelve thousand." He picked up the small portrait. "A miniature on ivory. Mrs. Henry, you say?"

"It's by Charles Willson Peale," Endicott prompted.

The principal nodded recognition of the name. "Eleven to twelve thousand as well, then."

"So, if a collector really wanted a certain piece," Koontz said, green eyes narrowed, "we could hold him up pretty good, couldn't we?"

Pope clenched a fist, as if longing to strike someone. But when he spoke, he sounded in control. "The keepsakes will remain in here throughout this gathering, guarded around the clock. The outer cabinet doors will stay open for viewing, the inner ones will be locked." After he carefully returned the antiques to their case, he and the guard locked the glass panels.

The attorney briskly rubbed his hands and said, "Now. Come with me, ladies and gentlemen. Mrs. Fansler has prepared a feast for us."

Cunningham grabbed his sleeve. "This is horseshit, Pope. How much is in that savings account? Millions? Billions?"

The stocky attorney stared icily. "All in good time, Mr. Cunningham. Mr. Endicott and I are carrying out Mr. Henry's directives. Your impatience will not persuade us to change the plan."

With a peevish frown, the big man eased his hand back.

Like a Scottish terrier who had bested a St. Bernard, Pope strode majestically out. The heirs followed, Brad offering Millie his arm, Letitia reaching for Scott's.

The scene at the long, cloth-covered dining table looked to Millie like a parody of the wealthy family at home as portrayed in period television dramas. The executors sat like parents at the ends, the heirs ranged like children along both sides. Millie's name card placed her near Endicott's end, with Scott to her left and Ross across the table. She gazed appreciatively around the large graceful room. A silver tea set topped a mahogany sideboard, a glass-fronted built-in cupboard held creamy tableware, and two drop-leaf tables flanked an imposing long-case timepiece on one wall.

"That clock's by Edward Duffield of Philadelphia," Ross said to Millie. "Beautiful workmanship, isn't it?"

"I don't know much about antiques, but I love old things. They make me feel as if I've stepped back in time."

He smiled, his skin glowing richly in the candlelight. "I know what you mean. It's nice to meet a kindred spirit."

"It must've taken you years to learn all you know, the makers' names and such."

"I suppose, but it was a labor of love." He donned wire-rimmed glasses and picked up the menu beside his plate.

Millie read aloud from hers: "Salmon mousse, roast quail, wild rice, vegetable *mélange,* spinach and hearts-of-palm salad, raspberry trifle. It sounds wonderful. I've never had most of this stuff before." Her stomach rumbled, reminding her how long ago and unsatisfying lunch had been.

"If Mrs. Fansler is skillful, you're in for a treat."

Remember how unfriendly she was. Which course do you suppose has the poison in it?

Millie mentally shushed Sylva, wanting to concentrate on enjoying this meal. Fansler set before her a blue floral plate holding a pinkish mound garnished with sprigs Millie recognized as dill weed. When all had been served and Pope lifted his spoon, she tasted the mousse, shivering with delight at its soft texture and delicate flavor.

Above the clinking of silverware, Pope's voice carried from the other end. "No, Mr. Bennett, these dishes aren't from Nathan Henry's day. The creamware in the cupboard—what's left of it—would have been in use then."

Scott leaned around Millie to ask a question of Endicott. "Have people lived here continuously since Henry died? If so, it seems lots of the furniture would've gotten broken."

The banker swallowed a bite of food before replying. "Mr. Henry decreed that a couple of his unmarried daughters should live here after he and his wife died. Upon the daughters' demise, it was left to the various executors' discretion whether to allow descendants to reside here. The original furnishings were to be retained where possible." He patted his mouth with his napkin. "That seems casual, given Henry's strictness about preserving the keepsakes, but he was evidently a complex man—easy and generous about some things, rigid and controlling about others.

"Once this gathering is over, the house and its contents are to go to the city for a museum."

"Henry must've been quite a fellow," Ross commented.

"If heirs lived here through the years, they must've been good stewards," Millie said. "The place looks wonderful."

"They generally were," Endicott said, pausing for a sip of water. "With one notable exception. Henry established a generous maintenance account, and one rascally descendant found a way to, shall we say, 'fleece' it. He remodeled the house, getting kickbacks from suppliers and contractors. The then-acting executors discovered the ploy, evicted him, and restored the mansion to its former condition. But doing so proved expensive. This was originally a much larger property. Most of the surrounding land had to be sold to keep the maintenance account solvent."

"Henry didn't anticipate anything like that, I'm sure," Scott said.

"He seems to've been overly optimistic—naïve even—about his own posterity's virtues. The house sat empty awhile. Then one executor moved here with his family to better look after it, and that became a pattern. Arthur's father, executor before him, did the same. And now Arthur."

"Mr. Pope grew up here, then?" Millie asked.

"Yes. He seems to almost feel he *is* a Henry."

"I notice he's protective of old Nathan's image."

Endicott smiled. "I'm afraid he feels I'm not adoring enough."

Fansler cleared dishes and served plates of golden-brown quail, wild rice, and a colorful mixture of snow peas, carrots, yellow squash, and zucchini. Millie savored several bites, then replied to a question from Scott about the English courses she had taken, her mind half on the conversation between Ross and Endicott.

"This dining table consists of several sections," the banker was saying. "The rest of the set are there by the clock. When completely assembled, the table seats twenty-four. Nathan's grandson had it made during the early nineteenth century."

Millie realized Scott had spoken again. "Sorry, I was distracted. What did you say?"

"Just—the Edgar Allan Poe home isn't far away." He dropped

his fork, which clattered to his plate. "Darn. Would you like to go see it. . . while we're here?"

A date? She'd only had a few since Jack had left, what with looking after Danny and scratching out a living. Would she remember how to behave? But exploring the city and seeing where a great writer had lived sounded fun. Also, Scott was good company, with a sense of humor she liked.

"Sure, if there's time. I didn't even recall that Poe was from Philadelphia."

"He wasn't. But he lived here a few years. Edited a couple of magazines, published a collection of his stories during that time."

"Leave it to an English major to know all that."

"We aren't just pretty faces, you know."

She smiled. Although she wouldn't have applied the word "pretty" to Scott, his face was pleasant and open, his self-deprecating manner appealing.

"You could join our ranks any time," he went on.

"So you're recruiting?"

"The world can always use another literate human."

"I *am* literate, already."

"I don't doubt that." He laughed.

"Could you guarantee me a good job? I hear some English majors end up as checkers at grocery stores."

"Could happen with any major. Besides, what do you have against grocery stores?"

"Nothing. They're among my favorite places. But I stocked shelves at a grocery one summer, and the salaries aren't the greatest." She took another bite of quail. "Grouch or not, Mrs. Fansler can cook."

"Yeah, this food's great."

Ross asked how long Endicott had been an executor.

"Thirty-eight years," the banker replied. "My bank has had

custody of the keepsakes for about fifty-five. They've had to be moved a few times over the centuries. Even banks sometimes go out of business."

"There must've been a lot of different executors," Ross observed. "How did that work exactly?"

"The will specified that the executors always be a lawyer and a banker. Arthur handled the estate's legal business and kept track of the heirs' whereabouts, births, deaths, and such. That apparently proved to be quite a chore. Especially since direct contact between executors and descendants was forbidden after the first three generations, until time came for this gathering to be announced."

Endicott smoothed his mustache with a slender index finger. "My own role has been mainly to oversee the savings account and care for the keepsakes. Following Henry's guidelines, of course."

"Imagine having charge of those wonderful antiques," Ross said, propping his chin on a graceful hand. "I'd have taken them out every day to gloat over them. My wife teases me about wanting to own every antique I see."

The banker smiled conspiratorially and again traced his mustache. "You do understand. The Henry keepsakes are exceptional. Real treasures."

"Your bank must've followed very tight security precautions with them."

"For many years, the keepsakes were kept in a safe within the bank's main vault." Endicott's manner became more animated, as with barely suppressed excitement. "I myself held the key to the safe, and only a few people had access to the vault's key. It was a good system, an excellent system."

Sobering, he looked away at the long-case clock. "Still, it wasn't foolproof. So about twenty-five years ago, the bank directors voted to install a time-locked vault and had that metal cabinet specially built for the keepsakes." His face lengthened.

"Each month after that, a different bank director would be in charge of the key to the cabinet's outer doors, though I retained the one to the inner ones. Both keys were then necessary in order to reach the keepsakes. It was the right decision, certainly. One can't be too careful with such special items."

"I concur, absolutely," Ross said.

"You must be sorry to give them up now," Millie said.

Endicott shrugged. "This is their destiny, the reason they've been cared for so well over the centuries."

"They're in amazing condition," Ross said. "Especially since most of those things wouldn't have been thought valuable when Henry died."

"Their upkeep was a legal obligation. It had to be taken seriously."

"And now? Are you still responsible for them?"

"Fortunately, no." The banker smiled smugly. "A bank director and I personally handed the keys to Arthur and a guard this morning. Much as I love the keepsakes, that was a relief."

Fansler removed dishes. To Ross's right, Eileen leaned across the table, smiling coyly at Scott. Her strapless bodice drooped, exposing some of its contents.

"If you draw something, Scott, you gonna sell?" She batted heavily fringed lashes. "I'll put mine up on eBay. Not if it's that map, though. I hope me or Daddy, one, will get that."

Scott said politely that he probably would have to sell, then replied to something Letitia said on his left. Crestfallen, Eileen toyed with the salad Fansler had brought her.

"You from Texas, too, Eileen?" Millie asked. The actress seemed a gentle soul, she thought, good-hearted though gullible. Was she now deserting Cunningham for Scott? "Your accent sounds like it."

"Yeah, Lubbock, but I live in L.A. now." Eileen struck a

pose, managing to look proud and defenseless at the same time. "My coach says I'm about ready to break into films. But first, I got to think of a good movie name. Eileen's okay, he says, but Goggins has to go. You got a neat name—Sharmilla Kristalynn. Awesome."

"Thanks. It's from a romance novel Mother read when she was pregnant. I'm not wild about it, myself."

Ross told Eileen his wife was from Midland, and they compared notes on west Texas towns. Millie heard Cunningham down the table loudly advising Letitia what to do with the money she would inherit.

"Investing's my business, and I can put you onta some good things. Wouldn't let just anybody in on them, but you being a relative . . . ."

Millie couldn't hear the low response.

"There's strangers out there," he went on, "dishonest folks who'll take advantage of you if you're not careful."

He wants her to let a relative take advantage of her.

Millie stifled a giggle. This time she heard Letitia's reply, that she already had plans for her money.

"Look what you did," Koontz growled near the other end of the table, displaying a smear of salad dressing on his immaculate sleeve. "You can just pay to get this jacket cleaned."

"I'm sorry," Peeples said with dignity. "But you needn't be so disagreeable about it."

"Wes loves making scenes," Johns said snidely. "After he came to live with us, dinnertime was always high drama."

"At least I wasn't a slug like you."

"Nobody wanted you around, Wes. Still don't."

"You twerps are both asking to get strangled." For emphasis, Cunningham jerked his shirt together over his paunch.

Startled silence followed his words, save for the tiny sounds of Fansler removing salad plates. Millie sneaked glances at other faces around the table, saw her own embarrassment mirrored there.

I owe you an apology, Sylva, Millie thought. *You warned me not to celebrate my new relatives' existence till I'd met them. But I refuse to let petty squabbles ruin this treat for me.*

Endicott smoothed the awkward moment, turning to Scott. "You're in academia, Mr. Wyrick, so I'm sure you'd enjoy looking over the Henry library. Nathan left a few good books, and later residents added others. Arthur has an impressive collection on history and antiques, though I do say it. I gave him several of the volumes."

"Great. I love poking into other people's libraries."

"So do I," Millie said, anticipating another pleasure. She moved an arm to let Fansler set a dish of trifle before her.

Talk turned to family. Scott said his aunt would have loved seeing Philadelphia, had she been herself. Millie told about speaking with Danny by phone that afternoon.

"Jeff's dad's taking the boys to a movie tomorrow night, and they have the camping trip Saturday. Danny was so excited, he barely realized I was gone." Millie tried a bite of the cake, custard, and fruit confection. "Mm . . . yum."

Ross asked Endicott if he and Pope would mind seeing their executorship end.

"To a degree. It's been . . . just an unusual and interesting job to me." The banker smiled confidingly. "But I'm a bit worried about Arthur. The Henry legacy has been his whole life."

"I suppose he'll have to move now?"

"Yes. He's been very comfortable here, having the Fanslers plus daily help, all expenses paid."

"So Mr. Pope may resent us heirs," Ross said thoughtfully, "for bringing all this to an end."

"'Resent' may be too strong a word." Endicott stroked his

mustache again. "But I'm sure he has mixed feelings."

The Fanslers are losing their home, too. Could explain their hostility.

Abruptly Pope laid his napkin beside his plate, pushed back his chair and got to his feet. "Let's adjourn to the library, ladies and gentlemen. It's time to begin the lottery."

"Yes!" yelled Cunningham. He looked around as if for a high-five partner, then settled for clasping his hands above his own head.

Chapter Six

The library must ordinarily have seemed welcoming, with its soft deep couches and lively color. Although Millie would not have chosen the combination of peach walls, maroon and white fabrics, and mustard-colored mantel, somehow it worked. Books abounded in glass-fronted cabinets, a splendid bookcase-desk, and two large wooden cases set at right angles to form an alcove. Millie imagined Mr. and Mrs. Henry seated in that nook of an evening, a taper burning on a candlestand between them, their children lying on the rug listening as one parent read aloud.

At present, however, the room had an "us against them" look, the heirs in three rows of folding chairs like recalcitrant schoolchildren, the executors facing them like teacher and visiting superintendent. Pope stood behind a portable lectern on a massive desk, shuffling papers in a folder. Endicott sat in a wing chair to his right. Beside the desk and in front of the banker, a pedestal as tall as Millie held an opaque blue bowl.

"Wasn't that meal delicious?" she said to Johns, who sat beside her in the back row. When she and Brad had arrived from the dining room, they had not found seats together. He now sat in the front row beside Letitia.

"It was okay."

"I loved the trifle."

Silence.

"Did you have a good trip to Philadelphia?"

"Fair."

"How'd you travel?"

"Flew."

Millie's other neighbor proved to be more talkative. Peeples said she was from Detroit, a retired physical education teacher now leading fitness classes for seniors.

"You look very fit yourself," Millie observed.

"Yes." The quietly confident tone belied the wrinkled face and sweetish lilac perfume. "I'm glad there's exercise equipment here, even if it's not state-of-the—"

Rap, rap. Pope struck the lectern with a letter knife. The chatter ceased.

"Ladies and gentlemen," he said. "My first duty is to give a brief history of Nathan Henry and his achievements." The attorney told how Henry had sailed from England as a young man, gained wealth as an importer and merchant, and joined other Philadelphia businessmen in subsidizing his adopted country's effort for independence.

Pope's bright eyes indicated his own interest in the subject, but his delivery droned. Cunningham fidgeted in the front row, as did Koontz behind him. Expressions and postures of others revealed boredom or impatience. Only Scott and Ross, ahead and to the left of Millie, sat alert. She herself thought that this ancestor, for all his egotism, sounded enterprising and bold.

"The Henry clan hasn't been prolific," the lawyer said. "Though Nathan sired eight children, one died at birth, one in the war and two in the yellow fever epidemic of 1793. One married but had no offspring. Two daughters never wed."

Cunningham feigned a snore, eliciting a snicker from Eileen beside him. Pope pulled out a handkerchief and wiped his perspiring forehead.

"Nathan's remaining son, Benjamin," he continued sternly, "had three children, but only John produced heirs. It's through Nathan's grandson John that all of you are related."

Pope could make discovery of a cure for the common cold sound dull.

Koontz crossed his legs and began to pat a foot against the back of Cunningham's chair. *Tap. Tap. Tap.* The larger man twisted around and shot him a dirty look.

Tap. Tap. Tap.

"Quit it, you little creep!"

Tap. Tap. Tap. Tap.

Cunningham rose and with a huge paw slapped Koontz's leg from his knee. The foot dropped to the floor, jarring Koontz and flipping him forward. His face struck the back of Cunningham's chair. The big man guffawed.

Pope whipped off his spectacles. "Gentlemen! Please!"

"Jeez!" Koontz said. He righted himself, pushed back his disheveled hair, and gingerly touched his mouth. "I'm bleeding, and my lip's sure to swell. You're a pig, Cunningham!"

His adversary winked at Eileen and took his seat. Pope frowned at Endicott. The banker nodded.

"You're all understandably eager for news of your inheritance," the attorney said, "but such outbursts are embarrassing and violate the spirit of a family gathering. As was made clear earlier, I'm following procedures dictated by Mr. Henry's will. So I must insist you control yourselves."

With a last stern look, he replaced his glasses and read the names of six heirs, not present, who would share in the legacy: Esther Davidson Bennett, Harley Goggins, James Douglass Ross, Daniel John Kirchner, Charla Ann Quint and Verlene Mathers Moriarty.

"Miss Quint is the aunt of Mr. Wyrick, Mrs. Moriarty no

immediate relation to anyone present." Pope stopped as if reluctant to go on. He meticulously straightened papers and returned them to the folder, a muscle working in one jaw.

Millie shifted in her chair. Beads of perspiration stood out on Peeples' doughy chin. Ross clenched and unclenched a graceful hand. Even Cunningham sat rigid and focused. At last Pope took a deep breath and spoke again.

"The savings account Mr. Henry established has grown handsomely over the years. Each living descendant will receive approximately half a million dollars."

For a moment, no one moved or spoke. Then Cunningham yelled, "Now you're talking!"

Arms like steel cables flew around Millie, compressing her chest and lifting her off the floor. She struggled, but the iron grip still held.

"He-elp," she whimpered, the feeble sound overwhelmed by whoops and cheers from the others. She kicked her dangling feet, thrust out against—nothing. Frantic, she drove a fist into her captor's shoulder.

As suddenly as Peeples had grabbed Millie, she let go.

"Sorry. Don't know my own strength sometimes."

Millie's feet touched carpet. Welcome air rushed into her lungs.

Half a million, Kirchner! You're rich, hon.

Could it be true? Would she no longer have to struggle to pay bills? Dazedly, Millie tried to absorb the news.

Cunningham jumped up and down, belly bobbing like a toy clown's. He grabbed Eileen, waltzing her awkwardly past the desk and around Endicott's chair. She stumbled along at first, then caught his spirit and emitted a high giggle.

Letitia hugged her brother. Scott and Ross gripped each other's hands and grinned. Even Johns let a smile curl his lip. The executors nodded indulgently. Finally, Pope called for order, and the heirs returned to their seats.

"Although Mr. Henry gave specific instructions about many details," the lawyer said, "he didn't say in what form you were to receive the money. In view of his silence about that, Mr. Endicott and I have decided to wire your shares to your banks. Let me know before you leave Wednesday where to send yours."

Scott raised a hand. "With that much coming to me, Mr. Pope, could you advance me enough for a plane ticket home?"

"I . . . don't think we can . . . divide—"

His fellow executor touched his shoulder. "My bank would be happy to arrange small loans. The legacy is excellent collateral."

"Thank you, Soames. Very helpful. Now we'll . . . draw for . . . the keepsakes." Pope's voice grew faint. His face paled. He clutched the folder, flipped it open, then closed it. He removed then replaced his glasses. "The absent heirs' nearest . . . relatives will choose for them. Miss Bennett for her mother and so on. Mr. Endicott will pick . . . for Mrs. Moriarity."

"So let's get to it," Cunningham growled.

The attorney sagged against the lectern. Endicott leaped up, grabbing his colleague by the shoulder.

"Arthur! Are you all right? Take some deep breaths."

Pope did so. Gradually color returned to his face. The heirs watched with expressions of concern or irritation.

"I'm all right now, Soames. Thank you."

"Let's leave the lottery for tomorrow, Arthur. Another day won't matter. The excitement's been too much for you."

"No." Pope stood upright. "It's just . . . warm in here."

Endicott sat again, carefully watching his fellow executor.

Pope explained that the bowl on the pedestal held sixteen metal disks, nine printed with numbers designating the various keepsakes, the others with dollar signs signifying that the recipient would receive only his or her portion of the savings account. He opened his folder, rustled through papers, frowned, and searched through them again. Turning, he whispered to the banker.

"I'm sure you had it just before dinner, Arthur," Endicott said aloud. "Remember, you gave Fansler our planning notes to dispose of."

"Oh, dear," moaned the attorney. "I must have handed him that too. He'll have burned it by now."

He turned again to the heirs, his cherubic face rosy with chagrin. "I'd meant to announce which number goes with which keepsake—Mr. Endicott and I assigned the numbers yesterday—but I'm afraid I've misplaced the list."

"Quit stalling, Pope," Cunningham grumbled. "You're yanking our chains."

"This won't delay the drawing, will it?" Brad asked.

"I doubt we could reconstruct the whole order entirely from memory," Pope hedged.

"What's it matter?" Koontz put in. "Just assign new numbers now."

The stocky attorney's mouth tightened. "We'll not start doing things haphazardly, Mr. Koontz. Not after all Mr. Henry's careful planning—plus our own, of course."

Endicott cleared his throat. "Here's an idea, Arthur. There's a copy of the list in my office. I'll call my secretary tomorrow and have her read it to me." He consulted his watch. "In fact, she's taking notes for me at a meeting I had to miss tonight and will probably return to the office to type them up. We could go ahead with the lottery, and I could phone her and post the list later this evening."

Relief spread across Pope's face. "Wonderful idea, Soames. Anticipation will add to the enjoyment anyway."

The banker rose and whispered something. Pope nodded and addressed the heirs again.

"I'm reminded that it was Mr. Henry's wish that you not reveal the lottery results till Wednesday, just before you leave. If anyone does so, I'm instructed to assess a penalty."

"What kind of penalty?" Koontz demanded.

"A severe one, loss of a portion of the offender's legacy." Allowing no more discussion, he turned to the bowl, reached a hand into it and stirred the contents. Metal clinked against pottery and other metal.

"Choose for Mrs. Moriarty, Soames. Then each of you, beginning with Mr. Cunningham, will draw in the order you're seated. If you're also picking for someone else, take an extra disk when you draw yours."

"Please God, let me win it," Peeples prayed softly.

Endicott stepped up, stirred the disks in the bowl and drew. Glancing without expression at the thin circle, he put it in a jacket pocket. Cunningham followed, grinning at his choice before slipping it into his pants pocket.

"Hey, Pope," he said, "okay if we trade numbers with somebody else? After we find out what goes with which?"

Pope frowned. "You shouldn't even say you have a number, Mr. Cunningham." He and Endicott held a whispered consultation. "But we'll let this lapse pass. Nothing in Mr. Henry's notes precludes a trade—on Wednesday."

With a satisfied grunt, Cunningham took his seat.

Actually, Millie thought, most heirs telegraphed clues to what they drew. Eileen's Cupid's-bow mouth pouted, twice. Letitia first smiled, then frowned. Brad glowered. Scott grinned both times. Ross nodded, then shrugged.

Koontz laughed aloud at his choice. Jauntily resuming his seat, the earlier unpleasantness evidently forgotten, he crossed his legs and kicked the chair ahead. *Tap. Tap.*

Cunningham whirled, grabbed the small man's shirtfront and thrust his face close to Koontz's. Eyes narrowed to slits, he spoke in a menacingly calm voice.

"I'm gonna say this once, you pint-sized piece of crap. A *fifteenth* of that money's more'n a *sixteenth*. Get me?"

Apparently, Koontz did. He uncrossed his legs and sat straight as a plumb line.

"Come now!" Pope said sternly. "Mr. Henry couldn't have foreseen that his heirs would be uncivil to each other, but I want your word, Mr. Cunningham, that you'll behave from now on."

Cunningham lifted a shoulder. "Whatever." The lawyer continued to eye him till he grudgingly said, "Okay, you got it."

Peeples drew next, squealing with delight. As had the others, she put her circlet away immediately.

Millie stood on tiptoe for her turn, her fingers questing among bits of metal, and peeked at her choices. Two dollar signs. Disappointed despite efforts not to be, she slid the disks into a pocket and resumed her seat.

Stilll, there's all that money. With Danny's share, a million bucks.

Yes, the money! A car, even a new one. A better place to live. Braces for Danny's crooked teeth. She supposed she should invest most of his share for college . . . .

Invest—that had been something *other* people did.

Her mother would have had a portion if she'd lived. It might have made a difference. She might have gone for treatment.

But maybe not. She might even have died sooner, with more money to support her alcohol habit. Tears of regret for her mother's wasted life gathered in Millie's eyes.

Johns drew, the only one to give no sign what he had.

"One more thing," Pope said, "then you may wander the grounds or otherwise enjoy the evening." Striding to a framed chart on one wall, he gestured at ruled lines interspersed with handwritten words and numbers. "The executors kept careful track of Mr. Henry's descendants. I'm sure you'll want to trace your lineages and see how you're related to each other.

"Ladies and gentlemen, I'm proud to present the Henry family tree."

✦ Chapter Seven

Most of the heirs and both executors left the room. Johns drifted to a bookcase and began examining books. Millie and Ross headed for the genealogical chart. Studying it eagerly, she found "Daniel John Kirchner" and his birthdate at the bottom, and above him her own name followed by "college student and health-care worker" and a date. Over her was "Wanda Michaels Johnson, waitress" and her mother's birth and death dates.

A whole life reduced to cold letters and numbers, Millie thought. Nothing of the mother who had shared a love of literature and learning with her daughter, reading aloud from library books as they huddled in blankets in unheated homes. Nothing of the romantic whose frantic search for love had found abuse instead. Nothing of the promising writer who had struggled to support both a youngster and an addiction by working dead-end jobs. Nothing of the child-woman who had slit her wrists, leaving that daughter alone. Millie longed to be able to share this good fortune with her.

She glanced over the other entries on the page and spotted a colorful trio a few lines above Wanda Johnson, two brothers and a sister—a brothel owner, a circuit-riding judge in Indian Territory, and a publisher of temperance pamphlets. Yet another ancestor had been a gun-runner during the Civil War.

A thrill ran down Millie's spine. *Her* family tree. An unbroken line of upstanding and shadier individuals whose lives reflected the times in which they had lived. This alone made the trip worthwhile.

Apology accepted, Kirchner. Don't overlook the chances for romance here either.

Millie shook her head. Much as she longed for a loving companionship of the sort Sylva had described with her Logan, she doubted she'd ever find it. Anyway, her mother would have been better off if she had managed to live without a man.

Johns walked up and began looking over the genealogy, one lip lifted in derision.

"There she is!" Ross stabbed a finger at the parchment a few lines from the top, his liquid dark eyes agleam with excitement. "My ancestor Zibby. See, here. Her name was actually Hepzibah, like Nathan Henry's daughter, but she was called Zibby."

The notation read simply, "Zibby, slave, 1841–1862."

"She wasn't even given the dignity of a last name," Millie observed sadly.

Ross nodded. Both were silent for a moment.

"She belonged to Nathan's great-great-grandson Emanuel Henry," he went on. "Emanuel raped her when she was a teenager. See, their son was the only one of his children who lived to grow up. Must be why Emanuel acknowledged him."

Millie stared. "You knew all that before you came? My mother didn't seem to know anything of her family history."

"Oh, yes. I first heard that story when I was a boy. My parents often told us tales about our ancestors."

"Then you knew about Nathan Henry's legacy before Mr. Pope wrote you?"

"Not exactly—just that we were supposed to inherit something or other. Nathan lived so long ago, and the details got garbled over the years. An uncle of mine was into genealogy, but his research hadn't gotten back that far before he died. I'd about decided the legacy was a fable, till Pope's letter arrived. Zibby and her son were several generations closer to me than Nathan was, and more . . . typical, so they had always seemed much more real."

"Spare us your sordid family stories," Johns said coldly. "We don't care about your slave granny."

"I do," Millie said, "and you're being rude."

"Don't worry about him, Mrs. Kirchner." Ross coolly addressed the shorter man, "You don't seem to be a happy man, Mr. Johns. I pity you."

Johns stiffened. A strangled sound came from him. "*You* pity *me*? How *dare* you?" Whirling, he strode from the room.

Millie smiled at Ross. "If it's any comfort, he's not singling you out. He's nasty to everyone."

To her surprise, the educator chuckled. "According to my wife, Alice, there are some people you just can't take seriously."

"She sounds like a wise woman. It's too bad your son couldn't come. Is it a long time since you've seen him?"

"Several months. James does some kind of government work he can't talk about. We don't hear from him as often as we'd like. But I guess that's every parent's lament."

"I really miss Danny. I suppose it's best he didn't come, though. He'd probably be bored a lot of the time."

They discussed historic events and ways their forebears might have been involved. Then Scott came in, tie loosened, jacket rumpled. He smiled tentatively at Millie. She smiled back, liking the way his broad shoulders filled out the old coat.

"I had to get some air," Scott said. "Pope was right about it being stuffy in here." He glanced over the genealogy. "You two worked out who's who yet?" He found his own name and traced the line upwards. "I see I'm descended from John Henry's daughter Mary." His finger followed another trail. "Millie, you go back to his son Samuel."

"And Mr. Ross to his son Thomas," Millie said.

"Please call me Hamilton, both of you."

"If you'll call me Millie."

"And me Scott. Aunt Charla worked on our family tree, but had only gotten back to mid-nineteenth century when her memory of even simple things began to fail. Now she won't—" Scott paused, his jaw set.

"Your aunt and my mother, gone in different ways," Millie said softly.

He gave her a grateful smile and started to reply, but broke off as Brad entered, smelling of tobacco. Greeting them all, Brad gave the chart a cursory glance, then flashed Millie a devastating smile.

"Fancy a stroll in the yard, fair lady?"

A cool walk did sound good. "Okay."

As they left, Millie glanced back at Scott. A frown shadowed his lean face. With anger? Or hurt?

★ ★ ★

Gilbert Johns strode through the archway and down the long hall. Voices buzzed in the rooms he passed, but he paid no heed. Contrary to what he had implied to Wes, he had had serious reservations about this trip.

For one thing, it disturbed his routine. It also required meeting a bunch of new people. He had known he wouldn't like them, only not that he'd loathe them so much.

But didn't he love the sound of getting half a million! And maybe a good deal more, depending on what that number he had drawn entitled him to.

At the rear of the mansion, he came to a set of French doors. Deciding that he might find a spot outside where he could be alone, he stepped through and nearly bumped into the butler, who was leaning against the side of the house smoking.

Fansler gave a start. "Good evening, sir." He stood back to let Gilbert pass, stubbed out his cigarette, and hastily went inside.

Gilbert stepped off a circular patio onto a clipped lawn illumined by a light over the back door. A few yards out, the rays dissipated. He found himself in near-darkness amid what Pope had described as "a yard that's unusually deep and woodsy for this part of Philadelphia."

He picked his way carefully among trees and shrubs. Of all the detestable people here, Cousin Wes galled him most. As kids, they had hated each other. Once the Johnses had taken Wes in after his parents' fatal boating mishap, the little interloper had claimed toys, goodies, and attention that might have been Gilbert's. Sharing a room had been a nightmare—Wes obsessed even then with tidiness. Worst of all, Gilbert's mother had insisted on dressing them alike. Wherever they went, people had exclaimed over the "cute twins."

Wes *would* turn up tonight in a dinner jacket exactly like his own.

Gilbert reached a sturdy iron fence at the side of the property, turned right, and strolled along it towards the back boundary. The patio light didn't reach here, but a three-quarter moon and rays from a neighboring house let him make out weed-free spaces between the railings.

"Fence looks clean enough even for Wes," he muttered.

At a sound from behind, Gilbert turned to see who was invading his solitude. He saw no one. Some animal, no doubt. Gilbert hated animals almost as much as people.

He and Wes had not seen each other much after high school, not since the funeral of Gilbert's father two years after the death of his mother. But today, the instant they had spied each other in the hallway, the old hatred had returned. In both, apparently.

Gilbert walked the length of the fence and back, dreading to go inside and face those people again. A cluster of lights in the center of the yard drew his attention. He headed for them.

The trip hadn't been too bad in some ways. He hadn't felt suicidal even once. And with half a million coming, he thought with a grin, he probably wouldn't! He would make himself take his antidepressant while here, as a precaution, though secretly he agreed with his father, who had thought the need of medicine meant weakness of character.

"Don't coddle the kid, Mildred," his father had often said. "He has to learn not to be a baby."

Today, that bottle of pills had disappeared, but fortunately Gilbert was a believer in redundant planning and had packed a backup supply. He had suspected Wyrick at first, but the roommate had vehemently denied having seen the medication, and on reflection Gilbert thought Scott wasn't the prankster sort. The thief must have been Wes.

Gilbert reached a brightly lit ornamental pool set in a wide band of gravel, pole lamps several yards apart surrounding it. Good, he thought, no one else about.

Spirits drooping, he stared into the shallow water, oblivious to the beauty of lilies and rocks at its edge. An entire week of this group's company lay ahead. He especially hated having a roommate, with no privacy even in his own room. At least he wasn't having to share with Wes.

Gravel crunched behind him. Gilbert ignored it, hoping the stroller would pass by and leave him alone. He waved away a swarm of gnats flitting about his face.

He recalled the step earlier. Was there another lone wolf out here trying to avoid people? Or had someone deliberately followed him? Wes? But why would his cousin want to see him, any more than he wanted to see Wes? Curious, Gilbert started to turn.

A hand grabbed his shoulder. Another shoved him hard into the pond. Water closed over his head. His shoulder and knee struck the rocky bottom. Momentary fear surged through him.

That gave way to anger. Wes was going to get it now, and good.

Gilbert thrust his face from the water, drew air into his lungs. His hands scrabbled for a hold on the slick rocks. Good, he almost had his knees under him. He would climb out and give Wes a real pummeling.

But the hands grabbed him again, forced his head under. His knees, not firmly set, gave way. He sank, a sharp rock stabbing his chin. Profane words tumbled over each other in his mind. No apology would suffice now—he would file assault charges. Cousin or no, Wes wouldn't get away with this.

Gilbert got an arm out of the water, grabbed his adversary's wrist and tugged. He couldn't loosen the grip. He grew alarmed, flailed desperately about. He clutched at the slippery bottom, seeking a handhold, some way to push himself up.

But the mighty fingers held tight. Was this Wes? Someone else?

Blood pounded in Gilbert's ears, his chest burned from holding his breath. The liquid over his head seemed impossibly deep, the grip on his neck heavy as an elephant's foot.

Gilbert Johns, loner and proud of it, wished desperately for a friend.

★ ★ ★

As Millie and Brad passed the parlor on their way to the back yard, she saw Wes Koontz standing in front of the metal cabinet, his arms gyrating melodramatically. A different guard, gray-haired and taller than the other, stood near Eileen, both listening to Wes without expression. Next door in the music room, Letitia sat at the grand piano. The opening notes of "Autumn Leaves" trilled down the hall after Millie and Brad. In the office, Soames Endicott perched on a corner of the desk holding a telephone receiver to his ear. The dining and sitting rooms were empty, the kitchen door closed.

Brad opened the French doors. Millie was about to step out when Peeples charged in, chest heaving, face damp with perspiration. Almost colliding with Millie, she stopped and raised a hand to her mouth.

"Hello—you two," she panted. "I've been—admiring the scenery. It's a—lovely yard."

"Pretty dark for that, isn't it?" Brad said with a grin.

"Oh, there's plenty of light. In places." Turning, Peeples moved lithely up the hall.

Pretty vigorous for an old lady.

Millie looked a question at Brad. He shrugged. They went out, and he shut the doors. At the patio's edge, he paused and touched her arm. Scents of his aftershave and tobacco mingled with the night air.

"I'm glad you came with me, Millie," he said softly, his eyes like sapphires under the bright overhead lamp. "I've been wanting to get to know you better." He leaned closer, and his lips brushed hers.

Something made Millie step back and say lightly, "Nathan Henry wanted his descendants to get acquainted."

"You know that's not what I meant."

"You seem like a nice guy, Brad. But aren't you rushing things a little?"

He frowned. "Then why'd you come out here with me?"

"A walk sounded good."

"Careful. Lavish praise might make my ego bigger."

"Is that possible?" She grinned to take the edge off.

To her surprise, he chuckled. The tension gone, they rambled around the yard talking about their plans for the legacy. A breeze ruffled Millie's hair, chilled her bare arms. The moon burst through frothy clouds, casting shadows like misshapen giants.

They picked their way through shrubbery in a dark area, making for a bright spot in the middle of the long lawn.

Thinking about Danny, Millie only half heard Brad's bragging about how he had "rescued" a more experienced lawyer in a trial. Would her son wake in the night and feel disoriented in a strange room? He had spent overnights with friends before, but never a whole week apart from her.

As she and Brad emerged from between tall cedars, Ross appeared in their path, head lowered, hands in pockets.

"Hello again, Hamilton," Millie called.

Startled, he looked up. "Oh, hi, Millie, Mr. Bennett." He went on towards the house.

Millie and Brad reached a radiantly lit backyard pool, a peaceful, serene setting. Then she noticed one thing wrong. Face down in the water, frighteningly still, lay a small man in a dinner jacket.

After one horrified moment, Millie grabbed the man's arm and helped Brad drag him out of the water. Soaking wet, he proved heavier than he looked, but together they got him onto the grass and turned him face upwards.

One of the cousins, Millie thought as she knelt and examined the man. Which one?

It must be Gilbert Johns. Hadn't she seen Wes Koontz in the parlor just before they came out?

No breath, no pulse. Lord, Millie thought, how long had he been in there? She leaned over him, starting to clear his airway as she'd been taught.

"Go call the paramedics," said Brad, pushing her aside.

"I know CPR."

"I worked one summer as a lifeguard." Brad straddled Johns

and prepared to resuscitate him.

Satisfied that he knew what he was doing, Millie left him and ran, heart pounding, towards the house. Wind stung her eyes, tugged at her hair. A twig grabbed her skirt, and she paused to work it loose. Once, she stumbled on the unfamiliar, sometimes pitch-black terrain. The way seemed longer, more treacherous, than during her earlier meander with Brad.

At last she reached the patio. Koontz stood near the entry, puffing on a cigarette. She ran past him and wrenched open a French door.

"Hey, sweet stuff," he said. "What's your hurry?"

"Gilbert," she flung over her shoulder and raced inside. Up the hall to the office she flew, pausing in the doorway to catch her breath. Pope, seated at the desk, looked up questioningly.

"Ambulance," she managed to say. "Drowned—Gilbert—"

The executor's eyes grew large, but he grabbed a wall phone and dialed "911." He relayed details from Millie to the operator, then replaced the receiver with shaking hands.

"What happened?" As he joined her at the door, heightened color painted his cheeks.

Millie shook her head, and they both rushed into the hall. Pope nearly bumped into Scott, who was coming from the direction of the parlor with shoulders slumped. She told Scott the news, and he gave a short whistle.

"Wow, no kidding?"

Nodding somberly, she turned to hurry after Pope. The three reached the French doors just as Koontz entered.

"What's Gilbert done now, committed suicide?" He winked at Millie. "That'd be just like him, when any normal human would be thrilled about getting all that money."

Pope and Scott ran on out. Millie explained.

"Gilbert really *did* kill himself?" Koontz's green eyes held alarm. "I didn't—I was joking. You know I was."

She ran after the others, Koontz loping behind. When they arrived at the pond, Scott was kneeling over Johns doing an expert press-release routine on his chest. Brad stood dejectedly nearby. He shook his head at Millie.

"No luck. Gilbert's not responding."

"I couldn't know— How could I?" Koontz babbled to Pope, who stood watching Scott in dismay.

Paramedics arrived shortly, but their efforts made no difference to Gilbert Johns. He was dead.

★ Chapter Eight

"What a horribly tragic accident," Pope said, as he and Millie walked back to the house. He ran a hand through his thinning copper hair. "Mr. Johns must have stumbled, fallen in, hit his head, and knocked himself out."

Millie didn't reply. The adrenaline rush had gone, and she felt drained of energy.

"The Henry luck's running true to form." Pope shook his head sorrowfully. "Such an unfortunate family."

Bad luck may not have been the problem.

Millie mentally shushed Sylva's voice. She didn't want to think about the other possibility that had occurred to her.

Uniformed officers arrived and took charge of the scene. One herded the mansion's residents into the parlor, cautioning them not to talk to each other.

"Wait," Pope said to Brad, Scott, and Millie as they were about to enter the big room. "Your clothes are a mess. You'll ruin that elegant carpet and furniture."

"No talking, I said," the policeman warned.

"I'm not discussing what happened outside," the attorney said stiffly. "It's my duty to preserve this historic old home. Fansler, bring three kitchen chairs and plastic sheets to go under them."

A man has died, and Pope's worried about a rug?

From the expressions on Brad's and Scott's faces, it appeared that question had also occurred to them. As if realizing how unfeeling he had sounded, the executor blushed.

"And some towels, Fansler. When you three are released by the authorities, put your soiled clothes in the basket upstairs to be cleaned. At estate expense, of course."

Millie ruefully eyed her borrowed dress. Would it be okay, with cleaning? She smoothed the skirt, noticing threads hanging loose where the bush had caught it.

You can afford to replace it.

Oh, she *could* do that now. She could manage lots of things that had been impossible before. The crisis with Johns had knocked even the news about the legacy from her mind. Her thoughts felt jumbled, torn between elation at her good fortune and shock over a man's death. She hadn't liked him, but he had been a fellow human, a relative even.

The Fanslers bustled about, handing out towels, spreading plastic drop cloths in a section of the parlor, and setting three enameled chairs on them. Millie toweled off her face and hands, then took a chair beside Brad, who was gloomily rubbing the grimy knees of his slacks. Scott shrank dispiritedly into a corner.

A solicitous Cunningham patted Eileen's neck as she wept on his shoulder. Near their couch sat Peeples, chin on hand, fingers trembling. Letitia perched on a love seat, picking at the beads on her white skirt, her lovely mouth tight with tension. Koontz drummed his fingers on a chair arm, ignoring the dark looks he got from others. Finally Cunningham rolled up a magazine and brandished it at him. Koontz's fair skin colored, but his staccato pecking ceased.

Even the executors seemed ill at ease. Pope's eyes darted from one heir to another, and Endicott fidgeted in his easy chair.

The Fanslers sat beside the guard, near the keepsakes cabinet, and made eye contact with no one. Ross occupied a sofa beside Pope, hands around his knees, staring at a table lamp.

He looked as preoccupied as he had outside, Millie thought. A question occurred to her: Ross must have passed near the pool just before she and Brad had reached it. Why hadn't *he* found the victim and pulled him out?

Police detectives arrived and held separate interviews with the mansion's guests. Called to the sitting room for hers, Millie arranged an extra plastic sheet Fansler had given her on the chair indicated by Detective Orville Nolen. He waited until she sat, then perched behind an elegant walnut desk facing her.

Nolen must be about forty, she decided, although his receding brown hair, flabby midsection, and drooping shoulders made him look older.

He questioned her courteously, writing in a notebook and occasionally peering up. Her hands quivered, though this wasn't her first time to face questions about a violent death. A boyfriend of her mother's had overdosed on their couch once, leading to a grilling for her mother and a frightening time for twelve-year-old Millie.

Then had come that awful night of her mother's suicide. The policemen had been gentle with young Millie, but pain and fear for her future had produced an emotional overload that had turned her numb. She hadn't cried, until later. Even now, the memory sometimes haunted her dreams.

"How'd you and your boyfriend happen to go to the pond?"

"Brad's not my boyfriend. We just met this afternoon. It was warm inside, so we went for a walk."

"You only met Bennett today? What about Johns?"

Millie explained about the gathering of heirs. Nolen's eyes lit in recognition.

"Oh, yeah, I read about that will. Made the paper here a

while back."

"It did?"

"Year or so ago, I think. You seem surprised. It's a pretty strange legacy, don't you think?"

"Yes, it is. But the executors said they had instructions to keep it quiet. I'm an heir, and I only learned about it myself three weeks ago. Are you sure it was Nathan Henry's will you read about, not Ben Franklin's? He made a similar one."

Nolen smiled. "I do know about that one, Mrs. Kirchner. Hard to miss, living in Philadelphia. This was someone else, and Nathan Henry sounds right. I recall it joined two famous names, like Nathan Hale and Patrick Henry." He looked around at the dainty room, the silk fabrics and delicate tables. "Nice. Must've been interesting stuff went on in this place two centuries ago."

As if recalling his duty, he shrugged and asked if Millie had seen anyone else in the pool area before finding Johns's body. She hesitated, then told about meeting Ross.

"That would be the black gentleman? Is he one of Henry's descendants?"

Millie nodded.

Nolen's eyes crinkled. "Bother you to learn you're related to a black man?"

"No."

"Might upset some. One of your fellow heirs, maybe?"

"You'd have to ask them."

"How about the victim? Any friction between him and Ross?"

Uncomfortably, Millie told of Johns's disparaging reference to Ross's slave ancestor, quickly adding, "But Hamilton—Mr. Ross—didn't seem mad. Amused, if anything. Anyway, Mr. Johns was rude to everybody."

Nolen's pale eyes narrowed. "You didn't like the victim, Mrs.

Kirchner?"

"Not really. But I certainly didn't kill him."

"Do you know of anyone who might have?"

"No."

"Who else didn't take to him, other than yourself?"

"Probably everyone here." As she recounted Johns's un-friendly exchanges with Koontz and Cunningham, her eyes fell on an arrangement of bottles on a table just past Nolen's shoulder. Obviously old, of all colors and shapes, the collection looked intriguing. She decided to investigate it when she had a chance.

The detective asked about people's movements following dinner, and Millie told what she recalled of each person's. At last he handed her a card, instructed her to phone him if she remembered anything else, and asked her to send in Ross. She got up, then immediately sat again.

"I've remembered something, Detective Nolen. It may not be important."

"Yes?"

"As Brad and I were going outside tonight, we met Vera Peeples coming back in. She seemed out of breath."

He asked a few questions and made notes.

"It probably doesn't mean anything."

His expression gave nothing away. "That all?"

"Yes."

Carrying her plastic, she went into the parlor and gave Hamilton the message, then took a turn through the downstairs, ending up in the deserted dining room. Dishes and cloth had been removed from table and sideboard, and the mahogany surfaces gleamed richly. She stood looking out a window at an eye-level bush outlined by lights from the neighboring house.

Now you've time to think about your new wealth, hon.

The money! She would actually have cash that wasn't already

spent before she got it. She could stop worrying about tuition hikes and Danny's outgrowing his shoes. They could eat out, somewhere besides fast-food places. She might even try to recreate some of the delicious dishes she had enjoyed here, assuming she could find recipes and ingredients.

And college. A half million wouldn't last forever, but she could afford not to work a while, could take a full load of classes. She would certainly get that double major in history and literature. For several minutes, Millie gave herself up to the sheer joy of imagining possibilities.

She stirred, reminding herself not to get carried away. She hadn't actually received any money yet.

Millie visualized the dining room as it had been earlier that evening, filled with people and food. Gilbert Johns had said little during dinner, and then only to fight with his cousin. Clearly he had been a loner, one who hadn't seemed to care about others or their feelings.

Yet he had been a person. One who was now dead.

Questions about that death rattled through her head. Judging from Nolen's queries, he didn't buy Pope's accident theory. A shiver went through her. The death could have been murder. Johns had not been liked by people here, although mere dislike seemed an insufficient motive to kill.

One person here had known the victim before, though. Wes Koontz. Was some unsettled score from the cousins' past behind the drowning? Had seeing Johns again triggered a long-festering rage in Koontz? Had he perhaps contemplated doing away with his cousin for years and chosen to do it here, with other suspects around?

But even with other possible killers about, Millie thought, Koontz still seemed the obvious suspect. And if he had planned to do murder here, surely he'd have had sense enough to hide his enmity towards his victim beforehand.

She paced, repeatedly circling the table while considering the question of opportunity. Koontz had been in the parlor when she and Brad had left the mansion. Then they'd wandered the yard a while before arriving at the pond. And when she'd returned for help, Koontz had been on the patio. If he had come outside just after them, he might have had time to slay Johns, hide among the shrubbery and reappear at the French doors.

But time would have been perilously tight.

Or the murder might have occurred even before Millie and Brad had gone outside. Koontz could have followed his cousin when he left the parlor. She and Hamilton had talked about the genealogy chart for some time before Scott, then Brad, returned.

If not Koontz, then who? Millie had told Nolen about the shoving match between Johns and Cunningham, but she couldn't believe that was the explanation for the death. In fact, Cunningham had had more problems with Koontz than with Johns.

The cousins looked alike, especially in their identical jackets.

Come on, Millie thought. Killing the wrong victim might be a staple of detective fiction, but probably seldom really happened.

Maybe the drowning had begun as a joke, with someone Johns had insulted tossing him into the pond to teach him a lesson. Things could have gotten out of hand and ended up differently than planned.

Millie stroked the satiny dining table, replaying in her mind the experience of finding the victim: the compact body in evening attire, a clump of lilies crushed by his weight; the struggle to pull him out; the discovery he wasn't breathing; the momentary awkwardness about who would give CPR; her rush to summon help; seeing Koontz at the back door; her sprint up the hallway to the office.

Something had been odd about the atmosphere inside the house . . . .

She had it. The quiet. Letitia had been playing the piano when she and Brad had left, but not when she had come back. Where had Letitia gone in the meantime?

"Any food left?" Brad called as he entered and gazed around the dining room. He looked his jaunty, confident self again. "That was a great dinner, but all the excitement's made me hungry again."

"The cupboard's bare—at least the sideboard is. Maybe Fansler can find you something, assuming he's through talking to the police."

"Good idea. Want to join me?"

"Maybe later."

He left. Millie continued to caress the table, seeking answers in its shiny surface. The more she considered who could have murdered Gilbert Johns, the more depressed she felt. As far as she knew, no heir besides herself could be ruled out. Not Koontz, not Ross, not Peeples.

Not Ed Cunningham, who for all she knew had disappeared right after the lottery. Not Eileen, whose movements after being seen in the parlor with Koontz were unknown to Millie.

Not Letitia. And not Scott. Millie hated suspecting her new friends but didn't feel absolutely sure of anyone.

She caught her breath. Not even Brad could be ruled out. He might have sent her for help in order to be alone with Johns—not to revive him, but to make certain he was dead.

★ ★ ★

Too restless for sleep, Millie changed into a T-shirt and shorts, put her soiled dress in the basket provided, and wandered the downstairs hall till both Bennetts hailed her from the parlor.

She went in and joined them at a tea table, nodding to the gray-haired guard beside the keepsakes case. Brad now wore a polo shirt and khaki shorts and smelled of quality cologne. The siblings' amiable smiles convinced Millie that she had been foolish to suspect either.

"Would you care for coffee, Mrs. Kirchner?" the butler offered. "We have both regular and decaffeinated."

"Yes, thanks. Decaf."

While her husband poured, Mrs. Fansler passed fruit bars and brownies. Millie took one of each, thinking that the couple proved the cliché that opposites attract: a balding, spare, impassive man; a dark-haired, plump, sullen woman.

"Great dinner, Mrs. Fansler," Millie said.

"Thank you." The words sounded chilly, automatic.

So much for the fat-jolly stereotype.

Scott peered in from the hall. "Coffee—just what I need. Regular, please. Hi, everyone." Looking relaxed in faded jeans and T-shirt, he moved a chair beside Millie's.

"You okay?" he asked. "Finding Johns must've been awful."

"I'm fine, just sorry we didn't get there sooner."

Brad arched an eyebrow. "I found him, too, you know."

"Aren't lurid crime scenes part of a big lawyer's job?"

"We don't do much criminal work. Anyway, an actual body is . . . different from photos." Brad swallowed hard.

"Sorry. You all right, Bennett?"

"Sure. Just didn't want you taking me for granted."

"How could I? Your ego's like a flashing arrow pointed directly at you."

"Behave, boys." Letitia laid a hand on Scott's arm. "You'll want to buy some new clothes now. I'd be glad to help you shop."

Millie sipped coffee, wondering if Letitia's interest in Scott was genuine or if flirting was second nature to her.

"How long have you two worked for Pope?" Brad asked the Fanslers.

"Twenty-three years, sir," the butler said.

"Don't say. You have a child, I believe?"

"One son, sir."

"How old?"

"Twenty-nine, sir."

"Where is he? What does he do?"

Fansler glanced at his wife, whose lips seemed to set more tightly with each personal question Brad asked.

"Frederick's currently in Chicago, sir," the butler replied, setting both carafes on a cart with the cookies. "He recently accepted employment with a moving company. Now, if you will please excuse me." Bowing, he followed his wife out.

"Wait'll my friends hear I got questioned in a murder investigation, guys," Letitia said, rolling her violet eyes.

Brad popped a bite of brownie into his mouth and dusted crumbs from his hands. "That was interesting. A grilling by police ought to be part of law-school curriculum. Gives you a different perspective." He asked what Millie had told the detective, and nodded at her response. "Good, sounds like our stories jibed."

"I was asked if Gilbert and I got along as roommates." Scott grinned. "That was fun to answer."

"I'm glad I didn't have to tell about Wes Koontz and me," Brad said. "Neatnik jerk."

"He doesn't seem very broken up over his cousin's death, does he?" Millie remarked. "Has he said anything to any of you about it?"

"I heard him tell someone that Johns would deliberately 'forget' to take his antidepressant," Brad offered. "Wes's theory? That Gilbert got the blues and killed himself."

"Suicide doesn't seem very likely," Millie objected. "Not just after learning about a big legacy. Besides, he didn't act depressed after dinner, just annoyed. And annoying."

Scott nodded. "I saw him come outside. He looked more thoughtful than sad."

Brad smiled in a superior way. "Don't expect logical behavior from a clinically depressed person."

"It seems an odd method to choose, too," Millie went on. "Drowning yourself in a shallow pool?"

"So the death was a freak accident, like Pope said." Letitia yawned. "I'm going to bed. It's been a long day."

They trooped to the front stairs and started up, Scott saying he'd found an Alexander Hamilton biography in the library to read. Millie decided a browse among books sounded relaxing, so she bid them goodnight and went to the library.

She found it deserted, folding chairs removed, tables and easy chairs rearranged. In a glass-fronted bookcase, she saw works from Nathan Henry's day, mostly travelogues and sermon collections. In other cases, novels, poetry, and manuals about various hobbies spoke of former residents' interests. Alcove shelves held books on antiques, biographies, recountings of military campaigns, and other historical works, many of which she had seen in her college library.

In a section on Benjamin Franklin, a book of the famous patriot's correspondence caught her eye.

"Eighteenth-century letters ought to put me to sleep."

As Millie went upstairs with her find, a wave of homesickness swept over her. She longed to hear Danny's voice, to tell Sylva all about her day. But even allowing for the one-hour time difference, it was far too late to phone.

In the bedroom Letitia stood brushing her silky curls, wearing a lavender gown and peignoir that must have cost the earth. She smiled.

"How about our relatives, roomie? Isn't Ed Cunningham

awful? And don't you shudder when Wes looks at you?"

"Yes, to both. Still, I'm glad to have relatives." She took her sketch pad from a washstand drawer, sat in the chair, and with quick strokes drew a Superwoman's body topped with a benevolent-looking crone's head.

Letitia crawled into bed and creamed her face. "I do wish there were more handsome men here besides my brother. Maybe if I can get Scott to buy decent clothes . . . ."

Annoyed for no reason she could pinpoint, Millie flipped the page and did another caricature. Letitia put away her face cream and leaned over Millie's shoulder. Seeing the drawing of a pig, snout in trough, fleshy neck and body encased in tight men's clothing, she shrieked.

"Cunningham! You're good, roomie."

Millie showed her the sketch of Peeples, and Letitia gurgled with delight.

"This got me into trouble in junior high," Millie confided. "Teachers took exception to my portraits of them. But I became creative about hiding places." She added touches to both drawings, put the pad away, and prepared for bed.

Letitia got paper and pen from her purse, scribbled intently, then announced, "Guess what, roomie? We'll each get about thirty thousand more from Gilbert Johns's share."

Millie didn't reply. Though she hadn't liked the victim, it seemed ghoulish to estimate the profit from his death. She turned to the first Franklin letter and read, imagining him seated at his desk, bifocals on nose, searching for just the right word.

But a different vision kept blotting that one out: a picture of a small corpse, wearing soggy evening clothes.

★ Chapter Nine

Little Millie jumped up and down in helpless anguish on the shore of White Rock Lake in Dallas. Her mother swam desperately across it, barely ahead of a pursuing shark that snapped at her heels. Razor-sharp teeth clacked ominously together, like someone rapping on a table.

"Miss Bennett, Mrs. Kirchner, breakfast will be served in half an hour."

Millie stirred. Where was she? What had happened to the shark? To her mother?

She opened her eyes, saw she was in bed, and realized the tapping sound in her dream had been a maid's knocking on the bedroom door. As the previous night's events rushed back into her consciousness, she groaned.

"Up and at 'em, roomie." Letitia playfully yanked the covers off. Bright-eyed, already coiffed, and dressed in a soft gray top and slacks, she stood above Millie, a picture framed by the bed canopy.

Never a morning person, and especially after such a brief sleep, Millie reluctantly rose and dragged herself over to the wardrobe. While she groped for a sleeveless shirt and shorts, Letitia smoothed bedcovers and prattled about how much she loved the early part of the day.

Murder under some circumstances made sense, Millie thought uncharitably.

She quickly bathed and dressed. Then she and Letitia went down to the dining room. The executors again sat at both ends of the long table, with Ross sitting near Pope and Peeples beside Endicott. A chair had been removed from one side, apparently to make the deceased heir's absence less noticeable.

"Good morning, Miss Bennett, Mrs. Kirchner!" Pope's heartiness sounded forced, and his face appeared strained and puffy. "Help yourselves to the buffet."

That yellow jumpsuit he's wearing makes him look like a giant lemon.

Millie stifled a giggle. She and Letitia filled plates from the plentiful assortment on the sideboard and sat near Ross. Moments later, Brad and Scott entered, greeted everyone, helped themselves liberally to food, and sat across from Millie and Letitia. Table talk concerned food, especially the scrapple many were trying for the first time.

Koontz stumbled in, got coffee, took a chair by Letitia and tried a weakly flirtatious smile. She didn't acknowledge him. His lip was indeed swollen, Millie saw.

Eileen and Cunningham appeared and heaped plates, he wearing a smirk, she looking half-guilty, half-defiant. Peeples beckoned, indicating an empty chair beside her, but Eileen circled the table and sat across from Ross.

"Look at the breakfast buddies I get stuck with," Cunningham said in a loud undertone as he dropped into the remaining seat between Peeples and Brad.

"Good, everyone's here," Pope said in his determinedly cheerful tone. "I trust everyone slept well in spite of last evening's tragedy."

"Yeah, a guy dropping dead on the premises sure brings on

the shut-eye." Cunningham shoved a hunk of toast into his mouth and leaned back, boxy shirt gaping at his belly.

Several said they had had trouble sleeping.

"Did my restlessness bother you, Hamilton?" Scott asked.

"Not at all," Ross said. "I hope I didn't snore. My wife says I do when I'm overly tired."

"Nope. You were fine."

Pope paused in raising his fork to his mouth. "I thought you were rooming with Mr. Cunningham, Mr. Ross."

"I changed," the educator said matter-of-factly. "Scott had no one with him after Mr. Johns . . . died."

"Fine by me," said Cunningham. "What Ross has might've rubbed off on me. Or is he color-fast?" He leaned around Brad to grin at Eileen.

She smiled uncertainly.

Pope sputtered, "Really, Mr. Cunningham—simple courtesy—"

"Don't bother, Mr. Pope," Ross said. "My new roommate and I have much in common. Intelligence, for instance."

Apparently unfazed, Cunningham said, "I like not having a roomie. Never know when somebody'll want to stay over."

Eileen blushed and seemed unsure where to look. But she rallied and leaned towards Millie. "What you gonna spend your money on, Sharmilla?"

"Millie, please. I need a car and may buy a house. But I won't spend it all at once." The discussion seemed academic just now, with the drowning and its cause looming like a thundercloud over all they did.

"I'm gonna buy clothes—lots. And get a new acting coach. I don't think the one I have is much good."

"Did you do any performing in high school?"

"A couple plays, and one in community the-ate-er since. People said I was great. I waitressed in Lubbock awhile, but figured I better make it in Hollywood before I completely lose my looks." Eileen self-consciously touched her neck, where a double chin had begun to form, and lowered her voice. "Ed knows Stephen Spielberg. He's gonna get me in one of his films."

If he knows Spielberg, I'm the next big rock star.

At a sound across the table, Millie turned. Peeples was trying to lean around Cunningham towards Eileen, but he thrust his bulk forward, blocking her. She flashed him a look of pure hatred. He grinned.

Pope announced that the group would tour the mansion that morning and nearby Independence National Historical Park in the afternoon. Millie's mood, already helped by food and coffee, lightened.

"A cool front came through overnight," the executor went on, "so we should have a pleasant stroll to the Park."

"Walking?" Koontz moaned. "Shit."

"Great, I can use the exercise," Peeples said.

"Now Mr. Endicott has an announcement," Pope said.

All eyes turned to the banker. He deliberately folded his napkin and laid it beside his plate before speaking.

"I wasn't able to post the list of numbers and keepsakes right after the lottery as promised. The meeting must've lasted longer than expected—my secretary didn't answer when I phoned the office. Later, of course, Mr. Johns's death drove such thoughts from my mind. But I'll call her this morning and get the information."

"More delay, huh?" Cunningham said. "We ever gonna find out what we won?"

"Certainly," Endicott said stiffly. His eyes turned steely. "And let me say, Mr. Cunningham, that being an heir conveys no license to be disrespectful to fellow legatees or to the executors. Arthur may be unwilling to dismiss you from this gathering, but I feel no such compunction."

"What's all them fancy words mean, banker?"

"Be polite or leave."

Cunningham snorted, but resumed eating.

About time Vulgar Vern got some of his own back.

"Thank you, Soames," the attorney said with a grateful smile. "One other thing, ladies and gentlemen . . . ." He hesitated, a flush tinging his cheeks. "There's an amethyst snuff bottle missing from the display in the sitting room. I'm sure someone took it as a joke. But it's part of the household inventory meant for the museum that will be here once this gathering ends. We must have it back right away."

Strange prank, Millie thought. Who would even notice such an item missing, except Pope or a servant? The sitting room had been occupied for interviews all last evening, but maybe she could examine that collection some time today.

The announcement over, Pope brightened and rose. "Follow me, ladies and gentlemen. We'll begin downstairs."

They went next door to the kitchen, Brad walking with Millie, Scott and Letitia following. Mrs. Fansler, her hands floury from rolling pastry dough, nodded coldly as they entered. Pope pointed out the latest in food-preparation and storage equipment, then started towards a closed door at one side of the big room.

"Both the kitchen and adjoining servants' apartment—" At a glare from the cook, he did a quick about-face. "But we needn't invade the Fanslers' private quarters . . . ."

"What Arthur started to say," Endicott said smoothly, "is that all this area was originally a large conservatory. Meals in Mr. Henry's day were prepared in a detached kitchen some distance from the house to lessen fire hazard."

Pope led the way to the sitting room, where he pointed out a portrait of Prudence Henry, Nathan's wife, a sweet-faced but simple-looking woman. Millie drifted to the table that held the crescent-shaped grouping of bottles and fingered one beside a gap where the amethyst one must have sat.

Then they moved next door to the office, where the attorney reverently pointed out a two-section chest filled with cubbyholes. "Mr. Henry especially valued this paper press. It was a gift to him from his wife and children."

"Why didn't he make that one of the keepsakes?" Brad asked, as he touched the cabinet's glowing surface. "It'd look great in my office. One of the partners uses antiques. Says they give the place class."

"It is lovely," Endicott agreed. "But Mr. Henry must've felt a bulky piece like this would be too hard to transport, especially if its new owner came from a great distance."

In the main hall, Pope pointed to the largest portrait, that of a corpulent, bewigged gentleman who looked smug and self-satisfied. "Nathan Henry himself," he said proudly.

A prig. Just the way I pictured him.

In the parlor, a uniformed brunet now guarded the keepsakes. Pope instructed the heirs to take chairs and stood in lecturing mode in the center of the room.

"This mansion was built in 1768–69 by Robert Smith, the carpenter-architect who also did Benjamin Franklin's house—which sadly didn't survive to the present—and Carpenters' Hall in Independence Park. This house and the grounds are much as they were in Nathan Henry's day, except for needed modernization and the sale of several acres necessitated by the actions of one Chauncey Watson—a nineteenth-century Henry descendant and, frankly, a scoundrel.

"Watson sold furnishings and did unauthorized remodeling to get payoffs from architects and builders. Happily, his changes were reversible, and much of the furniture was recovered. But those costs nearly wiped out the maintenance fund. This was prime property even then, however. The land fetched an excellent price."

Millie's eyelids drooped, the result of too little sleep, a warm room, a dull speaker, and a familiar tale she had heard from Endicott. When Pope paused, she started guiltily. Glancing around, she saw others yawning.

"What happens to the maintenance account now?" asked Brad.

"It goes to the city along with this house." The lawyer went on to speak glowingly of what the new museum would mean for historians.

Cunningham sighed heavily, rose, and began to pace. Others openly fidgeted. Pope stopped mid-sentence. Apparently abandoning whatever else he had meant to say, he gestured up at a white plaster ring several feet in diameter, centering the pale blue expanse overhead.

"Something you may not have noticed last night is this unusual wedding-ring ceiling. Also, the drawing on that wall is the builder's original rendering of the house. Besides being a prominent Colonial architect, Smith was active in the Revolutionary cause, so the sketch is valuable in itself."

"I can't believe I didn't notice that rendering yesterday," Letitia breathed into Millie's ear as they followed him into the hall. "I may sneak that out in my luggage."

She brought enough suitcases to carry off half the house.

Pope led them along the main hallway into the stairway hall, passing a painting of a woman wearing a gray stuff dress, a black shawl, and a forbidding expression. Brad nudged Letitia.

"Clearly you're related to that lovely creature, sis."

She made a face at him.

"That's Hepzibah Henry," Pope explained with a smile. "One of Nathan's two unmarried daughters who lived in the mansion just after his death."

"Miss Hepzibah Henry was quite a religious woman,"

Endicott said dryly. "But perhaps not a happy one."

On the second floor they saw the gallery, an expanse of hardwood floor with chairs and tables along both sides, used in earlier days for receptions and balls. Then came Pope's apartment, consisting of sitting room, bedroom-study, and bath, all in earth tones. A tan telephone sat on a bedside table. Millie noticed it had two lines, one the same number as the office phone. She guessed the other was private.

"Most of this furniture's mine," the executor said with obvious pride. "It's all of the same period as the house. A few things are copies, but very good ones."

Ross caressed the piecrust edge of a table and knelt to inspect its base. "Fluted column rising from carved urn on the shaft, C-rolled arch on the leg. Genuine. Made in Philadelphia, around . . . 1760?"

The attorney clapped his hands. "Well done! You know your antiques, Mr. Ross. Do you have one like it yourself?"

"No, but I've been admiring one in a shop." Ross rose, a grin lighting his pleasant features. "Now I can buy it."

Next door they saw a smaller suite currently occupied by Endicott, neat yet without the personal touches of a long-time occupant seen in Pope's.

The lawyer opened another door, then shut it quickly, but not before Millie had seen inside. Discarded clothes littered floor and furniture, and the tumbled bed looked as if wildebeests had mated there.

"I'm dreadfully sorry if I've embarrassed you, Mr. Cunningham," a pink-faced Pope said. "I'd assumed the maid had attended to all the rooms up here."

"Don't bother me," Cunningham said, grinning at Eileen. "We had a good time here last night, didn't we, doll?"

She looked at the floor.

"These rooms all have interesting characteristics," Pope said hurriedly, "but if anyone doesn't want his shown, please let me know."

No one spoke. Most moved on after the executors, but Millie noticed Eileen hung back and slipped into Cunningham's room. Millie heard drawers open and close, as if Eileen was looking for something.

Most rooms fell somewhere between the sloppiness of Cunningham's and the rigid tidiness of that shared by Brad and Koontz. All had period furnishings, though some were very plain—brought from the third floor, Pope said, to replace things Watson had sold that could not be reclaimed. In Millie's and Letitia's room, he opened the deception bed, saying it was an excellent example of its type.

At the rear of the building, the attorney noted that the back steps between the second and third floors were temporarily closed, awaiting replacement of a broken stair. He led the group back to the front staircase and up to the third level.

"As you'll see," he said, "the rooms up here are no longer used except for storage. In Mr. Henry's day, they would've been occupied by servants and poor relations."

They saw a prim governess's room and adjoining nursery, where wooden soldiers and tin wagons sat beside cloth and wax dolls. Then they peered into several rooms full of broken furniture, tools and other discards.

"The family didn't throw things away," Pope said in an understatement. "Perhaps Mr. Henry's preserving the keepsakes influenced them. Or maybe there's a 'pack-rat gene' in your heritage." He smiled at the feeble jest. "I've glanced through the stored items, and most aren't valuable. I just wish . . . ." He colored, then finished lamely, "They'll be examined thoroughly when the city takes over, of course."

Reaching the back of the house, he opened the last door.

Millie's jaw dropped. Luggage filled the room: huge steamer

trunks, serviceable valises, dainty cosmetic cases, stacked on the floor and in shelves lining the walls. Some items were battered and torn, others in excellent condition, as if cherished by their owners. All had a dusty, abandoned look.

The lawyer chuckled. "These didn't all belong to the Nathan Henrys, or even to later generations of the family. Can anyone guess why others' bags would be stored here?"

"Who cares?" Koontz said, brushing lint from his navy trousers. "I hate this dusty place."

"Bet I know," Scott said. "People used to make long visits— weeks, even months—when they had to come a long way."

"Oh, you're right," Millie said. "And some visitors probably died here?"

"Exactly!" Pope said in delight. "If no one claimed their baggage, it ended up here. Well done, you two."

"Big deal," Cunningham muttered. "For once I'm with you, Koontz." He left, the smaller man following. Others trailed out, too, leaving Pope, Ross and Millie in the room.

"Could I possibly look through the stored things while I'm here?" Ross said. "With one of you executors present, of course. I'd love to see what was saved over the years."

The lawyer's eyes widened with something like alarm. He shook his head. "It'll be a busy week, I'm afraid."

"Then could I return before the mansion goes to the city, and bring my wife? Alice would love to see it."

Pope hesitated. "Newark *is* close. Yes, bring her, do. But as for looking through . . . ." He paused, seemed to reach a decision. "We may be able to work something out." The men left, chatting about possibilities for a future visit.

Alone, Millie imagined herself a governess bringing her bag here for storage, while listening for sounds of quarreling from the nursery. Then she saw herself as a lady's maid come to search trunks for a certain gown, to be cleaned and pressed for an upcoming ball.

But as she absorbed the atmosphere, spectral visitors seemed to watch her, wraiths of unrealized hopes and plans imprisoned in dead owners' unclaimed luggage. She decided that the next time Danny begged for a ghost story, she would describe this eerie place.

Chapter Ten

The three walked down the front stairs, Ross stopping at the second floor to go to his room, Millie and Pope continuing to the first. At the bottom, they met Fansler.

"Sir," he said to the attorney, "there's a reporter here from the *Philadelphia Tribune* asking to talk with the heirs. I said he'd need to see you. He's in the library."

"The *Tribune?*" Millie said. "I thought the *Inquirer* was your big daily."

"It is," Pope said with a sigh. "I gave their man an interview and convinced him not to bother you heirs. The *Tribune* is a weekly that does restaurant reviews and pieces on locally prominent people. I'll talk to the fellow."

Millie went to the office and dialed Jeff's number. She had delayed calling in case the boys were sleeping late, but now got no answer. At loose ends, she went to look at the bottle collection. In the sitting room she found Peeples perched on a love seat, staring with defeated eyes at the assembled glassware. When Millie said hello, Peeples flinched and looked up, startled.

"You seem worried, Miss Peeples." Millie touched her shoulder. "What's wrong?"

"I—of course I'm upset. Someone died here last night."

"Besides that, I mean. You don't look well."

Peeples pressed her lips together, then spoke. "I guess I'm not. The rich food . . . the excitement . . . ."

"Perhaps you should rest before lunch."

"Maybe." She didn't move.

Millie examined the bottles, whose hues ranged from aquamarine to cobalt to amber. Labels pasted on or embedded in the glass said they had held substances as varied as bluing, stove polish, and massage cream. The oldest dated from 1870. Millie wondered if the snuff bottle was older and more valuable, also why the thief hadn't rearranged the remaining bottles to hide the theft. She frowned.

"That's the second bottle that's disappeared here. Gilbert Johns lost some pills yesterday." She glanced up, saw the other woman looked ashen. "You really aren't well, are you? Shall I get you some water?"

"No, I'm—all right . . . but maybe—I'll go to my room for a while." She left.

Soon, Fansler entered. "Mrs. Kirchner, Mr. Pope has decided to let individual heirs decide about speaking to Mr. Judd. If you wish to do so, he's in the library."

Millie considered. Maybe she could learn something from the reporter about how the police were viewing the drowning. If he became obnoxious, she could end the interview. She entered the library, where a slender man about her age lolled in a wing chair, running a hand through unkempt red curls. He jumped up and offered her a hand.

"Sharmilla Kirchner? Philip Judd, *Philadelphia Trib.*"

"Millie, please. Hello, Mr. Judd." They shook hands and sat in facing chairs. Millie noticed her feet didn't quite touch the floor. For the first time, it struck her that all the mansion's seating was unusually tall.

"You found Mr. Johns in the pool?" Judd's voice was thin

and reedy, his tone friendly.

"Mr. Bennett and I did, yes."

He asked knowledgeable questions and jotted illegible-looking notes on a steno pad, squirming almost constantly the while. Finally, he paused, gave her an appraising look.

"How'd you feel about Gilbert Johns, Millie?"

"I hadn't known him long enough to feel much of anything."

Judd drummed a palm on his thigh. "Impressions, then. How'd he strike you?"

She shrugged. "Seemed uninterested in the rest of us."

"A hermit type?" He scratched the back of his neck.

She nodded.

"How'd he and his cousin—Koontz—get along?"

"Not very well."

Judd asked about the victim's relations with other heirs. Millie responded noncommittally. Though she hadn't liked Johns, she saw no need to trash him in the media. The reporter kneaded an eye, blinked several times, changed hands, and rubbed the other eye.

"What's your view of the death, Millie? Accidental?"

"I'm not sure. People *can* drown in shallow water . . . ."

"How about suicide?"

"Mr. Johns hadn't seemed depressed. What do you think? Does it sound like suicide to you?"

"Nope."

"Do the police think it was?"

"They don't tell me their thoughts." Judd grinned, a likable grimace. "You strike me as an intelligent woman, Millie."

"Thanks."

"How do I impress you?"

"Like someone who wants a story, Mr. Judd."

"Call me Fij."

"Fij?"

"My childhood nickname stuck." He ran a hand through his curls. "My middle name's Irving, and Fij is my sister's version of my initials. Plus, I was fidgety as a kid."

Was? Give me a break.

Judd hitched his chair closer and lowered his voice. "Screwy will your ancestor made. His execs took pains to avoid publicity over the years, but I unearthed it when I did a piece on early Philadelphians and their current-day descendants. Quite a haul, that savings account."

"Your article must've been the one Detective Nolen mentioned seeing."

"Had to be. I was the only one who covered the legacy story early on. 'Course now that Johns has kicked, other reporters are interested." He meticulously straightened a pants leg. "It was great local-feature stuff even without the drowning. I'd planned to interview all you guys anyway. Now with the murder . . . ."

"That hasn't been established, has it? Is there something you haven't told me?"

"Come on, Millie, I said you were smart." He uncrossed his legs and re-crossed them. "The possibility—likelihood—can't have escaped you."

She didn't reply. He asked about her life in Dallas and got brief responses. Finally, he thanked her and asked her to send in another heir.

"Any particular one?"

"Surprise me. I'll talk to them all eventually."

In the parlor she found Scott debating the comparative merits of the Denver Broncos and the Philadelphia Eagles with the dark-haired guard. Noticing how the dark red of Scott's shirt brought out his dark brown eyes, she passed on the message.

"The press," Scott said, eyebrows raised. "I might've known."

"Suit yourself about talking to him." She smiled. "He has no subpoena power."

Grinning at her comment, Scott left. Millie turned to the young guard.

"Must be boring, watching a cabinet all day."

He shrugged politely. "Beats being outside on a day like yesterday."

"Is it nice today? I haven't been out yet."

"Must be ten-twelve degrees cooler, at least."

"Great." Millie studied the keepsakes through their protective glass, visualizing the Henry family seated together in this room. Self-important Nathan sat in the salmon easy chair, the keepsake candlestand and a lit taper beside him as he read the letter from his acquaintance, Franklin. On the yellow silk sofa, scrawny Hepzibah made a misstitch on her sampler, and Mother Prudence made her take it out. At the mahogany card table, middle son Benjamin pored over the map of Pennsylvania, the Wedgwood bowl filled with flowers at his elbow.

Behind Millie, someone cleared his throat. She turned.

"Detective Nolen would like to speak with you, madam," Fansler said. "He's in the office with Mr. Pope."

When she reached the office, the executor had left. Nolen stood alone at the desk. He and Millie sat, and he took her back over her statement of the previous evening, concentrating on her recollections of others' movements. She guessed he was trying to clear up discrepancies between versions. When he closed his notebook, she asked a question.

"Do you think Mr. Johns was murdered, Detective Nolen?"

"We haven't ruled anything out yet, Mrs. Kirchner. Either out or in."

She had known he wouldn't tell her. But something in his expression suggested murder had been ruled more "in" than "out."

★ ★ ★

When Millie returned to the parlor, she found Koontz, Peeples, Eileen, and Cunningham studying a list on a wall beside the keepsakes cabinet. Joining them, she read:

1. Map of early Pennsylvania
2. Wedgwood bowl
3. Benjamin Franklin letter
4. Set of samplers
5. Walnut candlestand
6. Silver inkstand
7. Pennsylvania rifle
8. Elizabeth Ross quilt
9. Ivory miniature

"Oh," Peeples said in a small voice. She appeared less ill than earlier, though still pale.

"Not bad, not bad at all," Cunningham said, folding his fleshy arms and rocking on his heels.

"What'd you get?" Eileen asked. "Oh, I forgot, we can't tell. Poo!"

He winked as if to imply they could work something out.

"Anybody know what Gilbert had?" she went on. "If it was a number, we ought to draw again. That'd give the ones that got cut out another chance."

"A second lottery!" Peeples gave her roommate a quick hug. "That's a great idea!"

"What makes you think we'd agree to that?" Cunningham slid an arm around Eileen's waist to pull her away. "People who have numbers won't risk losing them. Forget it, babe. It ain't gonna happen."

She shook off the arm. "People with dollar signs should get a chance, at least. Anybody know if he had a number?"

No one spoke.

"Whoever got the quilt," Peeples said eagerly, "I want to

buy or trade for it. I got something good, myself."

"Yeah, what?" Cunningham said.

"You know I can't say now."

"Then screw you, you old bag."

Peeples narrowed her eyes, drew back a beefy arm and slapped him hard. "I've heard about enough out of you. And stop hanging around this sweet woman, you horrid man."

Cunningham staggered, caught a chairback, and steadied himself. With a snarl, he flung himself at Peeples, caught both her hands, and thrust his face near hers.

"Touch me again, you'll go outa here feet first yourself."

She yanked away her hands. The two stared at each other. Then she said quietly but firmly, "You're the one who'd better watch his back."

Good thing Endicott insisted on politeness. Otherwise I'd think I heard cross words just now.

"Vera . . . Ed . . . ." Hands to mouth, Eileen looked from one to the other.

Koontz laughed aloud. "What a bunch of losers." He grinned at Millie and added, "All except you, sweet stuff." He strutted from the room, whistling under his breath.

Millie followed, leaving Peeples and Cunningham trading insults, and collected the book of letters from her room. Returning downstairs and finding the sitting-room empty, she sat in a needlepoint-upholstered chair to read. Minutes later, Ross entered, carrying a large book. He took a seat on a nearby sofa and glanced at the cover of Millie's.

"Ben Franklin, eh? Quite a fellow, wasn't he?"

"I still can't believe a relative of mine knew him, buddies or not." She noticed the title of Ross's volume. "You seem to know all about antiques already."

He frowned. "Not everything. In fact, when I looked at the keepsakes just now, something surprised me. Think I'll research it a little." He leafed through the tome.

Marking her place, Millie shut her book. "I'm curious about something, Hamilton. When Brad and I met you last night, you were coming from the pool area. Didn't you see Gilbert Johns lying there?"

"No. I must've passed within feet of him, but I was deep in thought, wondering what Alice would be doing."

"And you didn't see anyone else around?"

"No. The police questioned me repeatedly about that."

"You and your wife must be close. I envy that."

"She's a wonderful woman." He smiled fondly. "I should phone her, but I can't decide whether to mention the drowning or not. It would worry her, I'm sure."

Brad came in and asked Millie to join him in a game of table tennis against Letitia and Scott.

"I'm rusty, but I'll play." She put down her book.

Ross laid his beside hers, saying he would watch.

When the three entered the game room, Letitia stood beside the Ping-Pong table chattering to Scott, who listlessly bounced a ball on the tile floor.

"The guy had trunks of money," she was saying, "but no taste whatsoever. He insisted on displaying his ceramic pigs— hundreds of them—all over the house. I ask you . . . ."

Ross took a seat at the card table beside Eileen. She smiled at him. Peeples, her opponent at checkers, nodded curtly. As Millie took her place, she caught phrases of the women's conversation.

From Peeples: ". . . not good enough . . . your whole life ahead . . . ."

From Eileen: ". . . maybe not as young's you think. . . ."

Scott slashed a vicious serve into Millie's quadrant. She barely managed to return it.

"Look alive there, partner!" Brad said with a frown. Then

he winked at her and mouthed, "That's okay."

He proved to be a fast, competitive player but a demanding partner, his frequent "coaching" comments adding to Millie's nervousness. She found her skills returning, however, making her competent though clumsy. Letitia was an able player, only a bit slow in reacting. Scott, surprisingly adept and graceful, accepted her occasional lapses cheerfully. The score changed sides often, at last tying at game point.

Millie served, dropping the ball barely over the net. Scott reached for it but missed.

"You've just been toying with us till now." His broad grin belied the accusation. "Pretending you were no good."

"Yep, I set you up." She smiled back.

Several serves and returns later, Brad smashed the ball at Scott, who drove it hard at Millie. It glanced off the table, but she caught it with a backhand. It struck the edge on the other side and bounced past Letitia.

"We win!" Brad yelled, hugging Millie to him. "What a team we are."

"Luck had something to do with it," she said, politely extricating herself.

"Luck had everything to do with it," Scott teased. "Good game, everybody. Even if Millie turned out to be a hustler."

"Not a very good one, since we weren't playing for money," she said, returning his grin. She wiped perspiration from her brow, thinking that the game might have been even more fun if she'd partnered with Scott, who seemed less invested in winning than Brad.

Koontz entered, face flushed and perspiring. He got a soft drink from the refrigerator and joined the trio at the card table.

"Been walking?" Eileen asked, eyes on the checkerboard. "Thought you didn't like that."

"This was different. I was checking the value of something."

Koontz smiled smugly at Ross. "You were wrong. I can do much better than you said."

"I assume you mean by selling a keepsake," Ross said coolly. "I did warn you I wasn't an appraiser."

Peeples's hand hesitated on a checker. "Remember, I want first chance at the quilt."

"Will you shut up about that quilt?" Koontz touched the frosty can to his cheek. Ignoring her dark look, he addressed Ross. "I found a dealer that knows somebody who's in the market for exactly what I drew."

"Congratulations. I'm sure you'll get everything that's coming to you." Sarcasm rumbled in Ross's voice.

"Hey . . . ." A streak of color crept up Koontz's neck. "You know—somebody said you were by the pool when Gilbert—" He pointed an accusatory finger. "You killed him, didn't you?"

Ross pushed the hand aside. "Ridiculous." He bent to examine the checkerboard, dismissing the conversation.

Peeples watched both men with open dislike. "If he didn't kill him, you did," she told Koontz icily. "You and your cousin obviously hated each other."

Koontz slammed his soft drink onto the table, spraying her with dark liquid.

"Bitch! For once, Gilbert was right. He said you looked like a thousand-year-old hippo and behaved like a whiny brat. I hope that quilt rots before you get your hands on it."

Nope, no incivility here.

"That's uncalled for, Mr. Koontz," Ross said. "You owe the lady an apology."

"I can fight my own battles, thank you," Peeples told her defender, wiping cola from her forearm.

A bell sounded for lunch. They all trooped from the room.

Nothing like a nice aperitif of vitriol to whet the appetite.

★ *Chapter Eleven*

Over hearty oxtail soup—another food Millie was enjoying for the first time—and salad, Pope told more about the Henry family. Nathan's grandson John, he said, was a city leader when the water system that ended a string of yellow-fever epidemics was built. Later individuals included an abolitionist in the 1830's and her great-nephew, Ross's slaveholder ancestor.

"The Henrys, like many families of the period, were sharply divided on the slavery issue," the executor noted.

He and Ross discussed the point at length, Millie and Scott occasionally joining in. Most others at least feigned interest. Cunningham stared pointedly out a window. Pope finished his lecture, then paused and looked embarrassed.

"Ahem . . . .This may seem a small thing to all of you—but a . . . a salt cellar's missing from the kitchen. Mrs. Fansler is sure it was there before our tour today.

"She thinks—ahem—someone took it as a prank. I'm asked to say she'd appreciate your—er—bringing it back."

The heirs looked at one another.

"Who'd steal that?" Brad said. "She must've misplaced it."

Cunningham made a fright mask of his face. "Tell the old biddy I'll come get the pepper shaker, too, if she's not careful."

Endicott gave him a warning look.

"Mrs. Fansler is proprietary about her kitchen," Pope said. "We don't want ill feelings about such a small item, but this thievery—joking or whatever—must stop."

Another bottle, Millie thought. Medicine, snuff, now salt. What was going on?

After lunch the group gathered cameras and sunglasses and set out, the executors and Ross striding together in the lead, Koontz trudging gloomily at the rear. Letitia, chattering nonstop, held onto Scott's arm. Brad walked with Millie, swinging an elegant leather camera case and telling her how the legacy would improve his life.

The day was overcast and cool, a strong breeze whipping Millie's ponytail. Passing restored brick and stone houses on the way east towards the Delaware River, she felt excited and eager. In a short while, she would see sights she had only read about in books, places where rebellious colonists had debated their relationship with a king, signed a fateful declaration, forged a constitution . . . .

Her train of thought was broken as snatches of intense whispering reached her from behind. ". . . been thinking . . . steal my bracelet? . . . real mean . . . give it back!"

Millie turned. Eileen, pink Spandex pants glowing in the sun, was waving a slender wrist in Cunningham's face.

"Got no idea what you mean." He batted her hand away.

Eileen whimpered. Peeples, trotting behind them, grabbed Cunningham's arm and wrenched it behind his back.

"Ow! You old witch!"

"Hit her again, and I'll kill you." The words were low, almost conversational, but firm.

"Aw, don't take it personal," Cunningham said. "I didn't hurt her. We're tight, aren't we, lover?"

Eileen looked uncertain. "It—didn't sting bad, Vera. Let him go. You're not my mom or anything."

Reluctantly, Peeples released the arm. A triumphant Cunningham folded Eileen's hand in his big paw. Millie glanced at the executors, but they were talking with Ross and didn't appear to have heard the exchange.

A bracelet, she thought. Had Eileen been searching for that earlier in Cunningham's room? Another item missing, not a bottle this time, probably not valuable monetarily. But who was committing the thefts, and why? Cunningham, maybe, trying to stir up trouble?

It would be in character.

Just past Front Street, the party crossed over busy Interstate 95 and reached Penn's Landing. Pope pointed out the spot where William Penn had stepped ashore in 1682. The attorney waved an arm towards the area's various museums and attractions, saying they hadn't time to see these now but that they might like to return individually.

"The Workshop on the Water's my favorite," he added. "They still build boats the old-fashioned way there."

Brad snapped Millie's picture in front of the workshop, which he and Scott made a pact to tour later. They retraced their steps west past Front and strolled along Walnut Street to Second, where Pope showed them City Tavern, a reconstruction of the famous gathering spot of Revolutionary leaders. They entered Independence National Historical Park through a hedge around the perimeter, passed several historic buildings and paused at a spire-topped structure fronted by a cobblestone court.

"Carpenters' Hall," Pope said reverently, "is where the First Continental Congress met. The architect-contractor members of the Carpenters' Company were among the most active supporters of the Revolution."

"Big deal," Cunningham said. "Ancient history."

"History's precisely the point, Mr. Cunningham," Endicott

said evenly. "None of us would be here without it, in more than one sense."

Nodding appreciatively at his colleague, Pope resumed his lecture. Only Millie, Ross, and Scott appeared interested, however. Eileen worked at a cobblestone with the toe of a gold slipper, Letitia eyed a group of nearby college-age men, Brad and Peeples took pictures, Cunningham leaned against a wall, and Koontz stood with arms folded and eyes closed. Millie suspected Nathan Henry would be scandalized by his heirs' lack of enthusiasm for their heritage.

Among those thronging Carpenters' Court stood a rangy man in a gray suit, surreptitiously watching the Henry party. When he turned towards Millie, she recognized the heavy chin and thin brow. Winston Akers, the antiques dealer. This couldn't be mere coincidence. But what was he doing here? As Pope led the group into Independence Hall, he followed and joined the same tour group they did.

Millie and the others followed the young woman in the gray-and-green National Park Rangers uniform. In a long hallway, Millie visualized a breathless messenger, wig awry, stock tie flapping, racing along the passage to bring war news to the Second Continental Congress. In the Assembly Room, she imagined James Madison and Gouverneur Morris conferring in whispers over wording of a Constitution article, while calm, regal George Washington presided in the Rising Sun chair.

"Check out that inkstand," Scott murmured behind Millie. "Looks just like Henry's."

Jolted back to the present, she followed his gaze to the presider's table where sat the Signers' Inkstand. Made of lustrous silver, it held two quill pens.

"Glorious," she breathed. "I can't believe I'm actually *here.*"

"Awesome, isn't it?" Scott smiled. "You seem to love history as much as I do."

Pleased he had noticed, she said, "Why do you suppose we're so attracted to the past?"

He considered. "Partly love of story, I guess, the same thing that draws us to literature. One of my earliest memories is of begging Aunt Charla to read to me."

"You're right. History *is* just a collection of stories. I learned to read when I was four, from hearing the same book read over and over and asking what the words were. Those squiggly marks began to make sense."

He whistled softly. "A prodigy. You're full of surprises, Millie."

"I could say the same about you. Who'd have guessed you were an expert at table tennis? Especially since Brad beat you at it when we first got here."

"Yesterday, I was almost terminally nervous. Today, not so much. But I often play Ping Pong with a buddy after a grueling day of studying or working."

"My favorite way to relax is to sit and do nothing for a few minutes."

"That's good, too."

Millie moved away along the wooden railing, for a better look at the presider's chair. Akers pushed through the crowd to her.

"You thought any more about my offer, young lady?" he asked with a fawning smile.

"So that's why you're here. But how'd you know *we'd* be coming here this afternoon?"

"I didn't, of course. I was here on business and happened to see your group. Naturally, it seemed a good chance to talk to you. Mr. Pope refuses me entry to the mansion."

"I'm afraid I can't help you. I won't be getting a keepsake."

"Excuse me, then. Thanks." He moved off towards Brad.

Pope spied him and frowned angrily, causing the dealer to withdraw a few feet. The tour ended in a second-floor gallery similar to the mansion's, only larger.

The heirs and executors next strolled to Liberty Bell Pavilion. From there they crossed a quadrangle to the Promenade of States, a line of brick arches, each centered with a colorful seal, honoring the thirteen original states. Behind each archway, a brick enclosure surrounded by tall bushes housed a concrete bench. Set into the promenade's pavement were fifty-six bronze tablets representing the signers of the Declaration of Independence.

"Signers' Walk," Pope said, indicating the plaques.

"How many geniuses did it take to come up with *that* name?" muttered Cunningham.

The heirs examined the state seals. Some took photos.

"Can we go back now?" Koontz whined.

"You read my mind," growled Cunningham.

Pope acquiesced. "The buildings close soon anyway, though the park remains open at night. We haven't seen everything, but you'll doubtless want to return some time."

On the way back, Millie walked beside Ross at the end of the straggling line. The two talked easily, and she found him knowledgeable about more than antiques.

Akers approached them from behind and made his pitch to Ross, who politely declined. The dealer worked his way up the line, getting a snub from Peeples and a courteous head-shake from Scott. But Cunningham and Koontz engaged him in conversation. Pope glanced back, saw Akers, wheeled, and marched towards him, fury radiating from his squat body.

"Mr. Akers! Once this week's over, you may contact these people. But you will not hound them now."

"I'm not 'hounding' anyone," the dealer said stiffly. "Naturally, it's to their advantage to talk to me."

When Pope remained adamant, however, Akers left.

Reaching the mansion, Millie went to her room and tried

to nap, but her thoughts kept returning to the drowning. She wished she could believe it had been either an accident or suicide. If it had been murder, for greed or out of anger, the culprit must have been one of her new relatives. She thought about the way Nathan Henry had set up his legacy, with money being divided among *living* heirs. Cunningham had stated it concisely: One-fifteenth was more than one-sixteenth.

A shudder went through her. It would be a miserable week if every waking moment must be filled with suspicion.

Who could she really trust among these newly-found relatives? Ross, with his learning and aplomb in the face of rudeness? Peeples or Eileen, appealingly vulnerable in different ways? The self-centered but likeable Bennetts?

Scott, with whom she shared interests and a similar sense of humor? And whom, she had to admit, she was finding more and more attractive?

As Millie watched her roommate move energetically about, humming, choosing garments for evening, evidently untired after the long walk, doubts about her returned. Letitia might be strong enough to have drowned the smaller Johns.

But that luscious white beaded dress she had worn last evening had shown no trace of a watery struggle. Nor had anyone else's attire, now that Millie thought about it, though she hadn't been looking for such signs.

The Bennetts and their mother stood to inherit three shares of the Henry wealth. Maybe even that didn't satisfy these siblings with expensive tastes. If they weren't well off already, they must be deep in hock. Neither seemed a likely murderer, yet slayings had been committed by more improbable killers, often over far less money.

One fact Millie could not dispute: Letitia had wasted no time in calculating how much richer she would be as a result of Gilbert Johns's death.

✦ *Chapter Twelve*

Unable to sleep, Millie went downstairs and telephoned Jeff's house. Ring after ring produced no answer. Deciding the family had gone to a movie or a mall, she tried the nursing home and learned that Sylva had gone shopping with a group in the home's van.

Homesick and low-spirited, Millie went back upstairs, bathed, and dressed in a pale yellow dress borrowed from her friend Jennifer, also the source of last evening's attire. She went down to dinner with Letitia, who smelled like hyacinths and looked enchanting in a gauzy print of blues, mauves, and greens. They were passing the room occupied by Brad and Koontz when angry voices came through the closed door.

"Leave a mess in here again, Bennett, and you'll move out! Go sleep in the kitchen, for all I care!"

"If you can't co-exist like a normal person, *you* should leave."

"You think living in a pigsty is normal, do you?"

"Think you're a picnic to live with, Koontz? Your snoring sounds like a logging crew clear-cutting a forest."

"That does it! I'm asking for a change in my room."

"Great, I'll second it. I hope you get put with Cunningham. Then you'll see what messiness is."

Letitia grinned. "I'm glad we get along, roomie."

At dinner, Millie was placed between Cunningham and Koontz. The latter still looked out of sorts after his tiff with Brad, but he soon rallied and began to brag loudly about a date he had made for that evening.

"Terri's really something. She's got these huge eyes and the prettiest little nose. As for her figure, well . . . ."

". . . getting all that money." Millie caught the end of something Cunningham said. "You gotta be careful not to let it get away from you. Need to keep your kid from frittering his away too."

Busy savoring a velvety spinach souffle and its accompanying mushroom sauce, Millie didn't reply. She could get used to such victuals, she thought, then remembered with a thrill that she would now be able to afford them.

"I've been an investment counselor for twenty-two years," Cunningham went on in a kindly-uncle tone. "Be glad to give you the benefit of my expertise."

She continued eating.

"A single woman and a kid especially need to watch out. You don't got a man to take care of you, you know."

News flash, from Sensitive Sam.

"I'll check on investments when I get back to Dallas."

"Won't cost you a cent to get some tips now."

"No, thanks."

His fleshy face creased in a frown. He made the same offer to Ross, seated across from him, and got another no. When he tried Peeples, across from Millie, her look would have cut sheet metal. This time, Pope overheard.

"Leave your fellow heirs alone, Mr. Cunningham," he said coolly. "Anyone who wants your help can ask for it."

Brad leaned around Eileen and Koontz to invite Millie for a stroll after dinner. "If you're rested from this afternoon, we could walk over to the Bourse. That's that Victorian building near the Liberty Bell that Pope said has been restored and turned into a shopping mall."

Recalling her reservations about the Bennetts, she hesitated. Letitia spoke from down the table.

"Do come, roomie. We're going too, aren't we, Scott?"

He turned from listening to Eileen, whose cleavage was again on display in a black low-cut dress.

"Oh? Okay, sure."

Four sounded like safety in numbers. Millie agreed.

"How's about you and me doing the town, foxy lady?" Cunningham said, craning his neck around Millie and Koontz to speak to Eileen. "Let's live it up, since we can afford it."

"I got stuff to wash out," she said, a Scarlett-O'Hara tilt to her chin.

Millie wondered if she was still miffed at Cunningham over the bracelet or had just decided to concentrate on Scott instead. She felt a twinge of jealousy but told herself she had no claim on him.

After dinner the foursome started off, Millie and Letitia in light wraps. The wind had abated, and the night was clear and quite cool. A three-quarter moon danced reflections of itself in the windowpanes they passed. Millie and Brad walked in front, the other two behind, Letitia prattling about plans for her own business. She would have an upscale clientele, using antiques as appropriate in decorating schemes.

"I adore the mansion furniture," she said. "And I'd give anything to have that architect's drawing."

They crossed Walnut Street and cut through Independence Park, where darkened buildings squatted like giant Monopoly pieces and the spire of Carpenters' Hall rose ghostly against the night sky. They were crossing Chestnut Street when Millie heard footsteps behind them, loud in the deserted area. She turned.

"Miss Peeples. I didn't realize you were coming this way too."

The heavier woman came up to them. "It's a nice night for a walk. I asked Eileen to come, but she wouldn't."

They entered the Bourse building, a huge space done in Victorian opulence: rich reds and golds, iron grillwork, frosted glass, and ornate staircases up to tiers of stores. They split up, the younger four agreeing to meet for coffee later. As Scott walked away with Letitia, he threw a rueful glance back at Millie. She hoped it meant he'd prefer a change in partners.

Shaking off a lonely feeling, she browsed through boutiques and bookstores, happy in the knowledge that she could now shop such places any time she chose. Tonight, though, she bought only an Encyclopedia Brown mystery for Danny. Just before the arranged meeting time, she ran into a package-laden Brad.

"Tightwad," he teased. "A brand new half-millionaire, and all you could find to buy is one skinny book."

"I need to feel the money in my hot little hand before I splurge."

"How adorably old-fashioned. Don't you know we're becoming a credit-card society? That cash is disappearing?"

"It's done that all my life. When it even showed up."

"That refrain's getting old, precious." He touched her hand. "Let me teach you how to be rich."

She laughed. "Are you Bennetts already independently wealthy, or used to spending beyond your means?"

"Just incredibly good at managing money."

"But you have to have some before you can manage it."

Letitia and Scott came up just then with arms full of parcels. The four entered a café and sank into a booth by a window looking out into the mall.

"I told Scott how much we'll each get from Gilbert's share,"

Letitia said, checking her reflection in the window.

"Isn't my sister cold-blooded?" Brad said.

"Just realistic. Looks like you've spent freely tonight yourself, dear brother. Judging by those sacks."

"So did Scott. Or are those all yours, sis?"

Scott grinned. "Most are hers. I bought a shirt."

"And I had to browbeat you into buying that, my pet." She straightened his collar, her fingers lingering on it.

Scott looked uncomfortable. Millie fought a trace of annoyance at the ease with which both siblings assumed others would welcome their attentions.

The four had coffee and chatted companionably, then walked back through an eerily quiet Independence Park. Entering the mansion, they peered into the parlor, where the gray-haired guard sat alone reading a newspaper. Upstairs, Scott carried Letitia's purchases to her room, told everyone goodnight, and sauntered up the hall.

Letitia watched him retreat, her radiant smile fading, then entered her room, banging the door. Left in the hall, Millie and Brad looked at each other. He shrugged.

"Good n—" Millie began, but Brad stopped her with a gentle kiss. Surprised, she didn't at first resist as he drew her close.

"Tomorrow," he said huskily, "let's shake the group, go somewhere alone, just you and me."

She pulled away, moved both by her lingering suspicion and a reluctance to form a romantic tie with him. Handsome as he was, she wondered why she didn't feel a stronger attraction.

"I like you, Brad, but this isn't a good time for me to get involved with anyone. I'm sorry, truly."

Astonishment, then irritation, flashed in his eyes. He started to speak, evidently thought better of it, said a distant goodnight, and headed for his room. Millie entered hers and found Letitia frowning at herself in the mirror.

"What's the matter with me, roomie?"

Hearing that question from those lips, Millie chuckled. "You're kidding, right?"

"Why's Scott so standoffish? Guys would kill for an evening with me, and he doesn't even kiss me goodnight."

"He probably has a girlfriend in Colorado."

Letitia waved her hand, dismissing the possibility. "Out of sight, out of mind."

"Absence makes the heart grow fonder."

"Roomie, I can usually make men forget other women. You think Scott's gay?"

"He may just be reluctant to get close to anyone till we know how Gilbert died."

Letitia's eyes widened. "You think he suspects *me?*"

"No, but it makes sense to be cautious just now."

Letitia stared. "You don't trust me either?"

"I—yes, of course I do!"

"You don't." Grabbing a robe, Letitia flounced out.

Nice, Kirchner. Soon, nobody'll be talking to anybody. If Henry thought you'd all become friends in this crazy situation he created, he was loonier than a Canadian lake.

Millie prepared for bed, then took out her frustrations in her sketch book. She drew Detective Nolen as a sad-eyed bassett hound, Eileen as Miss Kitty entertaining the boys at the Long Branch, and Fij as the Roadrunner, limbs barely visible through the dust of constant movement.

Tired of drawing, she thought of reading and realized with irritation that she had left the book of Franklin letters in the sitting room. She tried a mystery novel she had brought, but soon the previous restless night took its toll. She never knew when Letitia returned to their room.

Neither did she know that, even as she drifted off, another heir was meeting his death.

★ ★ ★

Wes Koontz stepped briskly away from the Henry mansion. He hated physical exertion, but this walk should prove profitable. If he didn't make it back before Fansler locked up, he could always ring the bell and say he had gone out for air and lost track of time.

A man with a dog passed him, but the street was otherwise deserted. Wes hated the old-fashioned houses of this area, anything to do with history. Hearing people "ooh" and "ah" over antiques turned his stomach.

Usually.

He swung along, anticipation easing the remnants of afternoon weariness. Since childhood he had felt that he was special, with a great destiny ahead, that feeling fueled by rumors within his family of a mysterious inheritance due them. Even his mother's pessimistic warning not to count on anything had gone unheeded. But finding himself at thirty-three still living a mundane life, he had begun to doubt.

Then Pope's letter had arrived, suggesting that someone in the eighteenth century had indeed insured a rosy future for Wes in the twenty-first. The phone call tonight was more proof that Fate was finally coming through.

Hurrying along St. James Place under clear moonlight, Wes glanced at his watch. Plenty of time before the appointment. He felt keyed up, high on adrenalin. But then he slowed to an amble. He shouldn't arrive breathless, mustn't appear too eager.

So far this trip hadn't been too awful, even living with the Roommate from Hell. Wes could stand anything a few days, knowing he would be leaving much richer.

The attractive females here didn't hurt either. Too bad they were involved with other guys, the stunning Letitia paired with Wyrick, her pretty roommate with Bennett. Millie was too wise-ass for him, anyway. Even sexy Eileen, who had listened to his complaints about Bennett last night in the parlor, seemed to prefer Wyrick or that tub of lard Cunningham over him.

He didn't intend to be lonely, however. Even if Terri had stood him up tonight, he knew other women in Philly. Wes crossed Walnut, found an opening in the low hedge, and entered the historical park.

Something puzzled him. How did this collector know which keepsake he had drawn? Had one of the dealers Wes had visited this morning passed on the information?

Whatever. The man, or woman—from the caller's voice he couldn't be sure—had promised to pay handsomely to avoid having to bid at auction. But Wes had news for him or her— this antique would not come cheap.

Without crowds, the park seemed other-worldly, like a planet that no longer supported life. And scary. He passed the Todd House, whistling to bolster his flagging courage.

At least this unorthodox meeting place would make the negotiations private. Yep, the trip was turning out okay.

Too bad about Gilbert, of course. Still, he would likely have done himself in some day, and this ended the suspense. Odd that he had chosen the very evening he had learned about the money, but that was Gilbert for you, never a normal reaction. His career choice, pharmacy though he hated medicine himself, was a case in point. Wes had decided that dispensing drugs to others had made his cousin feel superior. At least Gilbert's death meant more money for Wes.

Library Hall rose huge and silent on the right, then Philosophical Hall. As he passed the latter, something burst from deep shadow, like an apparition pouncing out of the past. It bolted past Wes, skimming his pantleg. He started, stumbled, nearly fell.

The black cat streaked away. Wes righted himself, less and

less sure that this clandestine meeting was a good idea. The moon and street lamps gave light for walking, but also made bushes and buildings loom threateningly.

He passed Liberty Bell Pavilion, reached the quadrangle that led to the state archways, and stopped. Now that he thought about it, the voice had seemed familiar. Maybe there was no buyer. Another heir could have been pulling his leg.

Bennett? He might find this hysterically funny.

Yet if the caller was on the level, this was a chance to make a killing. Wes couldn't simply re-schedule the meeting, since he didn't know how to reach the purchaser.

"Can't talk over the phone," the whisper had said. "Meet me at Independence Mall, eleven o'clock, Signers' Walk, behind the Delaware arch. Don't tell anybody, or it's no go."

Secrecy was fine with Wes—this was no one else's business, anyway—but he'd make this collector pay dearly for dragging him down here so late. He racked his brain, trying to identify that voice. One of the dealers he had visited? That flittery reporter Judd? Winston Akers?

That afternoon, Wes had told Akers which item he had drawn, and the dealer had made an offer, much too low. Had he reconsidered? A covert meeting sounded like Akers's style.

Wes reached the promenade, started along the line of archways that stood like gallows awaiting doomed felons. He tried to tread softly, but to his intent ears his footfalls sounded like sonic booms. With each step, the keepsake's price rose higher in his mind.

As he approached the Delaware arch, he wondered why the caller had chosen that one. Coincidence or design?

The executors and other heirs knew Wes's home state, as did Judd—it had been mentioned in their interview—but they shouldn't know his lottery result. On the other hand, Akers and a few dealers knew which keepsake he had but shouldn't know of the Delaware connection. None should know both.

Wes peered into the nook, eager to learn who the enigmatic buyer was. He saw no one. Either he had arrived first, or the call had been a prank. He slipped inside.

"Over here." Someone seated at one end of the concrete bench softly hailed him.

Relief flooded Wes. "Oh, it's you. Why didn't you identify yourself on the phone?"

"You'll see. Now for my offer." The voice dropped so low that Wes had to lean close to hear. The collector stood and extended a hand.

Something long and metallic flashed. It plunged into Wes's stomach.

The assailant jerked the knife out and shoved it into Wes's chest. It glanced off his breastbone. He tried to get away, but he was trapped against the brick wall. He clutched at his attacker's arm, at clothing, at air.

Stab, jerk. Stab, jerk. Stab, jerk. Blows rained on his body. Weakening, he fought to stay alert. But years of avoiding exercise had poorly prepared him to fight, especially against an armed adversary.

His destiny, originating two hundred years ago in an ill-starred will, caught up with him as blackness closed in.

✪ Chapter Thirteen

Next morning, stunned silence greeted Pope's melancholy announcement. He stood at the head of the table, appearing to have aged ten years overnight.

Millie's stomach rejected the crisp bacon and blueberry waffle, and she pushed her plate away.

The initial shock past, all the heirs began talking at once.

"Koontz dead?"

"How horrible!"

"A mugging? In Independence Mall?"

"What the hell was Koontz doing down there last night?" Cunningham spoke above the rest.

"I've no idea," Pope said, shaking his head. "But it was a wicked attack, a great many stab wounds. Probably the thief was high on something. He stole Mr. Koontz's watch and money but tossed his wallet down. The police identified him from papers in that."

"It's dangerous here," Peeples shuddered. "This town is a murder mecca."

"Now, Miss Peeples," Endicott soothed, looking pale but composed. "Philadelphia is as safe as any modern city."

Is that supposed to be a comfort?

"I'm afraid the scheduled tour of Valley Forge will be delayed," Pope said, "till after the police, FBI, and National Park investigators have interviewed everyone."

"The FBI?" Letitia said in alarm. "Why them?"

"The Bureau's involved because Mr. Koontz's death occurred on federal property."

"You know," Scott said thoughtfully beside Millie, "maybe it wasn't a simple mugging."

"What do you mean, Mr. Wyrick?" Endicott asked.

"It's awfully coincidental that two cousins died on consecutive days, both in a city where neither lived."

"That's so," Millie said. "Why did Wes go down there again, anyway? He complained all yesterday afternoon about having to walk so far then."

"Let's not be alarmist," Pope replied with evident discomfort. "It's bad enough that two people have been killed without making their deaths into a conspiracy."

Millie's throat tightened. What if the same person had murdered both? And wasn't finished yet?

She had to remain calm. Pulling her plate closer, she forced herself to pick at the cooled food. Glancing around, she saw an apparently blissful Cunningham comforting Eileen, her fair head burrowed into his shoulder, tears dropping on the flattering rose dress she had proudly said was a gift from Peeples, bought last evening. Letitia chewed her lower lip, Ross shifted restlessly, Peeples twisted her hands in her lap, Scott looked pensive. Brad stared at his untouched food.

Brad, Millie thought. He had disliked his roommate, had argued with him yesterday.

She didn't like what she was thinking.

"How'd they know to call you, Mr. Pope, after they found Wes?" Scott asked.

"This address and phone number were in Mr. Koontz's

wallet, to help him find the place Thursday, I suppose."

Scott spoke in an undertone to Millie. "Does the fact that it happened at the Delaware archway bother you at all?"

"Because Wes was from there? It is odd, but I've no idea what it means."

"Me either. It just seems strange."

Scott could even be guilty himself, Millie realized, though if he had killed Koontz and was managing to look so puzzled the morning after, he was a consummate actor. But uneasily she admitted that she couldn't be sure of him.

"I wondered why Wes wasn't in our room all night," Brad said slowly. "I assumed he'd switched to another room, or had stayed out so he could claim he'd spent the night with a woman."

"He mentioned having friends here," Scott said. "Maybe somebody he considered a pal, wasn't."

"Possible," Millie murmured, miserable over the suspicions of new friends that crowded her mind.

Peeples stopped wringing her hands. "We're going to draw again, aren't we? For the disks Johns and Koontz had?"

The attorney's eyebrows shot up. He glanced at his fellow executor, who nodded slightly.

"I suppose we should," Pope said. "But this seems hardly the time to discuss another drawing."

Eileen lifted her head. "Vera's right. Everyone who has dollar signs should get another chance."

Her roommate frowned. "*Anyone* who wants to can put back *whatever* they drew and try again. Right, Mr. Pope?"

"I guess so, Miss Peeples. I guess so."

★ ★ ★

After breakfast, FBI Special Agent Wallace Kopechne, INHP Criminal Investigator Ross Tilbury, and PPD detective Marcy Cheatham questioned Millie in the sitting room. Stocky, brusque Kopechne took the lead, while the others—soft-spoken, florid Tilbury and stolid, unsmiling Cheatham—put in an occasional query. The FBI presence made Millie especially nervous.

In response to questions, she said she had not seen Koontz leave last night but had been out herself most of the evening. No, he had not mentioned plans to return to the park but said he'd be seeing someone called Terri. No, he had not gotten along well with fellow heirs. Pressed for specifics, Millie mentioned his quarrels with Brad, Cunningham, and Peeples.

"But those were petty disagreements," she added. "Nothing someone would get killed over."

"Ever listen to the news, Mrs. Kirchner?" Kopechne said without smiling. "People get murdered these days over tennis shoes. Or because they looked at somebody wrong."

As Millie described her own movements and what she knew of the others', she realized that, depending on when Koontz had died, all those who had gone to the Bourse could be without alibis. Including her.

The interview over, she went to the office and phoned Dallas, but Jeff's mother said the boys had already left on their camping trip. Gloom settled over Millie.

"Sorry you missed Danny," Jeff's mother said. "I can give you a cell-phone number for one of the Scoutmasters."

"I'll take it just in case, but I won't interrupt the outing. Just wanted to hear Danny's voice. You say they're due back late tomorrow?"

"Right." She read off the number, and Millie wrote it down. "Don't worry about him. The adults who went along are very responsible."

"I know. Thanks, Ruth. I really appreciate your looking after Danny this week."

"He's a good kid. And he and Jeff are joined at the hip, as

you know."

Millie had better luck at the nursing home. She waited briefly, then heard Sylva's welcome voice.

"Kirchner? About time you checked in. How're things going up there?"

"Great in some ways, not so hot in others." She told about the money she and Danny would be getting.

"Wonderful! Oh, hon, I'm so glad. That'll let you take things much easier. Now, what's this about some things not being so hot?"

"It's just . . . two heirs . . ." Millie stopped. She probably shouldn't burden Sylva with this news.

"Two heirs what?"

"Nothing. How's the weather there?"

"It's Dallas in June, so it's hot and sticky. Give, Kirchner. I get to hear every detail, remember?"

"But you came along with me," Millie said lightly. "And I'm enjoying your comments on everything."

"You flipped out, Kirchner? I'm the one who's senile."

"I hope I'm as keen as you when *I* hit seventy. Of course I'll have to get sharper before then."

"Flattery won't distract me. Tell me what happened, or I'll take to my bed with severe depression and blame you."

"You don't want—oh, all right. I'll probably get no peace till I tell. Two heirs have died."

"What?"

Millie explained.

"A drowning and a mugging? But you think they're connected? Couldn't it be a horrible coincidence?"

"It could, sure."

"But you don't believe it."

"No."

"So who do you think's responsible?"

"I've been trying to work that out. I think one of the remaining heirs may be killing to decrease the number of people who'll share the Henry millions."

Silence followed, then Sylva's voice quavered, "Oh, hon . . . hon, that would be awful. It would mean somebody . . . someone else could be murdered."

"Thanks. I'd been trying not to think about that."

"Millie, dearest! You must stay alert, watch your back every second! Goodness, I'm so sorry I got you into this."

"You didn't. I wanted to come."

"But if I hadn't—"

"Put the money for air fare in my checking account?"

Sylva hesitated. "If I hadn't urged you to go—"

"Don't blame yourself, Sylva. That's wrong."

"Millie, dear, if anything happens to you—now I won't sleep at all till you're safely back."

"Listen, I've probably exaggerated. Johns's own cousin said he was suicidal. As for the stabbing, that was probably someone after drug money."

"I appreciate your trying to make me feel better. But, as the kids say, I'm not buying it."

"Please don't worry. Now I'm concerned about you."

Millie calmed the elderly woman by promising to call the minute she knew anything more. Terrific, she thought as she hung up. If Sylva gets sick now, it'll be my fault.

She went to the sitting room to get the Franklin book.

It wasn't there, nor was the one Ross had been reading. She went to look in the library, and, sure enough, someone had returned the letters volume to its alcove shelf. Millie curled up in an easy chair and immersed herself in a letter Franklin had written his wife from Paris discussing a concern about the couple's house being built in Philadelphia.

Ross entered and sat in a wing chair. "Too short," he

muttered, "but why?"

He rose and circled the room, paused near Millie, rubbed his chin, and touched a table. He turned to look at another against the far wall and shook his head.

"Something the matter?"

He jumped. "Oh, Millie. No . . . it's just that candlestand keepsake. Can't think why . . ." He sat down again. "Shocking news about Mr. Koontz, wasn't it?"

"Yes. You have any ideas about who did it?"

"A junkie, as Mr. Pope said. These days, people get murdered for a couple of dollars to feed a drug habit."

"You don't think the two heirs' deaths are connected?"

Ross smiled. "Coincidences happen, Millie, probably much more in real life than in fiction."

"But why would Wes go there again, alone and so late?"

"I can't imagine. I saw him just after dinner as I was leaving to visit an old college pal in town. He said he was seeing someone too, implied it was a woman."

"You went out yourself? Were you late getting back?"

"After midnight. I hadn't seen Gregory in years, and we talked till quite late."

Fansler entered. "The reporter—" he began.

From behind him, Judd interrupted. "Thanks, Fansler, old boy. I'll take it from here."

Eyes narrowed in distaste, the butler bowed and left.

"Millie, Mr. Ross, hello." Judd pulled a silk side chair near Millie, straddled it backwards, opened a notebook on his thigh, and poised a pen to write.

"Can we help you?" Millie asked.

"Koontz. Give me your impressions of him, both of you." With his free hand, Judd picked lint off his gray slacks.

Frowning, Ross stood. "Excuse me, Mr. Judd. I don't wish to discuss this matter with you." He strode out, his powerful back rigid.

The reporter looked at Millie. "Something I said?"

"Maybe he doesn't want to talk for publication." An interview didn't appeal to her either right now, but she still hoped to learn something from Judd.

"I could've used him on background, wouldn't have had to quote him by name. Ross have problems with Koontz?"

"No more than most others did."

He folded his arms on the chairback and drummed a finger against an elbow. "You, too?"

She hesitated. "Not really."

"Meaning?"

"I didn't find him as fascinating as he seemed to find himself, but we didn't have any battles."

Alternately rubbing a knee and passing a hand through his tangled red curls, Judd asked more questions. Millie responded briefly, hoping he would let slip something he had learned from the police or Park Rangers. But he proved discouragingly careful about what he said.

"Who did it, Millie?" Judd finally asked, flipping his pen against the notebook. "Which heir snuffed Koontz?"

"You don't buy the drug-addict theory?"

"Do you? Two heirs killed in a strange city, on successive nights?"

"Not really."

He stared at her, seemed to reach a decision. "Work with me, Millie. The authorities are close-mouthed on an ongoing investigation, but you're bright and on the inside, and I'm a good reporter. Together, we could figure out who the murderer is."

"What makes you think it's not me?" The offer sounded tempting, but she suspected collaboration would benefit him more than her.

His eyes appraised her. "If you killed someone, you wouldn't choose either of those ways."

"What method would I use?"

"Poison. Or a gun."

"Why?"

"Drowning and stabbing require touching the victim. You like to keep your distance from people."

She smiled. "Then, if I'm as smart as you say, a hands-on method's exactly what I'd choose."

"Don't try to trip me up with my own logic. You in?"

"I don't think so. I just want to go home to my son."

"When I catch the killer, you'll wish you'd helped."

"I'll try to live with the disappointment."

A slow smile spread across his features. "You fascinate me, Millie Kirchner. I'll be back."

"Thanks for the warning."

★ ★ ★

"They grilled me pretty hard," Brad said, "but I never saw Wes after dinner." He sat beside Millie in the parlor, toying with the strap of his elegant camera case. "Not that he'd have told me his plans. We couldn't stand each other."

Various heirs gave Brad sidelong glances.

"But I didn't kill him," he said hastily. He threw Millie a dark look. "I was in *my own room* by about ten."

Cunningham smirked. "Struck out, didja?"

"Mr. Koontz went somewhere right after dinner," Pope said, crossing one crepe-soled foot over the other. "He came back soon after in a foul mood. I got the impression that his plans had fallen through." He uncrossed and re-crossed his feet. "I gather someone called him about 9:30. You took the call, didn't you, Miss Goggins? I heard the ring in the library and started to the office to get it—Fansler was helping prepare today's picnic—but it quit."

"Can't stand to let a phone ring." Eileen smoothed the skirt of her rose dress. "I couldn't tell if it was a man or woman, but it sure cheered Wes up. He was glooming and dooming around before, but he came back from the office humming. Said money was falling in his lap."

"What d'you suppose he meant?" Scott asked.

Eileen smiled coyly at him. "I don't know, Scott."

"Where's that bus?" Endicott said, debonair even in putter pants. He pulled aside a drape at the front window. "Did Mr. Koontz go out right after that, Miss Goggins?"

"He went upstairs first. Isn't that right, Mr. Pope?"

"I believe so," the lawyer said. "I heard the front door open and close around 10:15. Whoever was leaving was whistling. I assumed someone was stepping out for air. But it must've been Mr. Koontz leaving for Independence Park." He paused, staring sadly at his hands. "Time of death was around eleven. I guess Miss Goggins and I were the last to see him alive, other than his killer."

"He came in here before going out that last time."

All eyes turned to the blond keepsakes guard—Fred, Millie had heard him called.

"I went off duty at nine," Fred went on, "but Jim—the night guard—told the guys at the office about it after the FBI questioned him." Fred gestured at the keepsakes case. "Koontz looked in there and wrote something on some paper, then left. Jim heard the front door right after."

"Someone else saw him alive, then." Pope sounded glad.

"Jim said a couple others went out about the same time," Fred continued. "He'd got bored and was pacing the hall. Said a good-looking, dark-haired guy left right after Koontz. One of the heirs—Jim didn't know his name."

Eyes swiveled towards Brad.

"Okay, I went out to smoke," he admitted, "but I wasn't gone long enough to walk to Independence Mall and kill Wes."

"Maybe you ran," Cunningham offered maliciously.

"Did anyone see you return, Mr. Bennett?" Endicott asked.

Brad scowled. "Not unless the ever-present Jim did."

"Never mentioned it," the guard said placidly.

"And you don't got a roommate now." Cunningham sprawled in an easy chair, hairy stomach peeping through his shirt. "Convenient, ain't it?"

Brad jumped up, sending his camera case rolling against Millie, and towered over Cunningham. "Where were *you* all evening? We haven't discussed *your* movements."

"I'd had enough of this crowd. I walked to a bus stop and went to a bar. Stayed till midnight."

"A crowded bar? Anyone likely to remember you?"

"Sure." But Cunningham's eyes shifted uncertainly.

"The butler left too," Fred said. "Before Koontz, Jim thought."

"Fansler went out?" Pope said.

"Yeah. You, too, soon after Bennett."

The attorney flushed. "I just went for a short walk. I was back by 10:45. Didn't Jim see me return?"

The guard shook his head. "You or the butler either."

"Why're you all acting as if you need alibis?" Peeples said. "None of us killed Koontz. You said so, Mr. Pope."

"Not . . . exactly. The police said the apparent motive was robbery, and I guess I . . . inferred the drug-addict part."

"Well, still—" she sniffed—"it makes sense."

"Where were you last night?" Cunningham snarled at her.

She wrenched back muscular shoulders in outraged dignity. "It's none of *your* business, but I went to the Bourse with the others. I got back about 10:30."

"Anyone see you come in?" Brad asked.

She glanced down uncertainly. "I . . . don't think so."

"Jim didn't mention any women at all," Fred said.

Cunningham chuckled. "'Pears to me the FBI's got all the suspects they need." He turned to Endicott. "How about the banker? Where was he while all this was going on?"

Millie half expected Endicott not to answer. He did, with a curled lip that implied contempt for the questioner. "I went home to see my wife and returned shortly before ten. Fansler saw me come in."

"*Mr.* Ross?" Cunningham said, voice dripping innuendo.

The principal, who was staring into the keepsakes cabinet, explained he had visited a friend. "I'm sure the authorities have checked my alibi by now."

"You're on, Wyrick," said Cunningham. "Where were you?"

"In my room reading, from around ten on," Scott said.

"Sure about that?"

"At last, the bus is here." Endicott turned from the window, grabbed a large binoculars case, and hurried out.

Peeples beat Cunningham to the seat beside Eileen. Brad and Millie sat ahead of the women. The driver explained he was late because another bus had been sent but had developed engine trouble. Stowing several hampers in the baggage compartment, Fansler climbed on and sat behind the driver. Pope counted heads. The bus pulled out.

They rode northwest on I-76, dark clouds threatening rain. Her mind on a theory, Millie tuned out Brad's long story of a bus trip he had made to visit a girl. Maybe she had too quickly dismissed the idea that Johns had been killed in error? The cousins had looked enough alike to be twins. Suppose the drowning had been a mistake, Koontz the intended target all along.

You read too many murder mysteries, Kirchner.

It did seem far-fetched, Millie admitted, staring unseeingly at the rolling Pennsylvania countryside. But if the killer had only been after Koontz, that could mean the rest of them were safe. Yet the problem of guilt remained. With all the comings and goings last night, it seemed that almost everyone had had an opportunity to kill Koontz. Even people seen coming into the mansion before eleven might have gone out again. Millie wished she knew when Fansler had returned and locked the front door.

At least Letitia appeared in the clear for Koontz's death. Millie doubted she could have slipped out of the room and back without her knowledge. Besides the two of them, only Ross and Endicott—and maybe Cunningham—seemed to have stories backed by others. Even those might not hold up, though, if witnesses were uncertain of arrival or departure times.

Eileen apparently had been at the mansion the whole night, though she might have left after Koontz and Pope. If Jim of the good memory had been in the parlor or answering nature's call, he might have missed seeing her go.

Assuming Koontz's 9:30 phone call had come from the killer, it appeared that almost anyone except Eileen and Pope could have made it. Millie's three companions had all excused themselves to visit the restroom while at the café. Had one of them phoned Koontz then? Telephone records should reveal if the call had come from the restaurant. But she couldn't figure out how to get that information . . . .

"He isn't good enough, dear," Peeples was saying behind her. "If you get tangled up with the likes of—"

A pause, then Eileen's voice, small and pleading. "Vera, try to understand. This could be my big break."

Peeples snorted. "I thought you'd come to your senses yesterday. You seemed mad at him then."

"That was different. I thought he took my bracelet. I was sure I wore it Thursday night, but Ed swears I didn't. I been thinking it over, and I guess he's right."

Millie didn't catch Peeples's muttered response. She realized that Brad had finished talking.

"That's nice," she ventured.

He roused from a lolling position. "I say I lost my return ticket and had to wire my folks for money, and you say it's nice?" He flung himself back, hands clasped atop his head. "Lord help me if juries listen as well as you do."

"Sorry. My mind wandered."

"No kidding."

To change the subject, she asked his theory of why Koontz had gone back to the historical park.

"Dunno." He still sounded miffed.

"Think someone lured him there with the phone call?"

"Maybe. A woman, probably."

"Why?"

He looked at her as if she were a dense five-year-old. "Wes considered himself a ladies' man and was happy after getting the call. It's the obvious explanation, isn't it?"

"Not necessarily. He did make that comment about money falling into his lap."

Brad went on, as if she hadn't spoken. "Now which woman? Not you or Letitia. He wouldn't have been thrilled to hear from Peeples, and Eileen was somewhere downstairs."

Millie pointed behind them, mouthing "Eileen."

Brad nodded and raised his voice. "It could've been that babe he mentioned seeing, the one from his past."

"It didn't have to be a woman."

"Sheesh." Brad slid down in the seat, propping jeans-clad knees against the back of the unoccupied seat ahead.

Millie looked out the window, now misted with light rain. A highway sign listed towns ahead, including King of Prussia. The quaint name reminded Millie of a reason she had wanted to make this trip, the chance to see other places. Her spirits lifted. The police, INHP, and FBI would surely catch the killer. For the afternoon, she would put thoughts of murder from her mind.

At least she would try.

★ Chapter Fourteen

The bus pulled into a parking lot beside a modern glass-and-steel rectangle, the Valley Forge Visitors Center. The drizzle had stopped, leaving the sky a wall of pewter. Past the center, Millie saw that the paved road led over rolling hills topped with lush grass and beckoning shade trees. It looks like any modern park anywhere, she thought with a prickle of disappointment.

In the center, they collected park maps and watched a film on the Colonial Army's 1777–1778 encampment, then rode a short way to a cluster of crude log huts, reconstructions of those occupied by one colonial brigade. Puffy clouds now divided slate sky above from pale blue below.

Millie's interest in the outing rekindled as the heirs stooped to peer inside the cramped sheds. Though the day was warm, she easily imagined herself a barefoot soldier shivering in a bunk while snow drifted through holes dotting the roof. Brad snapped away with a costly-looking camera. Letitia asked why all the structures had sunken earth floors.

"Digging below ground saved building materials and reduced the area exposed to wind," Pope explained cheerfully.

Peeples took a cheap camera from her capacious handbag

and made shot after shot of Eileen posing in a rough-hewn doorway. Cunningham watched with a sardonic grin.

"You a lez, Peeples?" he finally said. "You sure got a thing for your roommate."

She shut her eyes as if counting to ten. When she opened them, it was to Eileen that she spoke.

"You aren't worried about that, are you, dear? You remind me of my niece. She hooked up with a man like him who ruined her life. I just want to protect . . . ." Her voice trailed off.

Eileen looked from one to the other. "No, I don't think that. You're mean, Ed. Vera tries to mother me too much, but she's not like you said."

"Gawd. Women!" Cunningham stalked off.

Leaving in a huff? Pity.

The heirs watched a demonstration of cooking over an open fire by actors wearing eighteenth-century garb, then got back on the bus. It circled a tall archway monument, passed a statue of a horseback-mounted general, made a couple of sharp turns and came to a covered bridge.

"Built long after the Revolution," Pope said with a dismissive wave at the last feature.

They rode alongside Valley Creek, the placid wooded stream that had lent its name to a long-gone ironworks and a historically important site. Millie smiled. If only Danny were here to share this experience.

At Washington's headquarters, a two-story house rented by the general during the encampment, Millie visualized him and his aides poring over military maps in the parlor. In the outside kitchen, she imagined a domestic stirring soup in the big kettle hanging in the walk-in fireplace.

The bus passed Redoubt #4, an earthen fort near one end of the Colonials' inner defense line, and climbed a steep grade. "Mount Joy," Pope said. "Ironic name, at the time."

After another sharp curve, they stopped in a parking lot beside Redoubt #3, anchor of the defense line's southern end. Millie joined other tourists on a raised wooden platform overlooking a line of closely packed sod baskets taller than a man.

Her reverie about bygone days was interrupted by a little boy's peevish whine, "Scoot over some, okay?" Moving away, she noticed an attractive woodsy area across the paved road. Deciding it might offer the solitude she craved, she strode over to it and climbed wooden steps up to the beginning of a hiking path. The trail led around a large tree and to a huge fallen log that seemed perfectly placed for contemplation. Perching on it, she lapsed into a daydream about how the woods must have looked two centuries ago, more heavily timbered and with denser brush. It would have been quiet here except for the movements and low conversations of the defenders. A nocturnal animal might have prowled nearby, a keyed-up soldier firing towards the sound.

"So this is where you got to," Brad said, as he poked his head around the tree. "We're ready to go. Wait, hold it." He snapped her picture, then had her change poses.

"You'll spend your whole inheritance on film and prints," she chided good-humoredly as he made another shot.

"So? Jeez, it's pretty out here." They walked back.

The bus passed an artillery park with rows of cannons incongruously menacing amid a tranquil field. It meandered past more reconstructed huts and stopped at a picnic area across the road from General Varnum's farmhouse. One table was occupied, but Fansler commandeered two others and spread gay cloths on them. While he set out lunch and Pope "helped," actually getting in the way, the heirs stretched their legs. Endicott took tiny fieldglasses from his over-large case and trained them on nearby trees.

The sandwiches, salads, smoked turkey, pickled eggs, and devil's food cake tasted wonderful to Millie. Pope said they would stay an hour there to relax and digest lunch. Millie took the book of Franklin letters from her purse, thinking that this would be an ideal spot to read. The other picnickers tossed trash in a barrel and left. Straightening her wrap-around skirt, Peeples announced she would walk back to a clutch of flowering trees she had seen on the way. Scott followed, saying he wanted a closer look at the covered bridge.

"That's a long way back," Letitia objected.

"The road curves a lot," he said. "On the map, it looks like you can go cross-country just past Redoubt #3."

Ross stood. "Okay if I walk with you that far, Scott? I'd like to look around that earthwork some more."

"Sure."

Leitia frowned. "Guess I'll take a nap on the bus."

Cunningham stretched, exposing his belly. Muttering, "I gotta get away from this crew," he headed across the road to the farmhouse.

These new relatives of hers weren't exactly brimming with intellectual curiosity, Millie thought, smiling to herself. Most seemed unimpressed by the park's history. At least Scott shared her enthusiasm. And Ross, of course.

Endicott brushed crumbs off his lap. "Think I'll go look for birds. Care to join me, Arthur?"

"Go ahead, Soames. I'll help Fansler clean up."

The butler's eyes flickered, but he wordlessly continued stacking dishes. Cutlery clinked as Pope collected utensils. Binoculars in hand, Endicott set out in the opposite direction from Peeples, Scott, and Ross. Eileen took a compact from her drawstring bag and began repairing her face. Brad invited Millie to go for a walk.

"No, thanks. I think I'll stay and read."

"Scared to be alone with me?" His smile managed to look amused and offended at the same time.

Millie hesitated. "I really just want to relax."

Shrugging, he grabbed his camera case and followed Cunningham. Millie chose a grassy spot under a tree and opened her book. But Brad's question had reminded her of the topic she had tried to forget. Laying the volume in her lap, she leaned against the tree, thinking about the deaths.

An obvious motive for both was the savings account. But taking such risks for another sixty thousand when each heir would already get half a million just didn't seem to make sense. Another motive might be theft of one of the keepsakes.

Peeples said she would kill for that quilt.

Millie hated suspecting the aerobics teacher—most of the heirs, in fact—but Peeples appeared physically strong, probably strong enough to have committed the murders. Yet was she mentally tough enough? And why two killings over one antique? Too bad the victims hadn't revealed what disks they had drawn. Koontz had implied his was valuable; Johns had given no hint.

Tree bark pressed into the back of her head. She shifted positions. Actually, she realized, theft of the antiques could not explain the first death, which had occurred before the list of keepsakes and numbers went up. If Johns had had a number, even he wouldn't have known which item it was for.

A bird twittered somewhere. Clattering, scraping noises came from the bus as Fansler loaded picnic baskets.

Ross obviously wanted all the antiques and could potentially claim two, for himself and his son. Had he somehow seen the cousins' disks and killed them to trade his dollar signs for their numbers?

Pope and Endicott coveted the keepsakes too. Of course, neither executor could claim any.

Winston Akers might actually be after one antique in

particular, not all. He could have learned from Koontz yesterday which item he had, then phoned last night to entice the heir to Independence Park and overpower him. But again, even if Akers got possession of a disk, he couldn't claim an antique.

Millie drowsed in the sun, stumped by the many questions. Then there was the revenge motive . . . . She settled her head more comfortably against the tree trunk and closed her eyes. Soon, she slept.

★ ★ ★

Hamilton Ross watched Scott stride away towards the bridge, then climbed the steps to the wooded area. He needed to reflect on a problem, and the shady trail looked inviting. Rounding the big tree, he paused. This place offered seclusion. He sat on the log to think.

The trip had proved to be interesting so far. Predictably, some heirs weren't thrilled by his presence, but such boorishness no longer upset him. Alice had taught him that tolerant disdain could sometimes be a more powerful weapon than outright anger.

He missed her acutely—her calmness, her sense of humor, her teasing manner.

"Your out-of-town chickie threatening to sue if you don't ante up the child support?" she had said that Saturday morning as she'd handed him the letter with the Philadelphia postmark.

"Can't be that." Hamilton had kissed the hollow of her cheek, damp from some kitchen task. "I always send the checks on time."

Alice, never impressed by the legend of the Henry will, had always insisted they not live their lives in expectation, or let such prospects affect important decisions. She had been right about that, Hamilton thought now, and most other things.

As he had read Pope's letter aloud, she had clapped her hands.

But when told she could not accompany him, she had looked teary. She had put on a brave face, however.

"At least you'll get to see James."

Then they had learned that James wouldn't be coming.

Hamilton recalled Alice's chuckle as she'd said, "What color do you suppose this Nathan Henry was?"

"He died a wealthy man in the late eighteenth century, the ancestor of a slave-owner. White, I suppose."

"How many of his other heirs would you guess are black?"

"You think I'll be the only African-American there?"

Her dimple had deepened. "Won't you be an interesting surprise for your new-found relatives?"

Hamilton had telephoned her twice from Philadelphia, heard her beloved laugh, and imagined emotions playing across her lovely face. But the news of Johns's death had upset her so that he hadn't dared mention Koontz's. He wished she were here. Yet if she were, he would be worried for her safety.

He wasn't concerned about his own. He had been in the army and was now principal of a New Jersey high school. He had battle experience.

It was too bad about those young men, though he had not liked either. He had tried to assure Millie that their deaths were coincidental but didn't believe it himself. Johns could have been drowned on impulse—someone seeing him near the pool and shoving him in—but Koontz must have been lured to the mall. Premeditation.

Lost in thought, Hamilton failed to notice small sounds of movement through the woods behind him. A limb bent, then settled slowly back, leaves brushing leaves.

The suicide theory about Johns didn't wash. Hamilton couldn't imagine committing such an act himself, with all he had to live for: Alice, a son of whom he was fiercely proud, a job he liked—most of the time.

A twig snapped, yards to his rear. He turned, but the sun was in his eyes. He saw nothing but trees. A squirrel must have broken a branch, he thought.

He had his antiques too, so far only pewter tableware, a few hand-made razors, some silver coins, and a yarn winder. He'd been especially proud of the winder, agreeing with the dealer's eighteenth-century date but sure it was of New Hampshire origin, not Massachusetts. Now, of course, his collection would change amazingly. He'd be able to buy many other antiques, though nothing so wonderful as the keepsake he'd already drawn!

A woodpecker rat-tat-tatted the trunk of a maple. Hamilton stirred, then returned to his brooding.

The puzzle bothering him concerned the Henry antiques. He had studied the keepsakes shortly after the lottery, and a surprising detail in the letter had made him scrutinize the others more closely. Then something about the candlestand had sent him to Pope's volumes on antiques. He would study them more after returning from Valley Forge.

His mind full of wondering, Hamilton didn't hear the tiny warnings that might have saved him: footfalls on moss, a swish of air as the club swung high above his head.

It thudded hard against his unprotected skull.

✦ Chapter Fifteen

Millie opened her eyes and stretched, easing a kink in her spine. Bare tables dotted the picnic area, and quiet reigned with no one about. A glance at her watch revealed that she had slept three-quarters of an hour. Rising, she looked inside the bus. Letitia sat in a rear seat, yawning.

"Hey, roomie, what's up?"

"Everyone seems to have abandoned us."

"Like to take a walk?" Letitia came off the bus to join her.

"Better not. The others'll surely be back soon."

"Someone left a Frisbee over there. Want to toss it?"

They took positions, and Letitia pitched the disk. Awkwardly, Millie fielded and returned it. Her roommate caught it deftly behind her back.

"Show-off," Millie groaned. "You've done this before."

The saucer continued to fly, Letitia executing flashy maneuvers, Millie racing to keep up. Then an especially hard throw arced away from her. Arm outstretched, Millie lunged, missed, and sprawled hard in the grass. Letitia chortled. Millie was picking herself up, wondering how to quit gracefully, when footsteps pounded along the road.

Scott loped up, chest heaving, cheeks wan.

"What's the matter?" Millie asked.

Letitia grabbed his arm. "What is it, Scott?"

His anguished eyes moved from one to the other. Finally he gasped, "Murder—somebody's—murdered him."

Cold fear clutched at Millie.

"If you're kidding, Scott, it's not funny," Letitia said.

Millie felt sure he wasn't. "Who's been killed?"

"Hamilton . . . somebody beat—" Scott paused, throat working with emotion—"beat him to death. Brad and I found him."

Millie felt as if she had been punched in the stomach.

"Where's Pope?" he asked. "Brad went to call the rangers. I came to tell Pope."

"Stretching his legs, I guess," Letitia said. "You didn't see him on your way here?"

He shook his head. Millie stared, her mind struggling to absorb the news. Only a short time ago, she and Hamilton had had that enigmatic conversation at the mansion, and he had sat across from her at lunch. Now he was gone. Numbly, she staggered after the others, retracing Scott's steps.

"Ross was a mess." His voice broke. "He'd been hit a bunch of times. I got sick to my stomach . . . ."

"Anything around to show who did it?" Letitia asked.

"I wasn't looking for clues." Scott's face had regained color, but looked strained.

A vision of the amiable teacher, killed as some people slaughtered animals, rose in Millie's mind. It triggered another— of her mother lying across a sink of blood-stained water. Twin images of horror and loss flashed through Millie's brain, mingling into a single monstrous scene.

She wanted to cry, "STOP!" But she kept quiet, as on that long-ago night. After she had calmly answered police questions, after the gurney had taken her mother's gaunt body from the apartment, Millie had crawled under tumbled sheets on her mother's bed and wept long wrenching sobs. Loneliness and despair had lain like weights on her chest, threatening to crush her. As Hamilton's skull had been crushed today.

In the double-exposure picture in her head, ruby drops became scarlet splotches, then rivers of gore. Grassy ridges and groves of trees blurred before her eyes. Time shifted to slow motion. A dull roar sounded in Millie's head. Her breathing grew shallow, her legs rubbery. She felt herself fall.

Strong arms caught her, drew her close. A heart beat rapidly under her hand.

"You okay?" Scott's voice, gentle, concerned.

Millie's head dropped onto his sturdy shoulder. When her mother had died, she had had no one to lean on. Need had helped drive her into Jack's arms.

The world began to right itself. Her knees held her once more. The old habit of staying strong for herself and Danny returned. Millie raised her head, read tenderness in Scott's dark eyes.

Watch it, Kirchner. He might be the killer himself.

She couldn't believe that, Millie thought, didn't want to. And he seemed genuinely upset over Ross's death. But she pulled away from the embrace.

"I'm okay now. Thanks."

She knew she didn't sound all right. Scott eyed her anxiously.

"Guess you're not so tough after all, roomie," Letitia said.

No, she wasn't tough. She wanted to cling to Scott, let his warmth and strength envelop and comfort her. More and more, she felt drawn to him. Yet she dared not trust anyone, even him. The knowledge was painful, reinforcing her sense of loss.

They started walking again, more slowly.

"Where'd you meet up with Brad, Scott?" Letitia asked. "Last I saw of him, he was headed over to that farmhouse."

"I was sitting by the stream when he came walking up. He took some shots of the bridge, then we started back."

Millie forced herself to consider the mystery aspect, squelching the emotional turmoil churning her insides. "How'd Hamilton seem when you left him earlier? Think he was meeting someone?" To her relief, she sounded normal.

"An appointment? He wasn't checking his watch or anything. But he did seem to have something on his mind."

"Hmm. Did you and Brad meet anyone? Between the bridge and the redoubt?"

"No. But now you mention it, when we were nearly to the redoubt, I saw someone in the distance who walked like Fansler. I figured then he was still at the picnic site."

"Finding Ross that way must've been awful for you," Letitia said, patting Scott's arm.

He had had a horrible shock, Millie thought—assuming he was innocent, as she fervently hoped. She longed to put an arm around him. Of course, she couldn't. Eyebrow raised, she wondered how her roommate could be so calm. Was she mentally calculating her own profit from the third death?

At Redoubt #3, a crowd had gathered near the steps, watching park rangers cordon off the crime scene. Brad talked with another ranger, Fansler eying them without expression. A wan Eileen clung to Peeples, who made soothing noises. Endicott glumly stared at the ground. Pope looked pasty, wretched.

Cunningham rocked on his heels, grinning, arms folded. Millie had never liked him, but at that moment she loathed him.

Cars arrived, bringing personnel from the Upper Merion Township Police, the National Park Service, and the FBI. Millie watched woodenly as forensics people photographed and examined the crime scene and agents and detectives spoke with onlookers.

When Millie's turn came to be interviewed, NPS Criminal Investigator Victor Oblowski and Police Detective Myrna McCoy perched beside her on the wooden platform. McCoy was young and serious, Oblowski older, with a nervous tic of pursing and releasing his lips.

In answer to their questions, Millie told about Nathan Henry's will and the gathering, then detailed the other heirs' behavior towards Ross, particularly that of his assigned roommate.

Good. Let the authorities make Cunningham squirm.

McCoy and Oblowski moved off and conferred. Then Oblowski went to speak to an FBI agent interviewing Cunningham, while McCoy had Millie clarify or amplify points she had touched on earlier. Soon Oblowski returned.

"I understand two other Henry heirs have already died, Mrs. Kirchner."

Millie recounted the circumstances of the earlier deaths, then answered queries about her movements and what she knew of others' after the picnic. At last, the investigators said she could go "for now."

Finding the Henry bus in the lot beside the platform, Millie climbed aboard and fell into a seat, emotionally and physically drained. Through the window, she watched the goings-on around where Hamilton had met his violent death.

She herself had spent tranquil moments on that log, had experienced a connection to history there. Now whatever pleasure she had felt about being at Valley Forge seemed as far removed as the eighteenth century itself.

Eyes closed, Millie lolled against the seatback. A shudder went through her. It now seemed certain that someone was targeting the Henry heirs. Had the killer slaked his bloodlust? Would she be next? Had the victims been deliberate choices or random, whatever heir happened to be handy at the time?

Dallas and Danny seemed impossibly far away.

Anger replaced fear. Millie yanked the clip off her ponytail, letting hair cascade over her shoulders. Hamilton had been a likeable, calm, intelligent man, devoted to his wife. No one had a right to kill him. And for what? A few thousands more? She would accept Fij's offer, she decided, or if his interest flagged, she'd work on the case herself.

She opened her eyes and saw that Eileen now sat behind her. The actress had repaired her makeup, but her eyes showed traces of weeping.

"Eileen," Millie said, "before Hamilton's body was found, were you anywhere near this redoubt?"

"Me? Nah. Everybody had left or went to sleep after dinner, so I walked around a lot, looked at that farmhouse and them cannons. Then I saw people down here and came over."

"Did you see any of our bunch while you were walking?"

"Mr. Endicott, halfway between here and the picnic place, looking at something through them spyglasses." Eileen tapped a fingernail on a front tooth. "Oh, and when I came outa the john by the cannons, I saw Ed."

"That's not far from here. What time?"

"Musta been fifteen . . . twenty minutes before I saw the crowd here. Ed was talking to some guy—oh, you know, it was the one's been trying to buy people's stuff."

"The antiques dealer? Akers?"

"Yeah, him. They looked real friendly. Maybe Ed was planning to sell him that old gu—Oops!—what he drew."

"Which way were they walking?"

"Away from here." Eileen's hand circled, indicating the redoubt. She colored. "Guess you heard Vera and me talking before. I've decided to cool it with Ed."

So Cunningham and Akers had been near where Hamilton

was killed, Millie thought. And maybe at the crucial time.

"Did you say Cunningham drew the gun?"

Eileen nodded sheepishly. "Don't let on I told."

"I won't. Did you get anything good for you or your dad? I have an important reason for asking."

Eileen frowned. "Just dollar signs."

Cunningham swaggered onto the bus and winked at Eileen. She turned a frosty shoulder, and he dropped into a place at the front. Minutes later Brad got on and sat beside Millie, then Scott took the seat ahead, turning and smiling at her.

"You holding up okay?"

"Not bad. You?"

"Sorta numb now, I think."

As he spoke, Millie studied what she had at first thought an ordinary face. Now it seemed handsome in a rugged sort of way.

Uh oh, she thought. She mustn't let down her defenses just because he had offered her a shoulder in a crisis. Guessing wrong about anyone in this situation could mean death. She turned to the window.

Letitia got on the bus and sat next to Scott. He nodded to her, then asked Brad, "Have any trouble finding a ranger after I left you?"

"Nope. Wish my cell phone had worked. Must've let the battery run down. Anyway, I saw a ranger driving by while I was looking for a phone over by the artillery park and flagged him down. He called his headquarters, then we came back here. Passed Pope a couple hundred yards from here and told him."

"Which way was Pope headed?" Millie asked.

A slow smile lit Brad's face. "What's it matter, Sherlock? He'd hardly've stayed around if he'd killed Ross. Anyway, he went white as whipped cream when I told him.

"Soon after we got here, Endicott came ambling along,

started telling about a bird he'd seen over on that statue. He quit when he saw Pope's face. I told Endicott about Ross, and he stared like he'd been kicked in the gut. Bucked Pope up to have him here, though."

Brad said Eileen had arrived soon afterwards, then Cunningham, then Peeples, and finally Millie, Letitia, and Scott. As Millie watched Brad's beautiful eyes, her doubts about him returned. Clubbing a man to death would take daring and a cool head, both of which Brad seemed to have.

"As you can see," he went on, glancing darkly at the front of the bus, "Cunningham isn't broken up about Ross."

The big man heard him, turned and glowered. Peeples climbed aboard and collapsed into the seat beside Eileen.

"Awful, just awful." The older woman's wrinkles looked even deeper-etched than earlier. "Who'd do such a thing?"

"Come on, Peeples," Cunningham growled. "Don't go all pious on us. You probably offed the nigger yourself."

She half-rose and lifted her huge handbag as if to throw it, then seemed to reconsider and sat again.

"If any of us killed him," she said icily, "it was you. Everybody knows you didn't like Mr. Ross."

"Oh, now it's '*Mr.* Ross'? You about fell out yourself when he walked in Thursday night. I suppose you did your best to get me in trouble with the FBI and police. But I didn't kill him, y'see, so they got nothing to hold me on."

"Can you prove you didn't?"

He snickered. "Don't have to. It's up to the law to prove I did, and they can't. Great system, ain't it?"

"Would you two quit bickering?" Brad said. "We're all on edge without that."

"Oh, the gentleman lawyer's 'on edge?' Thought the more fighting there was, the better you lawyers liked it. Speaking of who coulda killed the nigger, Bennett, you're making quite a habit of finding bodies, aren't you?"

A flush tinged Brad's cheek. "Shut your face, Cunningham. If people who deserved to die always got murdered, you wouldn't be sitting here now."

Cunningham chortled and turned to the front again.

Millie changed positions, glancing back as Peeples opened her bag and took out a handkerchief. Something fell into the older woman's lap. She gasped, grabbed it, and thrust it back into the purse.

But Millie had seen it. The number eight disk. If she recalled correctly, that was the one for the quilt.

Had Peeples drawn it in the lottery after all? But if so, why had she been campaigning for another drawing?

Fansler, looking cool and unruffled, got on and strolled to the back. The executors boarded—Pope stumbling, Endicott looking strained but stoic—and sat behind the driver.

"We'll return to town now," the attorney announced wearily. "We'd seen most of the park anyway."

As they drove off, Millie imagined ragtag colonial soldiers marching away from Valley Forge after their harsh winter, no doubt glad to be leaving. She knew the feeling.

⭐ *Chapter Sixteen*

"You sure know how to plan a sightseeing trip, Pope."

Getting no response, Cunningham shrugged and looked out the window. Pope didn't appear to have heard the barb. He slumped in his seat like a well-used Raggedy Andy doll, as if the fact that the heirs were in danger had finally sunk in.

The sky was overcast again, the clouds a mass of ashy gray. Millie stared unseeingly at the back of her roommate's head, her mind on the puzzle. As far as she knew, any of the party had had opportunity to kill Hamilton, even Letitia before Millie awoke. Perhaps they all had strength enough to administer a beating if Ross had been caught off guard and therefore had not resisted.

But Millie doubted there was more than one killer, so anyone with an alibi for one murder must be innocent of all. She decided to concentrate on Koontz's death, since she knew most about people's whereabouts that night.

Some of the men didn't have roommates, but each of the women had someone who would have missed her if she had stayed out late. Millie herself was Letitia's alibi. And unless Eileen and Peeples had conspired to kill Koontz—a remote possibility, Millie thought—they were home free, too.

Only what if Eileen had spent the night with Cunningham again, or had claimed to be doing so?

"Hey, Wyrick," Cunningham broke across her thoughts, "if your two roomies got on your nerves, you didn't ought to've snuffed them. Bennett probably would've shared."

The back of Scott's neck tensed.

A bolt of lightning jabbed the smoky heavens. Thunder boomed, caroming like a billiard ball from cloud to cloud.

"Ross must've snored loud, huh?" Cunningham persisted. "Why di'nt you shove a pillow over his face in the night? Lots neater. I hear his head looks like a dog's dinner now."

"For once in your life be quiet, Cunningham," Scott said in a tight voice, the backs of his earlobes pink.

"That's enough, Mr. Cunningham," Endicott warned, his face pale and troubled..

The brawny heir grinned and sprawled across his seat.

"Not feeling faint any more, roomie?" Letitia turned to ask Millie. At Brad's questioning look, she explained. "Millie nearly collapsed when she heard about Ross."

"You really okay?" He slid an arm around her shoulder.

"Yes. But how about you? You found . . . the body."

"It was definitely worse than any grisly photo, but I'm all right."

He did seem fine, Millie noticed. Could he have killed Hamilton himself, then met Scott and taken pictures of the bridge as if nothing had happened? Photography was a good cover for going places without arousing suspicion.

As for Scott, maybe the emotion he had shown when telling of Hamilton's demise had been murderer's remorse. But she didn't want to believe that. He seemed too likeable, too decent. She felt a connection to him. Could her instincts really be so wrong?

Hello-o-o! Remember Jack?

Thunderclouds boiled outside, reflecting Millie's inner turmoil over having to suspect people around her, especially—she had to admit it—a man who interested her greatly . . . .

Think Cunningham. He probably could've killed three people and enjoyed it.

If only Cunningham *would* turn out to be the murderer, Millie thought. Or one of the non-heirs. Akers could have scaled the iron-rail fence around the mansion to get at Johns that night. Neither of the executors nor Fansler would have needed to.

Sudden rain drummed the roof of the bus and lashed at the windows. Thunder rolled like low-pitched kettledrums.

By far the most likely candidates were the Henry legatees, Millie had to admit. No one else could claim a share of the money or a keepsake, and vengefulness over losing a home and lifestyle seemed insufficient reason to kill. Or was it? She remembered what the FBI agent had said about people being slain over tennis shoes.

Could either of the executors have committed today's vicious attack? Pope appeared too mild-mannered, too incapable of hiding his feelings, Endicott too stuffy, unwilling to dirty his hands. Perhaps either could commit a white-collar crime, but this—

As for Fansler . . . .

The bus pulled up before the Henry residence. The heirs and executors raced for the door through slackened yet steady rain. Most went upstairs. Scott touched Millie's arm, saying, "Let's see if we can get some coffee."

Drawn to him, but wary, she decided she'd be safe here with people around. His smile, when she agreed, lifted her heart. They were approaching the open kitchen door when voices from within made them halt.

"That's the third one." Mrs. Fansler's voice.

"Yes. Now's not the time." The butler.

"He relies on us—"

"Too much!"

Scott coughed. The conversation abruptly ceased, and Fansler stepped out. At the sight of them, his eyelids flickered.

"Mrs. Kirchner, Mr. Wyrick." He glanced towards the kitchen, then asked politely but coolly, "Can I help you?"

"Could we get some coffee?" Scott asked. "If it's not too much trouble."

The butler visibly relaxed. "Certainly, sir. I'll serve it in the sitting room."

As Millie and Scott sat facing each other at a tea table in the appointed place, she said, "Wonder what that conversation was about."

"I've no idea." His brown eyes held hers. "This is the first time we've been alone, Millie. You always seem to be with Brad."

"And you with Letitia."

"I was taught to be polite."

"So was I."

They laughed. Scott laid a hand over hers, setting her nerve endings atingle.

"I like you, Millie," he said. "And respect you. Raising a son by yourself, holding down a full-time job, going to college. It must seem too much at times."

Millie nodded. "Sometimes. But it's all important. Danny, especially."

"Will you give up the job now?"

"I may, or at least cut back on my hours. But I need to think things out carefully. Don't want to live high at first, then end up with nothing."

"Yeah, I'm cautious, too, when it comes to spending money."

"What changes will you make, do you think?"

"I can look after Aunt Charla, for one thing. She had some

money saved, but it's about to run out. I could apply to get her on Medicaid, of course, but . . . she's always been so proud. Not that she'd realize now, I guess. Anyway, I'll probably buy a car, get a nicer apartment. And travel. There are lots of places I want to go."

"Me, too."

"We have a lot in common, don't we, Millie?"

"Yes."

Scott started to lean towards her, lips parted.

Just then, Fansler entered with a tray and said dinner would be served in an hour. Scott leaned back and removed his hand. Disappointed, Millie gave him a wistful look.

The butler set the tray on another table, poured coffee, and turned to leave. A question occurred to Millie.

"Mr. Fansler," she said, "the night Wes Koontz was killed, do you recall what time you locked the front door?"

He blinked rapidly, twice. "I've told the authorities all I can remember about that, Mrs. Kirchner."

"I know. Do you mind telling me?"

"I suppose it's okay. I went to the grocer's for a few items, returned about 10:40, got busy in the kitchen, and forgot to lock up till nearly one."

"Did you see anyone come in after you did, and before you locked up? Mr. Pope or—anybody?"

"No one. Will there be anything else?"

She said no and thanked him. He left. Scott gave her a puzzled look.

"What's going on?"

"I've been wondering if one of us could've killed Wes and gotten back in without alerting Fansler."

"Sounds like almost anyone could have. Hamilton said he let himself in and was surprised to find the door unlocked."

Suddenly tired of the topic of murder, Millie asked about

Scott's life.

He said his parents had died in a plane crash when he was eleven. Then he had lived with his aunt, a fifth-grade teacher who had encouraged his love of books.

"Money was scarce, but Aunt Charla insisted on saving 'for a rainy day.' She worried we'd have an emergency and end up losing our home. I worked from junior high on, delivered papers, did whatever I could to earn a buck."

"You win this time," Millie teased. "I didn't start waitressing till high school."

He smiled sadly. "I was almost through my bachelor's when Aunt Charla was diagnosed with early Alzheimer's. I moved her to Boulder so I could look after her. But one day while I was in class, she left the house and forgot the way home. Scared the heck out of me. I found a place where she gets good care, but I sure miss the aunt I knew."

Surely a man who spoke with such feeling about his aunt couldn't be a killer, Millie thought. Still, the victims of Ted Bundy and other serial killers had thought them nice guys, too. Finally, she decided not to drive herself crazy with speculation, but to try to relax and enjoy this time together. She just wouldn't let her guard down.

Millie told about losing her mother and living in a foster home. "I married partly to get away from there, partly because I'd just read *Wuthering Heights* and decided Jack was Heathcliff in the flesh."

"So you ended up with a kid."

"Two kids, really. The older one ran away. But the one that's left is a keeper."

His eyes softened. His sympathetic smile stirred something within her, made her long to pour out her worries and beg him to convince her he hadn't killed anyone.

Aware how crazy that would sound, she tore her eyes from

his. A glance at her watch told Millie it was nearly dinnertime.

They rushed upstairs. Millie showered and put on the taupe sheath, which had come back from the drycleaner looking fine, even its pulled threads mended. But she omitted the brilliant scarf in acknowledgment of Hamilton's death. She paused at a window to watch a robin resplendent in red, gray, and black plumage sun itself on the sill.

But it noticed the human presence and flew away, leaving her feeling unbearably lonely. Would she ever again cuddle Danny, hear his teasing giggle? Would she look into Sylva's faded blue eyes, hear her wry but loving voice?

★ ★ ★

Glasses and silverware clinked at an otherwise-quiet dinner table. The dwindling of chairs mutely announced three absences. Finally, Peeples spoke.

"Can we go home? Do a second drawing and leave?"

Several voices agreed.

"Good idea, Vera," Eileen said, pale despite heavy rose blusher and mauve lipstick. "I'm scared to stay here."

Roused from his reverie, Pope speared a grilled shrimp.

"I'm sorry, ladies. Mr. Henry stipulated a week for this gathering. We must honor his wishes."

Endicott cleared his throat. "Arthur, in view of the circumstances, perhaps we should end things early. The heirs are frightened, and one can hardly blame them."

"The will's clear on that point," Pope insisted.

"It *would* be a shame for you to miss Olde Fort Mifflin," the banker hedged, "and the period homes in Germantown."

"Lot of good sightseeing'll do us if we're killed in our beds," Peeples muttered, pushing food around her plate.

Pope's chin thrust out determinedly. "Also, having everyone here will help if the authorities need to question us again. I know everyone wants the killer caught."

"You're not likely to be murdered in your bed, anyway, Miss Peeples," Endicott said. "The deaths have all occurred outside the mansion."

True. Interesting point.

Peeples raised her eyes in resignation.

"That means the killer must not be one of us," Brad said cheerfully as he watched Fansler remove his plate.

Crash! The dish slipped from the butler's grasp, barely missing a water glass. He apologized and whisked away the dropped plate, then carefully removed the other dishes.

Letitia frowned. "Who else would have a motive, Brad?"

"One of the other heirs. Someone who didn't come."

"Hm-m-m, maybe."

"That's a nutty idea," Scott objected. "My aunt's in a nursing home, and you said your mom has a broken leg."

"Danny's a tad young," Millie said dryly.

"Mrs. Moriarty has a weak heart," Endicott said. "She didn't come this week because her little dog became ill, but she's hardly athletic enough to do any of those murders."

"Eileen's father?" Brad said. "Ross's son?"

"Leave my daddy outa this," Eileen said, eyes flashing. "You don't know anything about him."

"Hamilton's son is somewhere overseas," Millie said.

"So we've been *told,*" Brad persisted.

Pope shook his head. "When I phoned Mrs. Ross, she said her son was abroad and might not make it home to the funeral. She was devastated to learn of her husband's death, poor woman. Besides, are you suggesting young Ross came here to kill his own father, Mr. Bennett?"

"Stranger things have happened."

Millie imagined Alice Ross, a thoroughly nice woman from her husband's description, hearing that her Hamilton wouldn't be coming home alive. Another life destroyed by this murderer, Millie thought, her gorge rising.

"Maybe some of the killings were a cover," Brad went on, toying with a chocolate-coconut crepe.

"What in the world do you mean, Mr. Bennett?" Peeples huffed. "Seems to me you enjoy seeing all of us scared."

"The murderer might've really been after one particular person—say Ross—and killed two others first to make his death seem part of a pattern. You know, confuse the issue."

"Too chancy," Millie said. "He might've been caught before he got to the one he wanted."

Conversation lagged over second cups of coffee. Then Pope loudly cleared his throat.

"I must address another serious matter. Fansler reports the architect's rendering is no longer in the parlor."

Millie glanced at Letitia, who returned her gaze with a puzzled shrug. If she had taken the drawing she'd made no secret of wanting, Millie thought, Letitia hid her guilt remarkably well.

Pope looked sternly from one heir to another. "This can no longer be considered joking. If the missing things are returned now, there'll be no recriminations. Otherwise, I'll have to file a theft report." He stood, signaling that the meal was over.

Scott invited Millie for a stroll in the back yard. It sounded wonderful, but her doubts about him lingered. She suggested the game room instead. He wrinkled his nose.

"No privacy. Maybe the sitting room."

"Okay."

They walked to the sitting room, and Scott paused at the door to let her precede him inside. As she passed near him, his breath tickled her cheek, stirring desire. She took an easy chair, and Scott moved another close to hers. The mixture of attraction and distrust she felt overcame Millie, and she blurted the question that was uppermost in her thoughts.

"Who's the killer, Scott?"

She had half expected to startle him into an admission. His grin was disarming.

"Has to be Cunningham, don't you think? He was away from the house when Wes got it, nobody recalls where he was when Gilbert died, and he hated Ross."

Millie told Scott about Eileen's seeing Cunningham near Redoubt #3 a few minutes before Hamilton's body was found. She omitted any mention of Akers.

"See?" he said. "And Cunningham's as big as Ross. Doing that beating would've been easy for him."

"Couldn't almost anyone have done it? If the first blow stunned Hamilton?"

"Even Eileen or Letitia?"

"Maybe. But I'm sure Letitia didn't kill Wes."

"You actually considered her a possibility?"

"No more than anybody else."

"Me?" His serious dark eyes challenged hers.

"You less than some."

"But you do suspect me. You must not be too terrified, though. You're here with me now."

She shrugged, reluctant to pursue that thought. Another idea occurred, and she said, "When you found Hamilton, didn't you say there was lots of blood around?"

"God, yes. All over the place."

"I didn't notice any on anyone in our group."

He frowned. "That's true. And when I used to kill chickens for Aunt Charla, I always got splattered. Who could it have been, then? None of Brad's theories makes sense."

"I guess the murderer could've covered his clothes with something. Or taken his outer stuff off."

Scott looked skeptical. "Wouldn't a guy in skivvies attract

attention?"

"The underbrush was fairly dense there. He could've partly disrobed in the woods, sneaked up behind Hamilton and killed him, dressed again, wiped any spatters from his face and hands, and come out somewhere else." She considered. "He'd have had to risk being heard, though. Beating someone so viciously must've made noise."

Scott nodded. "Maybe it could've happened that way. Who could've gotten out of and back into their clothes fast?"

"Almost anybody but Eileen, I suppose. Her dress has a lot of buttons. But the rest of us wore casual clothes."

Talk veered to other topics, but Millie's thoughts stayed partly on that scene in the woods. Preoccupied, she sat without speaking for a few moments.

"Millie." Scott's voice, tender now, got her attention. "You're good at hiding your feelings, but I know you must be upset about all these deaths. I want to stay close to you . . . keep you safe . . . ." He put an arm about her shoulders and leaned closer. This time, his lips touched hers with warmth and passion.

Swayed by his gentleness and their growing closeness, she returned the kiss. But she recalled her suspicions and pulled away.

Jack the Ripper probably was a terrific guy at times too.

"Sorry, Scott. I . . . just can't. . . get involved." She wished she could take back the words, move into his arms again. But she mustn't. Too dangerous.

"Somebody back home in Dallas?"

A nervous laugh burbled in her throat. "I've had no time for romance."

"Then it's because you think I could be a murderer." His voice, still low, had acquired an edge. "For what it's worth, I'm sure you're not the killer."

"I am sorry, Scott. Things are strange right now." She couldn't leave it at that. She had to soften the rejection somehow. "Friends?"

"Not the 'let's just be friends' routine, too!"

She laughed. The corners of his mouth tugged upwards.

"Okay," he said, "for now. Let's go see who's in the game room. But this isn't over."

Millie smiled, thrilled that it wasn't. Assuming he didn't turn out to be the murderer, of course.

⭐ *Chapter Seventeen*

In the game room, Scott and Millie found Letitia and Brad playing table tennis, both now wearing shorts and T-shirts. Scott removed his jacket and hung it on a chairback, ready to challenge the winner. Saying she wanted to look at the keepsakes again, Millie went to the parlor.

Fij and Peeples sat on a couch, the latter speaking softly, the former writing in a notebook and squirming.

Good. You need to see him anyway.

Millie nodded to the current guard, who sat reading a magazine. As she studied the antiques through the glass, they took her back in time, and she imagined a long wintry night with the Henrys. An older son sat cleaning the rifle, while Nathan read aloud to the family by candlelight, the taper placed on the candlestand beside his chair . . . .

Candlestand, Millie thought, suddenly returning to the present. What was it Hamilton had said about it? ". . . too short, but why?"

Why, indeed? What had Hamilton meant?

Peeples left. Fij came over and tapped on the glass.

"Nice, aren't they? Which one'd you draw?"

"We weren't supposed to tell, but it seems nothing about

this week is going as planned. I won't be getting any."

"But you still get the money, right? Not too shabby." He passed a hand through his curls, leaving them a jumble of upright corkscrews. "How about an interview, Millie?"

"I do want to talk to you." As they walked to the other end of the room, she asked quietly, "You figured out who the killer is yet?"

He shook his head. "You working with me?"

"If you can help solve this thing fast, count me in."

"Great! Got any theories?"

"Too many. I suppose you know about Hamilton's death?"

"Yeah, a buddy of mine works at the V.F. Visitors Center, and he phoned me. I got what I could from the Merion County cops and a few spectators. Too bad. I liked Ross. Even if it wasn't mutual."

He threw a leg over a chair and perched his open notebook on its back. She took another seat.

"Shoot, Millie." He tapped his ballpoint on the book.

"There could be more than one killer, of course. But I think the same twisted mentality is behind them all."

"Check."

"I figure the murderer followed Hamilton and Scott, hoping to catch Hamilton alone and off guard. His sitting on that log gave the perfect opportunity."

"Squares with my thinking." Fij bent to scratch an ankle. "The murder was premeditated but involved luck, too, like finding a tree limb the right size. They found a bloody branch, by the way, off in some brush." He spread a hand, bent one finger. "Let's talk possibilities. You're clean." He folded a second. "Letitia probably is. Nobody saw her leave that picnic place, so she couldn't have left till everyone else had, and she was there when you woke up."

Millie nodded agreement.

He doubled a third. "Eileen's story checks. Witnesses saw her twice where she claimed to've been." He touched another digit but didn't fold it. "I like Cunningham for the killer, but Eileen's vague about the time she saw him near that artillery. Think she's trying to shield him?"

"I doubt it, or she wouldn't have mentioned him at all. What about Akers? Eileen said he was with Cunningham."

"The 'antiques dealer'?" Fij rubbed his thigh. "Apparently nobody's tracked him down yet."

"You don't think he really deals in antiques?"

"Oh, he's for real. Has a reputation for shady deals. He'd con Ross out of an antique, but why would he kill him?"

"That stops me, too. But Akers does seem awfully eager to get his hands on those keepsakes."

Fij tapped a thumb. "Peeples says after she left the picnic she found a quiet place and just sat there, thinking. The spot she mentioned is fairly near Redoubt #3, but so far nobody confirms her story. Or refutes it." He raised the hand, three fingers bent, two upright, and thrust it at Millie. "Two good suspects, Cunningham and Peeples."

"I can count. Go on."

He spread the other hand and tapped a finger. "Bennett. Some ditzy woman saw him photographing the cannons like he said, but she hadn't a clue about the time. Three real prospects."

"I don't think Brad's guilty. If he'd just beaten a man to death, it seems to me he'd have been noticeably upset when he met Scott soon after. But for argument's sake, okay." She cleared her throat. "What about Scott?"

Fij's brows drew together, as if her voice had betrayed interest. "He *claims* lots of people drove by the bridge but no one got out. Nobody backs his story." He touched another digit. "*Four* good suspects."

She shook her head. "Scott was really agitated over finding the body. I doubt he could've been so convincing if he'd actually killed Hamilton. Him or Brad either."

Fij pulled at an ear. "Never can tell. You got a thing for Wyrick? Or Bennett?"

Avoiding the question, she mentioned her theory that both of the executors and the servants resented the heirs' presence, because it ended the Henry trust.

"Weak, huh?"

He rubbed his chin. "Seems especially farfetched in the banker's case. A witness puts him and his binocs way north, near Redoubt #4, just after lunch. He maybe could've walked to Redoubt #3, killed Ross, and got back to Gulph Road by the time Eileen spotted him there, but he'd have had to really move."

"And Brad said he mentioned having been at that statue, which is farther south than Redoubt #3. What about Pope?"

"After putting the food away, he and Fansler went walking. Pope stopped off to watch boys playing war near Gulph Road. Says he was there most of an hour. No one corroborates that, though. In fact, nobody remembers seeing him till Bennett and the park ranger did.

"The butler says that after he left Pope he hiked south past Redoubt #3, followed the main road around to #4, stayed a while and walked back. I haven't found substantiation for any of that. Yeah, Fansler was in the vicinity, all right."

Millie mentioned Scott's impression that he had seen the butler near Redoubt #3 while walking back from the bridge. Fij held up both hands, one with all fingers raised, the other with two up.

"Seven fair-to-good suspects, though the resentment motive seems shaky for the execs and Fansler. Okay. Any points you thought of that we haven't covered?"

She shook her head.

"Guess I'll see you tomorrow, then." He rose. "You going to Mass or anything?"

"No. Don't you reporters even take Sundays off?"

"Not when I'm on something good."

"Did you by any chance murder three people just to get a hot story?"

He grinned. "On a slow news day, reporting's a nasty business."

★ ★ ★

When Millie got upstairs, Letitia was lying on the folded-out deception bed reading a magazine bought the evening before. She said both she and Scott had beaten Brad at table tennis.

"Big brother's game was off tonight. I guess finding Ross affected him more than he's admitting."

"You seem to be handling things okay, though."

"I'm scared, believe me." The violet eyes grew stony. "But I'm not about to let Cunningham get me alone."

"You're positive he's the killer?"

"Aren't you? I had wondered about Peeples before, but she at least seems sorry about Ross's death. Cunningham's all but turning handsprings."

Millie got her art supplies and sketched a group of generic faces, like the crowd at the crime scene earlier. Letitia took a bottle of capsules from a drawer, swallowed one, and offered them to Millie.

"Sleeping pill? After what's happened, I need one."

Millie declined. But later that night, watching Letitia slumber peacefully, she questioned that decision. Twice she rose and looked down on the backyard, where pole lamps made pompoms of light against a misty night. Nothing stirred amid the trees and shrubbery. She felt alone, isolated.

Early the next morning, she dressed quietly and went downstairs. Breakfast was not yet set out in the dining room, nor did she see anyone. She decided to phone Sylva, who should be up, even allowing for the time difference. Finding the office open, Millie dialed the number of the nursing home and soon heard Sylva's voice.

"Morning, Kirchner. How're things in Philadelphia?"

Millie had questioned whether to mention the latest death, but on hearing the dear voice she found herself spilling the whole story.

"Please don't have a heart attack or anything, Sylva—it's probably selfish of me to tell you—but I had to talk to someone. I don't know who to trust here."

"Don't ever be afraid to tell me anything, hon. I'd be more upset if I thought you were keeping something from me."

"Thanks, Sylva, for listening and for caring."

"Lots of folks care, hon. You just don't often let them get close. But caution may save your life this time."

"So you think I'm in danger?"

"I'm not in my dotage yet, Kirchner. Three out of ten people have been killed, and nobody seems to know why or by whom? Yeah, I'd say Pauline's in peril."

"Any suggestions? Other than coming home immediately, which sounds awfully appealing. Unfortunately, the conditions of the legacy demand we stay a while longer."

"Then you have to be mighty wary, hon."

"I was planning to paint a bull's eye on my forehead. But you may know best."

"Hon, I'm worried, but I trust your instincts. You're smart and resourceful, and you've weathered more crises than any young woman should have to. I love you, you know."

"Likewise, you impossible old bear. It helps to feel you're here with me."

"I wish I were."

"No, you don't. But I'll survive. I hope."

"Take care, hon. I mean that."

After Millie hung up, she walked up the hall to the parlor. The security guard was gone, presumably on a bathroom break. Eileen stood near the door, straightening the architect's rendering in its customary place on the wall.

"The drawing—*you* took it?" Millie said incredulously.

Eileen's hand recoiled, jarring the picture out of alignment. Her face turned a mottled red.

"Why'd you steal it, Eileen?" Millie asked. "Because you didn't draw a keepsake for yourself?"

"Wasn't me took the pitcher," Eileen said indignantly. "I just brung it back for somebody. Don't say nothing. Please."

"Who'd you return it for?"

A sly look came over Eileen's pretty features. "I don't have to tell you. You're not the cops or the FBI."

"No, but if I tell Mr. Pope I saw you return the drawing, he'll probably pass the information on to them."

Eileen studied her vermilion fingernails. "Well . . . okay. But you can't tell nobody. Vera musta stole it. I broke a strap getting ready last night. She'd gone downstairs, but I figured she wouldn't mind if I looked in her drawers for a safety pin. The pitcher was under some underwear."

"And you offered to bring it back for her?"

"Lord, no! Vera don't know I found it. I sneaked it out this morning before she woke up. I already returned the snuff bottle, got back a bracelet of mine, too."

"Was there a bottle of pills there? Antidepressants?"

Eileen frowned. "Maybe. The salt shaker was, but I figure nobody'll make a big deal over that." She lifted her blonde curls, let them fall again. "Vera coulda got in a lot of trouble over the other things, though."

"Why didn't you confront her, then urge her to return them herself?"

"She might not've done it, and there'd'a been a big fight. You're not going to tell, are you?"

Millie considered. Eileen could have stolen the drawing herself, gotten cold feet, and made up the Peeples story. But it might be the truth. And now the rendering was back—

"I guess not. But why would she take those things?"

"Maybe she thought stealing them would help her somehow to get the quilt. She wanted it real bad."

"I know. Eileen, do you know what she drew in the lottery?"

"She wouldn't tell me."

They went to the dining room, where Fansler was arranging chafing dishes, puffs of steam rising. He bowed to them and left. They poured coffee, Eileen lacing hers liberally with cream, and sat at the table.

"The night Koontz died . . ." Millie stopped, searching for a delicate approach, then finally said, "Did you stay in your own room?"

"Yeah, why?" Grasping Millie's meaning, she blushed. "You mean, was I with Ed again?"

"Sorry. I know it's personal, but it may be important."

"I stayed with Vera."

"And she was there all night? She didn't leave?"

"Sure. You think *she* killed Wes?" Eileen sipped pallid coffee. "Forget that. Vera's a busybody but real sweet. She would *not* kill *nobody*. And she didn't leave our room that night."

"You're positive?"

"Yeah. I'm a light sleeper."

So the women had alibis. That seemed to leave three males who could have killed Koontz: Cunningham, Brad, Scott.

"Do you think Cunningham really went to a bar Friday?"

Eileen tilted her chin. "I didn't see Ed after supper that night. I was ticked off at him."

Scott and Brad dragged in, bleary-eyed, and shared sleepless-night stories with the two women. Then Endicott came in, looking as tired as she felt.

"Morning, everyone," he said, uncovering a dish on the buffet. "I hope you all rested better than I did. Oh, you needn't wait for the others. Arthur told the maids not to wake anyone, so people will probably straggle in."

Millie lined up with the others, smells of sausage and French toast stirring her hunger. They were eating when bright-eyed Letitia entered, followed by a haggard-looking Peeples and Pope. Letitia heaped her plate, Peeples took tiny bits of foods, and Pope settled for coffee. After a few desultory remarks by various diners, Endicott addressed Pope.

"You know, Arthur, I've been thinking. The keepsakes guard has to stay with them, but what about getting a second security person to roam the mansion? Wouldn't that make everyone feel safer?"

Voices chorused agreement.

"If you'd all like that," the attorney said listlessly. "Will you make the arrangements, Soames?"

"Of course, Arthur."

Millie had finished eating and was getting more coffee when Cunningham entered. Grinning, he flung his arms wide.

"Beautiful morning, ain't it? I slept like a dead dog. Gee, some of you don't look so good."

Others glared, watching him pile a plate high.

"You know, Cunningham," Brad muttered, "you're so happy, you must either be Ross's killer or know who is."

The heavier man flopped into a chair.

"I'm right, aren't I?" Brad said.

"You're a riot, Bennett." Cunningham shook salt all over his food. Then he shoved a hunk of sausage into his mouth and spoke around it. "The best part is, you don't got a clue how funny that is." He chuckled. ""No clue at all."

★ Chapter Eighteen

"Would it be possible to see Henry's will some time?" Scott asked Pope, when Fansler had removed the dishes, and the diners were on their third cups of coffee. "It must be fascinating."

The attorney smiled, easing tension lines around his eyes. "Of course, Mr. Wyrick. We have it here." He pushed back his chair. "I'd planned to show it to you all last evening, but with the events yesterday . . . ."

"It's not filed with the court?" Brad asked.

"It was entered in probate, of course, but since it's historically significant we're allowed to show the original to you, then place it in the museum."

"I don't wanta see some old—" Cunningham's eyes grew crafty— "Guess I better, though. It may not say all Pope claims. Maybe he coulda paid for our trips but pocketed the money himself instead."

Pope flushed but didn't reply. Peeples professed no interest in seeing the will and went to get ready for church. The others went to the library, where Pope lifted a portrait of a simpering female in Victorian dress to reveal a wall safe.

"She was a great-granddaughter of Nathan Henry," he explained, "famed in her day as a hostess and fashion plate."

He opened the safe, removed several flat, wooden, glass-topped boxes, produced a key, unlocked them, and took out pages. After arranging these on a library table, he stepped back. "Here it is, written in his own hand, witnessed by friends."

The heirs crowded around, Cunningham at the forefront. But after studying the faded, cramped longhand a few minutes, he said to Eileen, "Screw this. Can't make out the scribbling. Want to get more coffee, babe?"

"I'm not your babe, but I guess I could drink a cup."

The remaining heirs moved among the pages, deciphering them. Brad commented on the insight they gave into Henry.

"Paragraph after paragraph of who gets what. Imagine putting in a will which nephew gets which pair of gaiters."

"But the part leaving the house and furnishings to the city isn't detailed at all," Millie said. "It mainly refers to an inventory the executors were to keep current."

"Mr. Henry loved this place," Pope said, "but he seemed to realize things would get broken and replaced during two centuries. He stipulated that his unmarried daughters should be allowed to live here after his death, but then wisely left decisions about the mansion to the executors. Passing it down through many generations would've proved unworkable, I think."

Endicott agreed. "Branches of the family might even have sued for the privilege of living here."

"If I do say so," Pope said, "we executors have been excellent stewards of the house. We've even bought furniture ourselves which will remain with it.

"But returning to your point, Mr. Bennett, Mr. Henry seems to've had the idea that his descendants would treasure anything he'd ever worn or touched."

Sarcasm from Pope? And about the great Nathan Henry?

"The language in the will isn't all that different from what you'd find today," Scott said. "Legalese is legalese."

His mockery was lost on Brad, who stabbed at a page with his finger. "Check the capitalization. 'Children,' 'Friend,' 'Home,' 'Death'—we don't usually capitalize those words. And Henry sure couldn't spell."

"Spelling and capitalization weren't standardized then," Millie said. "People worked out their own spellings and capitalized the nouns they considered important."

"Sounds confusing."

"You can understand what's meant, however," Pope said. "' . . . if my Wyfe shall dye before me . . .' clearly doesn't refer to coloring cloth."

Fansler entered and spoke softly to Pope, who excused himself and left. He returned shortly, saying the authorities needed to question the heirs again. Millie went to the sitting room, where she sat at a desk with two interviewers.

"It seems another of your number was killed yesterday, Mrs. Kirchner," Detective Nolen said.

"Yes, and the rest of us are plenty scared."

"That's understandable. Believe me, we're doing everything we can to solve these murders." The bags under his eyes recalled to Millie her basset-hound sketch of him.

The middle-aged black woman he had introduced as FBI Special Agent Arnetta Gathron took Millie back over points in her earlier statements, then zeroed in on the keepsakes. What disk had Millie drawn? Did she know what others had? How had individual heirs reacted on seeing the list of numbers and keepsakes? Was there friction over any item? Millie answered, including the fact she had seen Peeples with the number eight disk at Valley Forge.

Nolen's eyes widened a centimeter. "You say she acted surprised? As in, 'I'd forgotten I brought that with me?'"

"It seemed something more at the time." Millie wondered

why the sudden interest in the lottery. When a pause came, she asked about it.

A smile twitched Nolen's mouth. "We prefer to ask the questions, Mrs. Kirchner. Tempting as it is to turn the investigation over to you."

Something about Hamilton's death must have spotlighted the keepsakes, Millie decided. When they finished, Gathron asked her to send in Letitia. As Millie strolled along the main hall looking for her, she met a gangly uniformed brunet. He nodded impersonally and strolled on up the hallway, like a cop on a beat. Passing the parlor, she saw the regular morning guard beside the keepsakes cabinet. So Endicott had already added more security, she thought gratefully.

She found Letitia alone in the library staring mournfully out a window. After her roommate left, Millie took books on early-American furniture from an alcove shelf and curled up in a chair. She looked up all the indexed mentions of candlestands, but nothing in text or picture captions explained Hamilton's cryptic comment, " . . . too short, but why . . . ."

Millie sat idly flipping pages of one volume, while pondering those words. A subhead in bold print seemed to jump out at her: "Dimensions, an Oft-Overlooked Clue to Authenticity." She read the paragraph that followed: "An eighteenth- or nineteenth-century table should be about 26–29 inches tall, the right height for someone occupying a chair of that period. Twentieth-century chairs are built lower to the floor, so tables made nowadays are also shorter. The antiques forger may give himself away by using today's measurements on 'yesterday's' tea table."

Her mouth went dry. Now she understood why her feet didn't touch the floor when she sat in the mansion chairs.

If the candlestand keepsake was "too short," Hamilton must have suspected it was a modern-day forgery! Her head whirled with the implications.

"Hi, beautiful." Philip Judd, looking cool and casual in tan slacks and yellow pullover, spoke from the doorway. "I nosed around and picked up some more info." He dropped into a chair beside her and took out notebook and pen.

"Good. What?"

"When the police did background checks on you guys, they turned up a long record for Cunningham. Burglaries, petty cons, forgeries—mostly checks, but also a few 'antiques.' Nothing violent so far, but that big savings account might've made him change his methods." Fij crossed his legs and swung a foot back and forth.

Millie stared. "Counterfeit antiques. So he must know more about early-American stuff than he lets on."

"Probably. So?"

"So the authorities are asking more questions about the lottery. And Hamilton must've suspected something." She explained and showed Fij the passage about dimensions.

"Okay, but even if the candlestand's fishy, how does it explain three murders?" He beat the pen against his chin. "And even if Cunningham could've made a fake good enough to fool Ross— no mean feat, apparently—how would he've smuggled it in with such tight security around the keepsakes?"

"I don't know, but Cunningham and Akers were palsy-walsy at Valley Forge. Maybe they cooked up something together. Or—the night Johns died, Cunningham was seen talking to the guard. Maybe he bribed him to help make a switch."

Fij pulled at an ear. "The guard couldn't have opened the cabinet alone. Pope would've had to be in on it."

"Oh . . . right. In fact, we heirs weren't even told what the keepsakes were before we got here. So Cunningham couldn't have had counterfeits already made." She slapped the book. "But I can't shake the feeling that this is important."

She twirled a strand of hair. "Hamilton might've been killed to prevent his exposing the forgery. But why the two deaths earlier? And why would anyone choose the candlestand to steal? It's not one of the really valuable pieces."

Fij leaned closer. "You haven't heard all my news. The Fanslers' son has done time too, armed robbery and rape." He tapped the pen on his knee in time with the swinging shoe.

"Really. And I bet nobody knows what the son looks like except his parents and Pope. And maybe Endicott."

The foot swung faster, and the staccato pecks changed to double-time. "Yeah. He could've been at Valley Forge and you heirs wouldn't have realized it."

"Maybe that's where Fansler Senior went after lunch yesterday, to meet his son."

"And the night Johns got killed, Senior had to've seen him go outside—he was out there on a break himself—but didn't own up. A maid told me all this." The rapping slowed, then ceased. "Let's see, he went back in the house soon, so he couldn't have followed Johns and killed him, at least not then. Maybe he tipped off the son, and the son drowned Johns. Junior could've sneaked over the fence to do it. He'd know the layout of the place."

"The maid's just now mentioning all this?"

"Loyal to Fansler, I guess. And till Ross got it, the servants tried to believe the accident and mugging explanations for the other deaths." Fij scratched his nose. "Think of anything else, Millie? We're partners, you know."

She shook her head.

"How about going out with me once this case wraps up?"

The shoe swung again. Millie decided a whole evening of his squirming might bring out homicidal tendencies in her.

"Thanks, but I leave Wednesday. I doubt it'll be solved by then."

"You never know. Anyway, you could stay over."

"Not really. I have to get home to my son."

He left. Millie rose, planning to get another look at the candlestand keepsake. As she carried the stack of books to their shelf, Pope entered.

"Lunch is ready, Mrs. Kirchner." He added teasingly, "Quite a bookworm, aren't you? Three at once."

"Just browsing."

"Antique-collecting can take over your life. You'd be smart not to get into it."

That sounded almost like a warning, Millie thought as she accompanied him to the dining room.

As another possibility occurred, her stride faltered. It had been his responsibility to keep up with the Henry heirs through the years, noting milestones and changes of address. Could he really have been unaware of Cunningham's criminal record? Might the executor even have contacted him before the other heirs, hatching an elaborate charade to get those keepsakes? Could the two men's hostility towards each other be an act?

Pope, Cunningham, Brad—maybe even Scott—were all playing parts? Was the aspiring actress actually the most real person here?

★ Chapter Nineteen

At lunch a more cheerful Pope announced that a second guard had been added and that he had requested and been promised extra police patrols outside. The architect's drawing and snuff bottle had also been returned, he said. Peeples paused in lifting a forkful of chicken salad to her mouth and swiveled towards Eileen, who became busy buttering a slice of crusty bread. Peeples slowly chewed her food.

The others chatted as if reassured by the encouraging developments. But when Pope mentioned plans to tour Olde Fort Mifflin later that day, anxious voices protested.

"I understand your nervousness," he said, "but if I thought you were in any danger, I wouldn't suggest this trip. The fort's a much smaller area than Valley Forge, and there'll be lots of people around. A killer won't be able to get any of you alone there."

"The fort is interesting," Endicott seconded, "and today's an especially good time to visit. There's to be a reenactment of a Revolutionary War battle."

Discussion continued, but in the end grudging agreement came from the heirs. Being trapped inside the house lacked appeal, and Pope convinced them that the fort would be safe.

After lunch they waited in the parlor for a bus. Millie noticed Peeples' eyes strayed often between the returned drawing and Eileen. But the latter, animatedly discussing clothes with Letitia, avoided eye contact.

Millie stood near the keepsakes, her eyes measuring the candlestand against a similar one by Brad's chair. The tables did appear to be of different heights. And if one keepsake was a fake, what about the others? Tingling with excitement, she looked up and saw Brad watching her with a puzzled expression.

The bus arrived. Scott helped Millie on and sat beside her, his nearness thrilling even though troubling. Brad sat with Eileen, occasionally glancing darkly at Millie.

They headed south towards Philadelphia International Airport. Though the day was sunny and breezy, with streaky white clouds across a bright blue sky, and though she looked forward to seeing the historic site, Millie wistfully watched planes depart overhead.

"One of those may be headed to Dallas."

"Your son back from his camping trip yet?" Scott asked.

"Should be later today. I'm eager to talk to him."

They took a narrow country road, with weeds tall on both sides, passed a sign giving fort hours, and turned into a parking lot containing another bus and several cars. Nearby buildings included a decrepit brick, a white frame, which Pope said had once served as the fort's mess hall, and others behind a wire fence that sported a sign for the U.S. Army Corps of Engineers.

"The Corps and the Pennsylvania National Guard operate a military reservation near the original fort," Pope said.

The fort itself lay across the road from the parking lot, past a moat thick with lily pads. Brad photographed the exterior, while the others entered through an arched gate in the brick wall. Inside, a small town of red brick one- and two-story buildings, some with white columns, ranged around the edges of a sizeable arena. A young man in a Parks and Recreation Department uniform gave each heir a printed sheet and said the reenactment would begin in half an hour.

Millie skimmed the handout about how a garrison of exhausted men had endured weeks of cannon fire here in 1777, working at night to rebuild walls battered down by day. The heroic effort had delayed arrival of a resupply fleet and prevented British troops from chasing and crushing battle-weakened Colonial forces till winter snows made pursuit impossible. Thus, the rebels had been able to regroup at Valley Forge before fighting renewed in the spring.

"'The siege of Fort Mifflin,'" she read aloud, "'has been called the forgotten battle of the American Revolution, yet the stubborn defense of this hastily completed fortification against hopeless odds was one of the most courageous and inspiring actions of the entire war.'"

Scott gave a low whistle. "If the fort hadn't held, the whole Revolution might've failed. I'm a history buff, but I never heard about this before."

"Me, neither."

Scott couldn't be the killer, Millie told herself, not someone so sensitive and companionable. But suspicion ebbed and flowed through her mind, making her wretched even as they shared a pleasant experience.

The burned shell of a commandant's residence occupied the center of the clearing. Flanking it were two large grassy mounds, on the west a powder magazine, on the east a late-nineteenth-century torpedo casemate. Several Japanese youths posed for one another's cameras at the officers' quarters in the northwest corner. Brad snapped photos of soldiers' barracks nearby. Millie and Scott joined dozens of other tourists milling about the arena.

At the northeast bastion, the two climbed a gun platform

overlooking the Delaware River, which curved around the fort on the east, bound for Delaware Bay and the Atlantic Ocean. New Jersey lay across the river, Philadelphia and its environs to the north. Millie donned sunglasses against a bright sun, shimmering on the glassy surface of wide, placid waters. She imagined herself a fort defender, fighting on despite wounds, noise, and fear.

"Serene now, isn't it?" Pope said. He stood near her, hands behind his back, smiling at the panoramic view.

"Looks can deceive," Cunningham spoke behind them.

The attorney frowned as if the sun had been shut off, but recovered and laid a hand on Scott's shoulder. "Mr. Wyrick, you'll appreciate a tactic the British used." The two moved off, Pope telling Scott how the attackers had finally diverted the river channel and sailed near the fort under cover of darkness.

Head-gesturing at Pope, Cunningham smirked at Millie.

"You're cheerful," she said. "What's your secret?"

He laughed uproariously, as he had at breakfast.

"Secret— Brad was right this morning, wasn't he? You know something about the murders."

His grin turned to a sneer. He walked away.

Millie's pulse raced. Was he the killer?

Her stomach clenched with fear. If he was guilty, she had been foolish to challenge him.

Stick close to other people today, hon.

Pope completed his story and wandered off. Scott and Millie entered a chamber beneath the fort's outer wall, a bombproof room used as a prison during the Civil War. Just inside, Endicott was discussing a stack of crude cots with Eileen. Near the back wall, which was dotted with fireplaces and ovens, stood Brad and Letitia. Earnest frowns on the handsome faces said the conversation was serious. As Millie neared them, she caught part of Brad's speech.

". . . we should take the chance . . . got nothing to lose. . . ."
Letitia nodded agreement.

The siblings spotted Millie and Scott and moved farther away. Millie examined a semicircular fireplace midway up the brick wall, her heart pounding as she realized two people could have committed the murders far more easily than one.

Someone with nothing to lose could be dangerous, she thought. Very dangerous.

★ ★ ★

Ed Cunningham strolled into the bombproof chamber under the fort wall. *Jeez,* he thought, those bakeovens at the back were big enough to stuff a body into. He walked out whistling, full of nervous energy, eager to get the meeting over. Pretty day, he thought, though not even bad weather could have ruined his mood, as high as it had been on the day Pope's letter had arrived.

"Mail call, Ed," Pauley had said, tossing envelopes on the bar and hoisting his wizened body onto a stool. "It came just as I was leaving, so I brought yours, too."

Ed grunted and kept on dipping glasses into scummy dishwater and into a soapier rinse. He didn't smile, wouldn't give his squirrelly neighbor the satisfaction. Friends were a luxury Ed Cunningham couldn't afford.

He felt itchy to move on, now that he'd saved enough to replace the suitcase and clothes he'd ditched when the last game had gone sour. Who'd have thought the old lady'd get suspicious and call the cops so soon? But there were plenty of spots in the world where folks would believe a guy who dressed well and drove a sincere-looking car. A Mercury or Olds next time, he thought, nice and steady, nothing flashy.

Ed finished the glasses and flipped through his mail.

"Occupant" envelopes went into a wastebasket. He put aside two utility bills till he was sure when he would be leaving.

One bulky envelope was from trustworthy Aunt Teresa, actually his dead Uncle Al's third wife. Having always had a soft spot for Ed, she let him use her address, signed for any certified mail, forwarded anything he might want to see, and trashed the rest.

Her envelope held another, its fine paper fairly reeking of money. From a law firm in Philadelphia.

Somebody threatening to sue, of course. But Ed never worried about such letters. He could be long gone before official papers got served. He slit the envelope with the knife he used to cut fruit.

The contents were not a threat. Apparently Aunt Teresa had been right to believe that wild tale of a legacy due her late husband's kin. Ed himself had never put any stock in the nebulous riches. He took advantage of others' faith, but he had little himself.

He pored over the letter a long while, reading it through three times as his neighbor watched, squirming.

"Hey, Ed," Pauley finally said, "your rich uncle die and leave you money?" He chuckled to signal he was joking.

Ed looked up with a benevolent smile. Astonished at such unaccustomed good humor, his neighbor gulped his beer too fast and strangled.

"Not far off there, Pauley, not far off." Ed folded the letter and stuck it into his pants pocket. Whistling, he picked up the knife and began slicing a lime.

Encouraged by the grin, Pauley tried again. "Hey, why not let a pal in on it? I'll help you celebrate."

Ed studied the old barfly maliciously. "There's just one problem with that scenario, Pauley. We ain't pals."

Crestfallen, Pauley downed his beer, rose, and drew himself

up to his full five-foot-two.

"Kiss my ass, Cunningham," he said in his most imposing voice. Unfortunately, it broke on "Cunningham," ruining the effect. He strode from the bar.

Grinning to himself, Ed watched the exit. He should worry about making an enemy here! Now he was coming into money, he might not have to try another scam for a while, at least not in Kansas. He would have to deplete his nest egg to get to Philly, but what the hell? One new place had as many possibilities as another. New territory—new people—new contacts—new cons.

Things were turning out even better than he'd expected, Ed thought now as he circled the compound, too restless to stand with the people gathering at the north end. Anyway, he didn't care about this history crap. The down side of the trip was having to hear Pope's endless speeches and troop around to places that bored the shit out of him.

Ed paused at the northeast bastion and looked at the water again. Still wet. God, he hated sightseeing. But he would be leaving in a few days, rich. Learning about the half million had whetted his appetite for more. The rifle would of course go to the highest bidder. Best of all, he was about to arrange for a lucrative lifetime income.

Leaving the river view, he sauntered around the edge of the arena. A few spectators occupied the benches in front of the officers' quarters and soldiers' barracks. Others stood in groups at that end of the enclosure. Almost time. Good. He passed the meeting place, but it was too early to go in. He continued walking, grinning as he recalled his stroke of good fortune at Valley Forge.

After the picnic he had looked at the Varnum farmhouse, messed around at the cannons, thrown rocks at birds, and walked almost back to Redoubt #3. Overcome with heat and weariness, he had made for an inviting stand of trees a few yards off the road. Glad of the shade amid the grove, he'd collapsed on a moss carpet and fanned himself with a handful of leaves.

How long till the others would be ready to leave?

THUD! Thud! THUD!

What the—? Someone driving a stake? A baseball bat hitting the ground? The dull whacking sound came from the direction of Redoubt #3. It didn't sound exactly like soil being pounded, but it wasn't a metallic clang either. Kids playing, maybe, beating a stick on a tree stump.

Ed scrambled to his feet and peered out through bushy limbs. Nobody on the platform over the earthwork. The noise seemed to come from the wooded area across the road from it. He waited. Could it be animals fighting? But he had heard no frantic scurrying. Someone clubbing a dog to death? More like that. He waited, hardly daring to blink.

Presently, a figure emerged from the woods several yards beyond a set of steps, glanced furtively around, stuffed something into a bag, and walked unhurriedly along the road towards Redoubt #4. Full of questions, Ed followed, watching his quarry adjust clothing and smooth hair. They reached a bend where the road doubled back on itself. Then they left the paving and struck out across the grass. Checking his map, Ed realized they were heading for the covered bridge. The terrain roughened, became brushy. Walking grew more difficult. Ed tired and turned back.

Reaching Redoubt #3 again, he decided to see if he could learn what those sounds had been. He climbed the steps across from the earthwork and rounded a big tree, almost falling over the inert body of a man.

Hamilton Ross.

Blood splotched the trail, spotted a fallen log, spattered leaves, soaked Ross's green polo shirt, and dotted an outstretched arm. Clots encrusted what was left of the man's head, the face crushed, pale bone splinters protruding through his dark skin.

A little gore Ed could handle, but this . . . . His stomach lurched; his heart beat fast. Closing his eyes, he tried to imagine himself somewhere else—anywhere else. At last he felt steadier, and his nausea eased. Averting his eyes from the body, he turned and ran down the steps. Up the road he went to the haven of his thicket. He flung himself on the moss and waited for his heart to stop thumping.

Then he realized his danger. He had made no secret of hating Ross. If he were seen here, he would be suspect number one.

Ed scrambled to his feet and crept along to the edge of the grove. He took a deep breath, patted his hair into place, and made himself walk casually past the artillery field, change directions, and approach the cannons. He struck up a conversation with an elderly man, laughing genially so the old guy could later report how calm and relaxed Ed Cunningham had been, not at all like someone who had just beaten a man to death.

Ed walked back to the road, briefly followed a couple walking hand in hand towards Redoubt #3, then sped up and passed them. "S'cuse me, folks." Just beyond the pair, he stopped as if uncertain of his way. He consulted his map, shook his head, reversed himself and again passed the couple, this time shrugging and saying, "Wrong way."

There. They should mention him as a casual sightseer.

Nearly back to the cannons, he saw Winston Akers just ahead. What was *he* doing here? Ed had caught up to Akers, and they had had a profitable talk.

No doubt about it, he thought now as he circled the arena again, Ed Cunningham was in a lucky cycle. Not only had the uppity nigger got what he deserved, not only had Ed escaped a murder scene undetected, he had seen the killer. His blackmail ultimatum had even been received with resignation, as if expected.

But there had not yet been time to talk terms. That would happen during today's show, with everyone else's attention occupied by it.

A stir went up from the crowd. Ed turned and saw "soldiers" in Revolutionary War era uniforms and tricornered hats enter through the north sallyport. A few manned the main gate and fort walls. Others entered the soldiers' barracks and officers' quarters.

BOOM! Cannon fire exploded from the south, outside the fort. The battle was on.

Ed stopped near the arsenal in the northeast portion of the fort, turning to watch the activity at the south wall, as defenders fired cannons towards the river, reloaded, and fired again. Men in various stages of undress, buttoning breeches or pulling on shirts, ran from the barracks. Soldiers hurried to gun platforms and to the arsenal. It was too much for Ed. This was *too* good a view. He skirted the back of the arsenal and moved along the east wall.

As he went, Ed searched the crowd for one face. At last he spotted it, saw the murderer slip through a bunch of watchers, behind other spectators, and into the old torpedo casemate, jacketless and with his hands empty, as Ed had stipulated.

Moments later, Ed followed. He would ask for a hundred grand to start, he had decided, not so much the killer couldn't pay but enough to make it clear that Ed was sure of his information. He could raise the ante later.

Yes, Philadelphia was working out fine. Ed Cunningham would never have to resort to small-time swindles again.

His thoughts occupied with rosy plans, he entered the earth-covered mound and started up a narrow passage. A few feet along, where daylight didn't reach, the way grew dim, then opaque and black. He hadn't counted on this. Ed's palms began to sweat. He wished for a cigarette lighter, a match, something. Ever since his teenaged years, he'd relied on his size as protection, but dark places returned him to the night terrors of his defenseless childhood.

He touched a wall to steady himself and went into a crouch, eyes straining for a clue to what lay ahead. The atmosphere felt close, smelled stale. He paused, thinking he'd turn back, reschedule the meeting in a better lighted place.

But he hesitated. Privacy . . . schedule. And the lure of money was strong.

A sudden recollection of Ross's bloody head brought him up short. Cunningham turned quickly, sensing a trap.

The air behind him seemed to change, grow warmer. Something caught at his windpipe, jerked him to a halt.

It tightened on his jugular, shut off his breathing. Panic gripped him. He clawed at the wire encircling his neck, fingernails digging his own flesh. But it held fast, stifling him, making him crazy. He reached behind to grab at his assailant, but the attacker eluded his groping fingers.

Too late Ed realized that a lifetime of deceiving others had not kept him from being tricked himself. He had under-estimated this murderer. Fatally so. He dropped to his knees, succumbing to the darkness.

★ *Chapter Twenty*

Millie and Scott had joined the spectators near the barracks, not far from Letitia and Eileen. Pope and Endicott were standing in another group at the officers' quarters. On a bench near them, Peeples sat distractedly opening and closing one hand. Brad was waiting with his camera by the north sallyport. Cunningham was leaning against the arsenal.

Make-believe soldiers entered and took their places. A barrage of cannon fire began.

Millie held her ears. Her eyes and nostrils smarted from smoke and black-powder stench. The "injuries" and "deaths" reminded her of Hamilton and her mother. Even imagining herself a fort defender, buying time for Washington, didn't work this time. The reenactment blocked her own vision.

The bombardment continued for many minutes, then red-coated troops stormed the main gate. A melee of rifle fire and hand-to-hand combat followed. Men lunged at each other with knives and bayonets. Their emptied rifles became clubs. Faintly sick, Millie wished it over.

Finally, it was. "Survivors" and "casualties" bowed to cheers and applause and left the arena.

Millie looked around for the Henry party. Eileen and Letitia, as well as Endicott, stood where they had at the start of hostilities. Pope had moved yards away, near Brad. She didn't see Peeples or Cunningham.

The show over, some of the spectators left. Millie and Scott resumed their tour at an artillery shed in the south end, then entered the casemate to its northeast. At first, daylight through the open door allowed easy going up a long corridor, but soon the way dimmed, turned black. Disoriented, Millie faltered. Scott bumped into her.

Suddenly alarmed at being in this dark place, alone with someone who might be a killer, Millie drew away from him. She steadied herself against a wall, planning to let him move past her and then to creep back up the hall to daylight. She heard fumbling sounds beside her, then the striking of a match. Scott held it high. She saw him shrug and smile.

They were near the end of the passage, where a dark doorway loomed.

"Want to go back, or look inside?" Scott offered. "Probably nothing much to see in there."

Millie hesitated. Either he was no murderer, or else adept at pretense. Every part of her argued for the former. "Just a quick peek," she heard herself say.

Millie stepped through the door just as the match went out. Her foot struck a bulky object on the floor. Stumbling, unable to get her balance, she fell forward onto it.

"They should put a light in here," she said. "Or else not leave things for people to trip over." Then she realized her left hand was touching fabric, like a man's shirt. Her right lay on something hairy, warm.

A human arm.

She gasped, recoiled, tried to push herself upright.

"Where are you, Millie?" Scott asked. "What happened?"

Frozen, she heard another match scrape, then saw in its flame

Scott's eyes, large and concerned. She jumped up and grabbed his arm. Unable to speak, she pointed downwards.

He stooped, held the light low, then passed it back and forth over the crumpled figure.

"Lord—Cunningham!"

Millie saw that the man's hands were clenched at his neck, his tongue sticking out. She heard gargling sounds, coming from her own throat. Steeling herself, she knelt beside Scott. He held a palm near Cunningham's nose, then checked his wrist.

"No breath, no pulse," he said. "Think it was a stroke or heart attack?"

The match went out. Scott lit another and held it near Cunningham's cheek.

Millie gasped. "Look how he's clawed at his neck. I think it's murder. Can you try to revive him? I'll go for help."

"Good idea. Hurry back."

Leaving him striking another match, she retraced her steps along the hallway, touching walls to steady herself. She sped up as a beacon of daylight grew at the end of the tunnel. Emerging into blinding sunshine, she stopped, shielding her eyes against the glare. A middle-aged couple strolled past, and Millie hailed them.

"There's a problem in there," she said as composedly as she could manage, pointing at the casemate with a shaking hand. "I'm going to get someone. Could you please wait here and make sure no one goes inside?"

With puzzled expressions, they agreed. Millie ran towards the main gate, where the Parks and Recreation attendant was talking with a spectator. What had occurred inside that earthen mound? she wondered as she hurried towards them.

Someone must have jumped Cunningham during the mock battle. But who? She had seen the other heirs and both executors just before it started, and all but Peeples just after.

Peeples. She had not gotten along with any of the victims, and Cunningham had been her special nemesis. Had she, in spite of Eileen's defense, committed all four murders?

At least Millie knew Akers and the Fanslers were not guilty. The fort was a fairly small area, and she would have spotted any of them here.

But what about that mysterious Fansler son? She wouldn't recognize him if he were present.

Millie reached the gate just as a spectator moved off, and gave the uniformed guide her message. He frowned, asked a few quick questions, and told her to go back and watch the casemate till he got there. As she left, he was making a call on his cell phone.

She returned to the casemate entrance, where the middle-aged couple asked what was going on.

"Someone's been injured inside," Millie said. "You haven't let anyone in since I left?"

They shook their heads no. "But who got hurt?" the woman demanded. "And how?

"I guess we'll all know more once the emergency people get here." Millie hoped she sounded calmer than she felt. "Thanks for watching the door. I'll take over now."

The pair moved off a short distance but stood eyeing her and muttering to each other. Just then, Letitia and Eileen approached.

"I'll do your face before dinner if you like," Letitia was saying. "We'll bring out those pretty eyes—" She broke off as she saw Millie. "What's up, roomie? You're white as salt."

Millie whispered that she and Scott had found Cunningham inside and that he appeared to have been attacked. Eileen clutched her arm.

"Is Ed bad hurt? I want to see him."

"I think he may be dead," Millie said gently. "You mustn't go in."

"I was so sure he was the murderer," Letitia murmured, putting a sympathetic arm around Eileen. The actress hid her face against Letitia.

The Parks and Recreation attendant arrived, carrying a large flashlight and a first-aid kit. "Help's on the way. I've got people stationed at the exits to keep any more folks from leaving. Keep guarding this door." He went inside the casemate.

Brad came up swinging his camera case, and Millie told him the news.

"Cunningham!" he said. "There'll be no shortage of suspects this time. Everybody who ever met the jerk."

Brad looked genuinely surprised, Millie thought. Noticing Eileen's tears, he stammered a shamefaced apology.

She wiped her cheek, spoke between sobs. "I was—wasn't in—love with Ed—or nothing—but he—was nice to me—sometimes. Oh, I'm—so scared."

Scott came out, shook his head slightly at Millie, and said he was going to find Pope. Soon he returned, he and a shaky-looking Endicott supporting an ashen-faced Pope. They eased him onto the grass, and the banker dropped alongside his colleague. Millie fanned the attorney with the handout from her pocket until his color improved somewhat.

"I'll never forgive myself," he moaned. "I was sure you'd all be safe. I promised you—"

"Don't reproach yourself, Arthur," Endicott said, pushing a gray lock from his eye. "I'm as much to blame as you. Nobody could've predicted this."

"Apparently *someone* could have," Millie said.

Endicott sighed heavily. "Of course we'll cancel the historic-homes tour planned for tomorrow. And perhaps the rest of the gathering."

"You're right," Pope said. "I've been so wrong to. . . ." His voice trailed off.

A crowd had gathered in front of the mound. A man said loudly, "Did somebody get shot? Thought they weren't using live ammo in that battle."

"What's going on?" Peeples said, walking up to Eileen. "Why are you crying, dear?"

Letitia told her.

"Oh, no," the older woman said, gripping Eileen's hand. "I'm so sorry, dear."

Leaving Letitia's arms, Eileen ran to her roommate. Peeples rocked her like a child, silvery hair against gold, wrinkled face smiling behind the younger head.

Before long, paramedics and law enforcement people swarmed the area, inside and outside the mound. The Henry party waited in a group, watched by a uniformed policeman. Detective Nolen and Special Agent Gathron spoke with Scott, then with Millie on a bench near the barracks. She shuddered as she described for them her experience of falling on Cunningham in the dark.

"When did you last see him alive?" Gathron asked.

Millie told of seeing the victim in the arena, then recounted her conversation with him a few minutes earlier.

"And what did you make of that, Mrs. Kirchner?"

"Till then, I'd thought he was the killer. Now I wonder if he was blackmailing whoever it is."

She answered questions about where she had stood during the battle and where others had been. She hadn't seen anyone near the casemate during the reenactment, she said, but hadn't been looking that way.

"Was Cunningham friends with anyone here?" Nolen asked.

Millie mentioned his relationship with Eileen.

"I know he wasn't popular. Who'd he fight with most?"

She detailed his exchanges with Peeples, Brad, and Pope.

At last Gathron said, "So four out of ten of you have been killed in four days. And three of the bodies were found by some combination of you, Mr. Wyrick, and Mr. Bennett. Interesting, isn't it?"

Millie bit her lip. "You make it sound like some kind of conspiracy."

"I tend to notice coincidences," Gathron said with a wry smile. "Often, they aren't."

After she was dismissed, Millie joined Scott by the main gate.

"You okay?" he said, laying a hand on hers.

She nodded, comforted by his touch. "You?"

"Still alive. That seems to be a real accomplishment the way things are going lately."

From afar, they watched the swirl of activity around the casemate.

"The killer must be nuts," Scott said. "To keep on, after all the attention the other murders have gotten."

"Or desperate."

"Pretty daring to attack a guy with hordes of people around. But I guess the battle would've covered sounds."

"Especially inside that big mound of earth. The killer must've been waiting for Cunningham inside. The timing had to've been tricky, though." She told Scott her blackmail theory.

"Sounds like a real possibility." He searched her eyes with his. "Thank God you're all right, Millie."

"You, too," she said tremulously. "We'd better get out of here while we still can. And to think I was really looking forward to seeing Philadelphia."

They learned Cunningham had been garroted. As Millie sat beside Scott on the bus trip home, shadows lengthening across fields, her emotions were in an uproar. Terrified to remain longer, desperately missing her son and home, she nevertheless was glad of one thing:

She now knew for certain that Scott was not the murderer.

★ ★ ★

"It was awesome, Mom," Danny piped in Millie's ear. "We roasted wienies and told ghost stories, and I caught a fish, nearly a foot long! We ate it for supper, and it was great!"

"Terrific!" She could almost see his lively hazel eyes under their long lashes. "I'm glad you had a good time."

"We had watermelon, and Jimmy Peterson sprained a finger climbing rocks. When are you coming home?"

"Thursday at the latest—I hope sooner. I miss you."

"You're bringing me something, aren't you?"

"You bet. Bought it the other night."

"What is it?"

"A surprise. But I'll tell you something else nice—we're going to get money from that relative I mentioned."

"Awesome! How much?"

"Enough to buy you a bike. And me one, too."

His shriek nearly broke Millie's eardrum. "When?"

"The money will be sent to my bank in Dallas. We can probably go shopping next weekend."

They talked a while longer, mostly about the bikes and places they could ride on them. When Millie hung up, gray-green homesickness washed over her. Talking to Danny had been wonderful, but now uncertainty over when—or if—she'd see him again seemed unbearable. She dragged herself up the hall and started for the stairs. Maybe she would just announce tomorrow she was leaving. What could Pope do if she did?

Philip Judd came out of the game room. She groaned.

"Hi, gorgeous," he said with a grin. "Spare a minute?"

"Don't take this personally, but your face is the last one I want to see right now."

"How could I take that personally?" He scratched an ear. "Got to talk to you. Few minutes, okay?"

Reluctantly she went to the library with him and replied listlessly to his questions. He paused in pacing around her chair and rapped his knuckles on his forehead.

"Why didn't I go to the fort? I knew it was on your agenda, but I thought I could use my time better here . . . ."

"I wish you had gone. You might've had sense enough to count noses during the reenactment."

"Think Cunningham did the others, then somebody did him?" Fij circled her chair, one hand rubbing his neck.

She shook her head. "I think it's the same person."

"Peeples? You didn't see her right after the show."

"True, but it lasted half an hour or more. Time for one of the others to slip away and then back."

"You saw Letitia and Eileen together, the execs too. How about Bennett? Think anybody'd have noticed if he cut out?"

"Not likely. He was moving around to get good shots."

"Bennett could've done all those murders. He had the strength, the opportunity—"

"As far as we know. But I can't— Oh, I don't know what to believe."

Finally, she excused herself and went to take a long, soaking bath.

At dinner, though Fansler served flawlessly, worry shadowed his face. Millie wondered if even the servants feared for their lives. But his wife's cooking—crown roast, souffled potatoes and asparagus almondine—had not suffered.

"I was listening to a radio talk show just now," Brad said, "and the host called this place the 'house of death.'"

"The media are really pestering me," Pope said. "They love

serial killings, and they'll make this into a scandal."

"It *is* a scandal," Peeples said indignantly. "I'm going home tomorrow, and you can't stop me."

All the other heirs backed her. Pope frowned.

"Detective Nolen says they can leave, Arthur," Endicott said. "So long as he knows how to reach them."

"All right. Some of you might still be alive if I . . . ."

Millie saw her own relief mirrored in the others' eyes.

"Where'll you go, Mr. Pope, once this place becomes a museum?" Scott asked.

"I've rented a small house. But I must clear up things here first, like arranging about the victims' remains once they're released."

"You said the cousins had no close relatives except each other," Letitia said. "What about Cunningham?"

"I spoke to an aunt, actually a widow of his uncle. She didn't sound terribly upset over his death but was indignant to hear that she wouldn't inherit his share of the legacy."

"We gonna draw again?" Eileen asked in a newly confident voice, her appearance vastly improved by subtle makeup, a smooth chignon, and a simple, sophisticated navy dress of Letitia's. "Ed had the gun. What'd those other guys have?"

The executors looked at each other. "I suppose we can forget Mr. Henry's prohibition about discussing the lottery," Endicott said. "I saw Mr. Johns's disk when he drew—a dollar sign. I didn't see what Mr. Koontz or Mr. Ross got."

"Do you know what they had, Mr. Pope?" Brad asked.

The attorney shook his head. "If anyone needs to change flight reservations, the office phone's available."

"Do you have a computer handy?" Letitia asked. "I'd like to check flights online."

Pope's blank gaze answered her question.

"What about the second drawing?" Eileen insisted.

Peeples watched Pope keenly but didn't second Eileen.

"Tomorrow morning," he said, looking suddenly worn out.

Fansler served a crispy-pillowy confection of puff pastry, cherries and whipped cream.

"Mrs. Fansler's trying to kill the rest of us all at once," Scott said.

Millie grinned at the gallows humor. No one else did. But Millie felt light-hearted, glad she could share a moment with Scott without wondering if he was what he seemed.

After dinner, the heirs trooped to the office. Letitia and Brad got the phone first and took a long time working out a satisfactory schedule. Millie pulled Scott aside.

"The phone in Pope's apartment has a second line."

They found the executors in the parlor, both staring into the keepsakes case.

"It ends tomorrow, Soames," Pope said mournfully. "I feel as if my life is over."

Endicott laid a hand on his shoulder. "You've managed magnificently, Arthur. Mr. Henry himself couldn't have done better. I'll miss these beautiful antiques, though."

"So will I."

Millie asked Pope if she could use the phone in his apartment. He hesitated.

"The kitchen phone has a separate line. Use that."

Three lines. Koontz's call could've come from here.

In the kitchen, Millie and Scott found Mrs. Fansler piling leftover roast in a Tupperware bowl and supervising a maid's loading of the dishwasher. She greeted them with her usual scowl but pointed to a phone on the counter. Millie made flight arrangements, then Scott.

"So this is what being rich is like," he said when he had finished. "Flying, not hitching."

They thanked the cook, who nodded curtly. As they were

leaving, the butler came in carrying a stack of cups.

"Where'll you two go now?" Millie asked him.

His wife glowered at her.

"Mr. Pope found us positions with his friend." Fansler handed cups to the maid. "The house is compact, up to date. Even with daily help, this mansion's a big responsibility."

"So you're glad to be leaving?"

"Prepared, Mrs. Kirchner. We're prepared."

"Have you been happy here? Your son as well?"

The gaunt face softened. "Frederick couldn't play downstairs because of all the antiques, but he loved to run along the third-floor hall." Fansler frowned. "I suppose we indulged him. One tends to do that with an only child."

I must remember that once we get the Henry money, Millie thought. So far she hadn't had much chance to spoil her only child. "Mr. Pope must've been close to your son, setting up that exercise room for him."

The cook cleared her throat.

"Yes, well," the butler said, "if you'll excuse me, I'll just help finish up here." He picked up two full containers and headed for the refrigerator.

Scott and Millie walked hand in hand to the parlor and sat on a sofa, making plans to share a cab to the airport. He bent his head as if to kiss her, but just then Brad and Letitia appeared and suggested a Scrabble match.

"Scrabble?" Scott said. "Somehow, I'd never have picked either of you as devotees of that game."

"We played a lot when we were growing up," Letitia said. "It's still Mom's favorite game, and we've been playing with her since she's been laid up."

Reluctantly, Scott and Millie agreed, and they all went to the game room.

"Scott and I'll play you and Brad, roomie," Letitia

announced.

Millie saw Scott stifle a smile. They sat in captain's chairs at the games table, and Brad got the Scrabble set from a cabinet.

Both siblings proved to be better at the game than Millie would have anticipated. Brad did try to introduce "words" that no one else recognized but, when challenged, offered only token argument. Letitia complained prettily that she never drew decent letters; however, she managed to score well with those she got. Scott showed a talent for placing letters to make words both horizontally and vertically.

But Millie's abilities, honed through helping residents at the nursing home, stood her in good stead. A few women residents—including Sylva—played Scrabble nearly every day, and Millie often got drafted to help someone think of a word or to spell one. Since they all called on her from time to time, the game stayed good-humored and no one cried foul.

When the final scores were tallied, Millie and Brad had won.

"Told you we were a great team, Millie," he said with a wink. "It's two to zip, guys. Too bad you can't compete in our league."

"What's this 'our league' business?" Scott said with a grin. "Without Millie's plays, like adding "nex" in front of "us" to make a triple-word score, you'd have gotten your clock cleaned."

"Beauty and brains in one special package," Brad said with a suggestive look into Millie's eyes.

"I'd have done much better, Scott," Letitia said, "if I could've gotten some better letters. When we play with Mom, I almost always win."

"Dream on, sis," Brad said. "It's getting late, guys. Guess I'll go out for a last smoke." He gently took Millie's hand, turned it over, and kissed the back of it. "Thanks for the game, fair maid. See you tomorrow."

He left. Letitia glanced at Scott, who was gazing at Millie, hesitated, then wheeled and followed her brother. Millie and Scott returned the letter tiles to the box, put it in the cupboard, and went upstairs.

In the hallway outside Millie's room, they stood looking at each other a long moment. Then he leaned over and brushed her lips with his, tentatively yet eagerly. Millie returned the kiss. His arms went around her waist. She laid her hand on his chest, felt his rapid heartbeat. The embrace seemed especially sweet, now she knew he was innocent.

Minutes later, she entered her room. Letitia stood brushing her hair, seemingly lost in thought. Millie got her drawing tools and sketched the dead heirs: Hamilton clutching a bloody candlestand; Cunningham with a thin line tying his neck to one; Johns floating beside one of the small tables; and Koontz with one sticking out of his chest. Then she examined the four pictures.

Candlestands everywhere. She must have them on the brain. *A morbid pattern, Kirchner.*

Millie felt she was on the verge of figuring out something, but couldn't quite get it. She drew Pope as a snarling grizzly, very different from her original teddy-bear image of him, then Endicott as a shifty-eyed gangster, then the Fanslers as Dickensian rogues Mr. Jingle and Sairey Gamp. Unflattering portraits, all.

Was her subconscious trying to tell her something? That the four were in collusion? It sounded crazy, yet nothing in this situation seemed sane.

"It wouldn't work," Letitia said abruptly. "Being a professor's wife just wouldn't suit me."

Millie smiled, relieved to know she and Letitia were no longer in competition for Scott. She tossed aside the sketch pad and opened the book of Franklin letters. But her thoughts returned to the phone question. If the call to Koontz had come from

Pope's room or the kitchen, it must have been made by one of the tenants, or with their complicity, or during their absence. She decided she must manage a private talk with the cook.

But from what she had seen so far, it promised to be a one-sided conversation.

Chapter Twenty-One

With the prospect of leaving for home, most of the heirs seemed cheerful the next morning. Only Peeples appeared edgy, dropping her eyes when anyone looked at her.

"When we going to do the drawing?" Eileen said around a bite of banana pancake. "My plane leaves early afternoon."

"Right after breakfast," Pope said with a sigh.

"You must know what disks the victims had, Mr. Pope," Brad said. "Else how'll you know what numbers to put in?"

"You're right," the attorney conceded. "Disks were found on all of them. I guess with things disappearing here people were afraid to risk leaving them in their rooms. The original disks are evidence, but we've had duplicates made."

"So what do we have a chance at?" Brad persisted.

"Yeah," chorused Letitia and Eileen.

"Ahem. Well, Mr. Johns had a dollar sign as Mr. Endicott said, Mr. Cunningham the number seven for the gun, as Miss Goggins said, and Mr. Koontz the number nine, for the miniature."

"Mrs. Henry's portrait," the banker said. "Lovely."

"Mr. Ross had a dollar sign and the number four, for the samplers."

"Can't be," Scott said. "Ross had the eight, for the quilt. I promised him I wouldn't let on he'd told me."

So Scott had known all along what Hamilton had but hadn't told her, Millie thought with a dart of disappointment.

"You're the one who's wrong, Mr. Wyrick," Peeples said. "Mr. Ross deceived you. *I* have the eight."

All heads turned towards her.

"Why would Hamilton lie about that?" Scott asked.

Brad scowled. "If you drew the quilt, what was all that business, asking what everyone had and trying to trade?"

Peeples looked at her plate. "I . . . misread the list at first . . . thought the number for the quilt was a nine." She put a hand to one eye. "My vision isn't what it was. But yesterday I checked the list again and saw my mistake."

"You killed Ross so you could trade disks," Brad accused.

Millie decided she had to speak. "I saw the number eight fall from your bag at Valley Forge, Miss Peeples. You seemed shocked to see it."

"I drew it, honest," Peeples said, looking up with misery-filled eyes. "I just didn't recall I had it with me yesterday." She looked from one suspicious face to another, lifted her chin as if to brazen it out, then buried her face in her hands. The muscular body shook with sobs. The other heirs exchanged embarrassed glances. At last, her crying subsided. She raised her head, teary but resigned.

"You're right. I drew the five, for the candlestand. Somebody must've slipped the number eight into my bag at Valley Forge. I wanted that quilt so bad . . . when the disk fell in my lap, I just . . . but I didn't kill Mr. Ross."

Endicott frowned sadly at her, as if he wanted to believe her but couldn't quite.

"The police will have to know about this, Miss Peeples," Pope said somberly.

She nodded, squared her heavy shoulders and cleared her throat. "I may as well admit I took the architect's drawing and the other things, too. It'll probably come out anyway."

"You?" Letitia said. "But why?"

Peeples spread her hands, palms up. "I was getting better, my counselor said so. But here, the unfamiliar situation, the tension . . . ." She hung her head. "It's kleptomania. I've fought the problem for years."

Eileen put an arm around her shoulders. "It was me put the pitcher and bottle back, Vera. I found them in your drawer when I was looking for a safety pin."

Her roommate looked up. "I wondered, but finally decided a maid must've found them. Why?"

"I was scared you'd get in trouble."

The older woman gave the younger a watery smile.

After breakfast, they all adjourned to the library, which was arranged as on the first evening. Pope stood at the lectern, and Endicott took the chair behind the pedestal holding the opaque bowl. This time Millie sat between Letitia and Scott in the front row of folding chairs.

"I've placed five disks in the bowl," Pope said. "The numbers four, seven, and nine, plus two dollar signs. Since it's not clear if Mr. Ross drew the four for himself or his son, it seemed fairest to put back both." He glanced at the back row. "Miss Peeples, the number eight, please."

"Just a minute," Millie said. "That'll make six disks in the bowl then. But the victims had only five between them. There's one disk too many."

Color drained from Pope's face. His eyes flew to Endicott, who frowned thoughtfully.

"She's right, Arthur," the banker said. "But Detective Nolen said they found three numbers and two dollar signs on the victims?"

Wordlessly, Pope nodded.

"Let's see," Endicott went on, "I watched you put the disks in the bowl Thursday just before dinner—nine numbers for nine keepsakes, then seven dollar signs to bring the total to sixteen." He turned to the heirs. "How many numbers are you holding? Raise your hands." He lifted his own to indicate he held one for Mrs. Moriarty. Letitia raised one hand, Scott and Peeples two each.

"And three in the bowl," Endicott said. That's the nine. How many dollar signs have you?"

Millie and Eileen raised both hands, Brad and Letitia one each.

"Six," the banker said, "and two in the bowl. Mrs. Kirchner is correct. There's an extra dollar sign."

His colleague at first seemed struck dumb. Finally, Pope murmured, "How?"

Endicott tapped a finger on his chin. "You decided I should get a couple of extras made initially, remember? In case one got lost? It appears that some time between Thursday evening and this morning, someone got his hands on one."

"How?" the attorney repeated. "The spares were locked in the office desk, with our schedule and other papers."

"You're sure that drawer has been locked all the time?"

Pope rubbed his forehead as if to summon a genie. "Except when I was taking things out or putting them in. And only once was anyone else around when I opened it. You remember, don't you, Mr. Bennett, Miss Bennett? We talked a while after the lottery, when I was putting my folder away. And I took extra disks from my pocket and put them in, too?"

"Ye-e-es," said Letitia slowly, then more positively, "yes, of course." She turned to Brad, who nodded.

"Were the keys ever out of your possession, Arthur?" Endicott asked.

Pope stroked his chin. "No, they were always in my pocket except when I was using them or changing clothes." His eyes widened. "Wait, when I was in the office after breakfast Saturday—I was overwrought, what with Mr. Koontz being so brutally slain—I must've absentmindedly laid them on the desk. Anyway, I found them there later."

"Dear God, Arthur!" Endicott said. "Someone could have had all your keys—they might've stolen the keepsakes!" More calmly, he shook his head. "No, the guard would've still had his key. What a relief! That bit of security certainly paid off."

Peeples jumped up and marched over to Brad. "*You* did it! Tried to make me look guilty, and all the time it was you! I didn't even know there *were* more disks, much less where they were kept. But you Bennetts did. You may have done the murders together."

Brad looked daggers at her. "Ridiculous. Sit down, before I forget I'm a gentleman."

"Please, everyone," Pope said. "I know your nerves are frayed, but you can all be civil a few more hours."

With a final glare at Brad, Peeples resumed her seat.

Pope turned to the pedestal, took the bowl down, set it on the desk, and rummaged in it. He held up a disk with a dollar sign on it before dropping it into his pocket.

"Now," he said, "Miss Peeples, return the number eight. Anyone who wishes to may put back a disk and draw again."

Peeples dropped in two metal circles, announcing she was returning the number five to try again for the eight. Eileen eagerly tossed two into the bowl. Brad and Letitia followed, adding three between them. Millie pitched in both of hers. Pope looked inquiringly at Scott.

"Mr. Wyrick, I gather you'll not be drawing again for either yourself or your aunt?"

Scott nodded.

"What'd you get?" Peeples asked him.

"The Wedgwood bowl and the inkstand."

This man can keep a secret, Kirchner. Remember that.

Peeples sniffed loudly. "No wonder."

"Soames," Pope said, "are you not drawing again for Mrs. Moriarty?"

The banker half-rose. "I spoke with her by phone, and she wants to keep what I drew earlier, the Benjamin Franklin letter." He sat.

"You probably rigged the drawing somehow," Peeples said.

Endicott's lips tightened, but he remained silent.

"That comment is unworthy, Miss Peeples," Pope said coldly. He replaced the bowl on its pedestal, hooked a short arm up into it and stirred the metal bits. "I myself put the disks in the bowl Thursday, with Mr. Endicott watching. I mixed them around just before you drew, as I did just now, without looking into the bowl. You all saw me. There's absolutely no way either Mr. Endicott or I could've 'rigged' anything. Please draw first, Mrs. Kirchner."

Millie drew one circlet, disappointed again to see a dollar sign. Okay, she thought, she wasn't fated to own a keepsake. It seemed too bad, though. She had developed a fondness for all of them. She drew again.

"The number five, the one for the candlestand!" A shiver of pleasure ran down her spine. Even if the little table wasn't genuine, it must be an excellent copy. Hamilton himself hadn't been sure about it.

Letitia drew twice. The first time, she frowned, but the second, she flashed her beautiful smile and gave Brad a thumbs-up sign.

"The miniature," she announced. "It'll be a knockout with a black dress." She sat down, whispering to Millie, "Brad *said* we'd nothing to lose by returning the map disk."

Millie's eyes widened. So this second lottery was what the Bennetts had been discussing yesterday.

"The rifle!" Brad said as he drew. "Great!"

Eileen crossed her fingers, drew once and looked crestfallen. But when she chose again, she exclaimed, "One—the map! Goody, I'll give it to Daddy."

"Maybe I'll let Mom have the miniature," Letitia said doubtfully. "She'd let me wear it whenever I want."

Peeples approached timidly, her hand trembling on the bowl's rim. With an air of desperation, she plunged, withdrew a tightly closed fist and returned to her seat beside Eileen. Everyone watched as she shut her eyes, raised the hand to her face, and slowly opened it. The lids of one eye parted. Then both eyes flew wide.

"Eight! The quilt! I got the quilt!"

Eileen hugged her. Brad began to applaud, and one by one the others joined in. Smiling, Pope asked Scott to pick for Hamilton's son. He did and held up the number four.

"The samplers," the attorney said. "Very nice, especially since Mr. Ross had drawn those earlier." He looked a question at Endicott, then drew a long sigh. "That's everything, then. We're finished here."

Millie had been trying to work out the significance of that extra disk, but by the time the drawing ended, she still didn't see how it explained four deaths. She doubted the events were unrelated, however. And Pope's misplaced keys might turn out to be an important clue in the puzzle, as well.

★ ★ ★

After the lottery ended, Scott asked Millie to go walking in the backyard. Though she prized every moment they'd have together before parting for trips home, she remembered she had to do something. Giving him a hug, she excused herself.

"Okay, if it's absolutely necessary. I'll finish packing." Scott kissed the tip of her nose and went upstairs.

Millie was at the open kitchen door, hand raised to knock, when she saw Mrs. Fansler at the range struggling to thrust a frisky lobster into a steaming pot. A flailing claw hooked her hand. She pulled free, but the big lobster fell, sending a fountain of boiling water over range and tile floor. Some splattered the cook's hand.

"A-a-agh!" She screamed, jumping back. Her foot skidded on a wet spot, and her heavy body hit the floor.

Millie rushed in. Avoiding the puddle, she knelt beside Mrs. Fansler.

"Are you hurt? That was a nasty fall."

The cook lay unmoving at first, as if the wind had been jarred from her. Then she inhaled hard and said, "What are you doing here?"

"I was—can I help you up? Or call a doctor?"

"Where's Malcolm?"

"Malcolm?"

"My hus— Oh, he's running an errand. You'll do, then."

"Maybe you broke something and shouldn't try to stand."

Grabbing Millie's shoulder, Mrs. Fansler eased herself upright. She moved her hands exploringly over her hips and lower back.

"I'm okay."

"Want me to find Mr. Pope or a maid?"

"No, just sop up the water, so I don't slip again. Towel's over there."

It wasn't the most gracious request, but Millie wiped the floor and helped the cook pull herself up by the handles of the range drawer. It took three tries before she was standing.

"Thanks," Mrs. Fansler said grudgingly, rubbing her left hip. She lowered the fire under the lobster pot, which was threatening to boil over.

"Sure you don't want to see a doctor, get an X-ray?"

"Just help me in there, and I'll rest a little."

Millie supported her as she limped into a cozy bedroom done in blue and white chintz. Lacy white ruffles adorned lampshades, edged pillows on chairs and double bed, even lined the many picture frames on walls and endtables.

A mighty froufrou setting for Daisy Dour.

Most of the photos featured a young dark-haired man with a gap-toothed smile and prominent blue eyes. Millie helped the patient lie down, then pointed to a frame on a bedside table.

"Is that your son?"

The cook nodded. "That's Frederick."

Those protruding eyes would be hard to disguise, Millie thought. He might have been at Valley Forge—she could have missed him in that large area—but she felt sure he had not been at Fort Mifflin. The Fanslers must be innocent.

"Aspirin in the medicine chest," Mrs. Fansler said, eyes closed, forehead knit. "Glasses over the sink."

Millie fetched pills and water and watched the cook down two aspirin.

"This may not be the best time to say it, when you're in pain, but before I go, I want to tell you how much I've enjoyed your cooking. The meals have been wonderful."

The dark eyes opened, then narrowed.

"Really?"

"Would you share the recipes? I'd especially like to make the souffled potatoes and the trifle at home."

"I guess so." A trace of a smile lightened the stern countenance. "Glad you liked them." The cook motioned to a chair. "Want to sit a minute?"

Millie sat, they exchanged food likes and dislikes, and then she broached her question.

"Mrs. Fansler, did anyone come into the kitchen and make a phone call Friday evening? About nine-thirty? If you weren't in there then, could someone have done it without your knowing?"

The scowl returned. "Friday? Your second night here? I don't think—let's see, you were going to Valley Forge the next day, so I baked a cake and Malcolm made sandwich spread. No, I was in the kitchen all evening. Nobody came in."

Disappointed, Millie left, turning off the heat under the lobster as requested, and went into the parlor. As she looked at the keepsakes again, a thought fluttered at the edge of her memory. But it flitted away like an elusive moth.

The candlestand was now hers, she recalled with elation. It would look out of place with her sticks of furniture, but she could buy better things. Scott would enjoy the bowl and inkstand, and it seemed fitting that Miss Peeples should get the quilt.

The letter was what Millie had really wanted. Still, Mrs. Moriarty might appreciate it. As Millie read it again, that particularly clear phrase leapt out: ". . . continued to work till late in the Day . . . ."

Something seemed different about the wording from that in the many Franklin letters she had read recently. Still, she thought, it could be her imagination. She seemed to be suspicious of everybody and everything.

She had it. In the published letters, words ending in "ed" had an apostrophe replacing the "e," as in "pass'd" and "oblig'd." She had noticed the detail many times. But here, "continued" ended in "ed."

Of course, people at that time hadn't always spelled words the same way. But Franklin had been a writer and a publisher, so wouldn't his spelling have been more consistent than most people's?

Franklin had played with the language too, however. He had invented his own alphabet, using twenty characters of the English alphabet and substituting six others of his own invention. He had also liked unusual words, like "pejorate." Was this phrase in his letter to Henry simply an example of his experimenting with spelling?

Her mind puzzling over the discrepancy, she went upstairs to pack. It could mean nothing.

Or a lot.

★ *Chapter Twenty-Two*

A discreet tapping at the bedroom door interrupted Millie's folding of the borrowed yellow dress. The butler called, "You have a phone call, Mrs. Kirchner."

She tensed. Had Danny hurt himself skateboarding?

But it might be Fij calling with information. She hurried downstairs to the office telephone.

"Mrs. Kirchner," said a male speaker. "Akers here. I disguised my voice so the butler'd let me talk to you. Congratulations! Want to turn that candlestand into cash?"

Relief that it wasn't bad news about Danny coursed through her.

"How'd you hear about that? And so soon?"

"You interested in selling?"

"How much?"

"Seventy-five hundred."

"Hamilton Ross said it was worth at least thirty thousand."

"I'm afraid his estimates were badly overinflated."

"Why should I believe you rather than him?"

Akers coughed. "Ross was a talented amateur but not a dealer. You could try to sell it yourself, naturally, but finding buyers takes time. I'll pay cash in hand. Today."

"How do you know so much about what goes on here?"

"Call me if you decide to sell." He rang off.

Millie finished packing and set her bag beside Letitia's stack of luggage just inside their bedroom door.

During a lunch of lobster salad, homemade rolls, and strawberries in almond sauce, the heirs chatted happily about going home. When they rose from the table, Eileen spoke.

"Thanks for everything, Mr. Pope . . . in spite of . . . you know . . . ." She shook hands with the men, hugged Millie and Letitia, thanking the latter for the makeover, then turned tearily to Peeples. "Can I come visit some time, Vera?"

"Please do. And I'll call often." Peeples hugged her.

A taxi took Eileen away. Peeples and Letitia went upstairs to nap. Scott invited Millie to see Poe's home. Eager for more time alone with him, she started to say yes, but then remembered an earlier promise he had made.

"What about your plan to see that Workshop on the Water with Brad? If you still want to do that, maybe you and I could see the Poe home another time?"

Scott grinned. "I guess I did agree to do that with him. So long as you promise there'll be another time."

He and Brad set off for Penn's Landing.

Millie carried the Franklin book to the library and was putting it back on a shelf when she decided to check her memory about the spelling. Seated on a sofa, she scanned pages while doodling "'d" and drawing a candlestand on the piece of sketchpaper she had used as a bookmark. Every past-tense ending she found in the book used the apostrophe. That proved nothing, of course—Franklin would have written many letters in his eighty-four years—but it encouraged her doubts.

Brooding about the oddity, Millie absently stuck the paper in the book, put it on an alcove shelf, and pulled out several volumes on antiques. They dealt mainly with furniture and tableware, but in one she found a section on autographs and documents of interest to collectors. Skimming paragraphs, she read one chilling passage:

"If considering the purchase of an old letter, examine *all* elements for authenticity: paper, ink, style of signature and other handwriting, phrasing, even spelling."

Could the Franklin letter possibly be a clever forgery?

Millie put back the books, dropped to the alcove floor and sat cross-legged against the nearest wall. Could someone have substituted fakes for all the keepsakes? she wondered. But who? How? When?

Every scenario she came up with required help from a second party. Pope would have needed a guard's key. Ditto the Fanslers if they had found Pope's keys and made a duplicate. Maybe Endicott had copied both keys before giving them to Pope and the security company. But the bank had apparently made guarding the keepsakes a priority, so the director who had helped make the exchange would have had to be in on it. If a switch had been made during the trip from the bank, the armored-car driver would have known.

Besides, no matter who had replaced the antiques—if anyone had—she didn't see how that explained four murders.

Distractedly, Millie stroked a waxy leaf of the full-branched ficus tree directly in front of her. None of the heirs had known what the keepsakes looked like before they arrived. Unless . . . maybe they had been displayed and photographed at some time. But that would have violated Henry's secrecy order. Could this be another of the infamous Watson's schemes, one undiscovered in his day?

But he wouldn't have had access to the keepsakes. They had been stored in a series of banks since Henry's death. Millie stretched her legs, tucked her right foot under her.

The brutality of the Koontz and Ross crimes bothered her, too. Could the lawyer, the banker, or the servants carry out such acts? But she might have been too quick in exonerating the Fanslers' son, who had a history of violent crime. Many people at the fort had worn sunshades, and dark glasses could hide googly eyes.

Millie traced a vein in the leaf. Perhaps one of the guards was really an heir who had declined Pope's invitation to come. No, none of them was a young Caucasian male, as each of the guards was.

She let go the leaf, watched it shiver into place. Might one guard secretly be an employee of Akers? That seemed more likely.

Someone entered, sat at the bookcase-desk, opened a drawer, and shuffled papers. Pope, presumably. Millie kept quiet. She didn't want to talk to him now, while she was trying to work out this problem of the keepsakes.

A second person came in and walked to the desk.

"Excuse me, Mr. Pope." Fansler's voice.

"Yes?"

"I'm afraid I must ask you for some money."

A pause. "I'm not aware you have any coming, Fansler. Not till the first of the month."

"I have an urgent need, Mr. Pope."

"Your son again?"

"He's stolen money from his employer. The man's offered to let Frederick repay it and stay out of prison, but—"

"How much money?"

"Nearly twenty-five thousand."

A longer pause. "That's a great deal. Can't he simply give the money back?"

"There's none left. He's gambled it away."

Her thoughts divided between the puzzle and the men's

conversation, Millie suddenly realized she should have made her presence known earlier. Doing so now would embarrass them all. She decided to stay put till both men had left.

"What do you expect me to do, Fansler? I don't have that kind of money, not for a young man who won't repay it."

Silence. Then, "I'm afraid I must insist, Mr. Pope."

"Insist, Fansler? This is intolerable. Those few things I sold, no one will even miss out of all that junk. Yet you've held it over my head all these years."

Fansler cleared his throat. "I believe you have another worry, Mr. Pope." He paused. "Mr. Akers . . . ."

A longer silence this time. Millie's leg, curled under her, began to throb. She forced herself to stay very still.

Pope sighed heavily. "It'll take time. I don't keep that much in my checking account."

"Tomorrow?"

"It'll mean cashing in some CD's, but I guess I could manage it by then."

Fansler left.

"Swine," Pope growled. "I ought to murder the old—"

Millie bit a finger, a second pain to take her mind off the agonizing cramp in her leg. What did Fansler know that was worth twenty-five thousand? Was Akers the killer, hired by Pope? Had his attempts to talk to the heirs really been a way to gain their confidence, lure them to their deaths? Was the lawyer's evident enmity towards Akers part of an act? If she agreed to sell the candlestand, would the dealer suggest a private meeting place where he could kill her too?

Whatever the details, Millie knew she had to get out of here and tell Detective Nolen what she had heard. But she couldn't leave with Pope present.

Finally, when she was ready to scream with pain, the attorney rose and left. She made herself wait till he had time to get well away. Then, using a bookshelf as support, she got to her feet. The numb leg crumpled, and she slid to the floor. She pulled up again. This time, hanging onto shelves and furniture, she dragged herself to the door. She leaned against the facing, flexing her leg, trying to decide what to do. She had never had a cell phone—an economy she regretted at times, like now—and the phones here were in places where she could run into Pope or his blackmailer, Fansler. She must get outside, to another telephone or to the police station. Weren't emergency calls from pay phones free these days?

Feeling returned to her leg. She peeled herself off the door frame, exiting the library just as Pope appeared in the archway. His eyes widened in surprise. Clearly he guessed she had overheard his damaging admissions.

She tried to saunter past him, but he grabbed her arm, his doughy grip unexpectedly firm. His pudgy body blocked her path to the front door. She twisted away and fled up the stairs, planning to run across the second floor and down the rear steps, then climb the fence to freedom.

"Mrs. Kirchner, wait!" He hastened after her.

She pounded her way upward, Pope pursuing fast on his stubby legs. She thought she could outrun him. If only he didn't guess her intention and double back, catching her when she returned to the ground floor, as she eventually must.

Then she recalled that the fence was fairly high. She might get caught climbing it. Maybe he would have to pause to rest on an upper floor, and she could get down to the front.

Midway along the second floor hall, she wondered where the roaming guard was. She hadn't seen him since before lunch. Perhaps with the heirs leaving he had already been dismissed. Could she depend on help from either of the guards anyway, against the man who was paying for their services?

"Oh, Mrs. Kirchner," Fansler called from the rear of the

hallway. He approached her at a brisk, purposeful pace.

Millie hesitated. Maybe he would help. But he must have been blackmailing Pope for years and had just sold his silence about something else, probably the murders. Turning swiftly, she ran back to the landing just as Pope hove into view below.

"Wait, Mrs. Kirchner!" he puffed. "We need to talk."

She dashed up to the third floor, adrenalin pumping, breath coming fast. She would cross this floor and then try the back stairs. Maybe neither man would guess her plan.

Her feet faltered. The rear stairs between the second and third floors were sealed off because of a broken step. Now what?

She decided to hide among the clutter and think what to do. Entering a room piled high with cast-offs, she made her way through broken doll carriages, old lampshades, and decrepit ironing boards and squeezed behind a stack of rolled rugs at one wall. She crouched down, fighting a sneeze from the dust.

This had been a bad decision, she realized. If Pope and Fansler decided to search all these rooms . . . .

Minutes went by without the door opening. Perhaps the conspirators were watching both sets of stairs. Feeling safe for the moment, Millie relaxed against the carpet rolls. And with that release of tension, her subconscious abruptly popped out answers to some questions.

She knew who had replaced the keepsakes, and when. Also, how that fact explained each murder. What she still didn't know was how many people she had to fear.

A floorboard creaked in the hall, but from the rear of the mansion. Had someone unblocked the back stairway?

She peered from behind the rugs, seeking a weapon. She had learned to shoot from another teen while in foster care but saw no pistol or rifle handy. Anyway, a gun stored up here would likely be unloaded or rusty. That old electric iron could be thrown, though.

Millie inched along behind the musty pile, stifling another sneeze. She stretched an arm towards the trailing iron cord, almost touched the end. She squirmed forward. Her fingers closed on the plug. She tugged gently. The iron began to move.

Easy. Careful. She had it.

Footsteps came slowly along the hallway, stopping at the door to the room she was in. With a sick feeling, she realized that her tracks across the dusty floor made her location clear. Her sweaty fingers gripped the iron handle. Footfalls came towards her hiding place.

"Mrs. Kirchner?" a voice called softly. "Come on out." From the low tones, she couldn't identify the speaker.

Perhaps this was the break she needed, someone who would help her get word to Nolen. At any rate, she had been found. She hauled herself from behind the carpets and stood, the iron at her side.

Millie looked into the face of a murderer.

★ Chapter Twenty-Three

"Playing hide-and-seek?" Endicott said, surprisingly urbane in jeans and sport shirt. "I heard a noise, came out of the luggage room, and saw you run in here. Arthur agreed I could take a steamer trunk before everything goes to the city. Shouldn't, of course, but they won't miss one." His gray eyes sparkled with excitement. "I must show you something I found in one of the trunks, Mrs. Kirchner. You're such a fan of Ben Franklin, you'll truly appreciate it."

"Th-anks," Millie quavered, "but I . . . need to . . . go down-stairs."

"It'll only take a moment. It's a note that must've slipped behind the trunk lining. Not from Ben himself, which would've been too wonderful, but from his grandson Temple, who acted as his secretary." The banker's eyes traveled downward, then up again.

Had he seen her weapon? Millie slid the iron back, behind the curve of her thigh.

"The trunk's newer than Temple's day, so the note must have been stored there and forgotten. Do come see it."

Millie tried to move past him.

"I will. Later."

He put out a hand. "Indulge an old man. Please."

"I have to—finish packing first."

Abruptly, he grabbed her arm, wrested the iron from her, and flung it away. It clanged against a floor lamp. Dodging her flailing fists, he took her in a bear hug.

"Help!" she yelled, willing to take her chances even with Pope and Fansler.

"Shut up!" He slapped her hard across the face. "No one can hear you up here, anyway."

Lips and cheek smarting, she tried to jerk away. But with surprising strength he pinioned her tighter. She tried to call out again, but his arm choked off her breath. He half-carried, half-dragged her across the room, her toes stirring dust. Awkwardly he bumped her down the hall and into the baggage room and kicked the door shut. To her alarmed eyes the stacks of valises and bags looked more forsaken than before, the shadows gloomier.

He released her. Millie gasped for breath, then lunged for the doorknob, but he stuck out a foot and tripped her. Her head struck the door. She lay still.

"That's enough—silliness," he panted. "Get up."

Slowly she stood and saw, through a haze of pain, that he now held a pistol. She didn't know its make, but recognized the silencer as a staple of films and TV.

"You helped me—a lot," he said. "Thought I'd have to lure you up here with that story about the note in a trunk."

Despite the closeness of the room, Millie shivered. She rubbed her throbbing forehead, fighting panic. There was only the one exit. Maybe she could rush him, knock the gun away, and get out. But he could be expecting something like that. She didn't like her chances.

Should she shout again? But Scott and Brad were out, Letitia and Peeples asleep, Pope and Fansler uncertain allies. And another cry might make Endicott gag or shoot her.

Her life couldn't end this way. She had to get back to Danny, couldn't leave him motherless, even younger than her own mother had left her.

It's up to you, hon. Put that good brain to work.

Stalling seemed the best approach for now. Dropping her eyes in an attitude of submission, she swallowed to clear her fright-constricted throat. Then she looked up and spoke in what she hoped was a sympathetic tone.

"Those keepsakes must be really special for you to want them so desperately."

"Very. Seeing them every day, knowing they'd never be mine, was torture. Of course, I can't show them to people who'd truly appreciate their rarity."

"Then tell me about them. Make me understand."

He chuckled. "An obvious ploy. And futile."

"You replaced them all years ago, didn't you? Before the time-locked vault was added—when you could still visit them by yourself."

"Bright girl. You've worried me all along, hobnobbing with Ross, studying about antiques. But I didn't really think you'd put it together." He squeezed the back of his neck as if releasing tension. "When I found your doodles in that book of Franklin's letters today, though, I knew you were close."

The bookmark. She had been careless, dangerously so.

"I'm no expert, but those copies look great to me," she said. "Did you make them yourself?"

"Hardly. A contact in the antiques trade mentioned a skilled forger named Felix. I tracked him down, gave him photos and detailed drawings, then made the switch before the bank opened one morning. It didn't seem so risky then."

"You figured the heirs and any buyers would assume they had genuine antiques. Henry's will was their provenance."

"The old fool was right about his things being prized in this century. But not because he had used them."

"By the time you realized some of the fakes had flaws, the bank had tightened its security. You couldn't undo your crime."

He laughed, a high unnatural sound suggesting he was near the edge.

"Besides, I still wanted the originals. But everyone has problems. Yours is imminent death. When my trunk's hauled away, your body will be inside."

She recoiled at the image, heard her trembling lips say, "That can't work. How'll you explain my absence?"

"I'll say you had an errand to run before your flight. You'll become a missing person."

Scott wouldn't let it go at that, Millie thought, even if the others might. But she had to figure a way out, couldn't let this greedy, vain man destroy both her life and her son's.

"Now, move over there so I can pick your coffin." The banker indicated a spot near a set of shelves piled with small bags, which ran along the room's outer wall.

She did as he directed, watching as her captor prowled among the luggage. If he would look away, maybe she could grab something and heave it at the gun. But any move on her part might make him whirl and fire. She had to keep him talking.

"You killed Ross to prevent his exposing your theft."

He nodded, cold eyes shifting between her and various trunks on the floor. He opened one lid, then shut it.

"And Cunningham was blackmailing you."

"He saw me come out of the woods after I killed Ross, putting the plastic sheet and gloves I'd worn into a plastic bag inside my binoculars case." Endicott shoved the trunk aside and pulled another one over. "I'd taken the plastic things and a different gun along, since I didn't know what sort of chance I'd get at him."

"That case did seem big for those tiny fieldglasses. But didn't the police examine your bag?"

"Sure. But I'd already burned all the plastic and hid the gun—one untraceable to me—in that big brushy area between the redoubts."

"But surely there'd be traces, in your bag or where you dumped the weapon—Hamilton's blood, your DNA . . . ."

"I was *very* careful."

He began to pace back and forth across the front of the room. Millie watched him like a mesmerized rodent eyeing a snake.

"I didn't plan to kill anyone," he said as if explaining to himself. "Things just kept going wrong."

"You must've killed Johns by mistake, thinking he was his cousin. But why were you after Koontz?"

"That's more complicated. You know about the 'ed' spelling in the Franklin letter, of course."

"Yes."

"It wasn't a dead giveaway—Franklin may not have used the apostrophe every time—but I was afraid that if scholars examined the letter closely, which they would since Ben's such an icon, someone might wonder about that spelling and then about all the keepsakes." The banker banged his fist on a suitcase with a thump. "That damned Felix had an exact copy of the letter's wording and he still got it wrong." He resumed pacing. "The idiot had the nerve to demand more money not to expose me. He was the first one I had to kill."

Millie barely heard the last part in her excitement over noticing something. One end of the shelves beside her was in the front corner of the room opposite the door. On the top shelf, directly above the point where Endicott turned, sat a satchel at a rakish angle atop an overnight bag. Each time he pivoted, the movement rocked the valise.

If only it would fall . . . .

Not trusting herself to speak calmly in her eagerness, she nodded encouragement.

"The inkstand, the bowl, most of the counterfeits are first-rate. But if only one aroused suspicion . . . ." He stopped abruptly. The carpetbag shook but stayed where it was.

"I tried to draw the letter disk in the lottery. I found out that Mrs. Moriarty is nuts over her dog, so I sneaked over to her house here in town and spiked its food. I knew I could get Pope to let me pick for her if she didn't come."

Millie found her voice. "One in sixteen isn't very good odds."

"You underestimate me. I notched the edge of the letter disk so I could find it by feel, and I convinced Pope that I should choose first. Unfortunately, the one for the miniature also had a small nick. I got confused."

Dust tickled Millie's nostrils, giving her an idea. She coughed hard, hoping the power of suggestion would make him do likewise and the vibrations would knock the satchel from its perch. But he merely resumed his walk.

"Why didn't you just change numbers for the letter and the miniature before you posted the keepsakes list?"

"That might've gotten past Pope but not my secretary. She misses nothing. Anyway, I had more trouble than I knew then. Saturday morning before we went to Valley Forge, Ross remarked to me that the candlestand seemed short. I said it was the angle he was seeing it from, but I knew then that Felix had made another mistake. Moron!" Endicott let out a stream of curses.

Millie's wildly searching eyes had seen something else. On the end of the shelving nearest her, the unit had come loose from the wall. Instead of reattaching it, someone had wedged a chunk of lumber under the upright. She stifled a hopeful cry. If she could move that support, the resulting jar might topple the bag. She began to edge towards it.

He noticed even that small movement, and ran to her with nostrils flaring. His knuckles strained white on the pistol grip as he stuck the gun into her face. Fear paralyzed her. She wondered if years of obsessing over the antiques had unhinged him.

"What're you up to now?" His hot breath smote her cheek.

"Just flexing my leg." She forced the words through dry lips. "Got a cramp."

He retreated a step, slowly moved his weapon back.

"Koontz actually drew the disk for the letter, didn't he?" she said.

"Little Miss Brainy." He resumed his search for a trunk. "I did see Koontz's disk during the first lottery. He didn't know what he had, but later I told him that I'd recalled what his number and Mrs. Moriarty's were for. I offered to trade him what she'd won for the letter, plus pay him twice what Ross had estimated the letter was worth."

Scarcely daring to breathe, Millie slid her foot slightly to the side. This time, she got away with it.

"I claimed I had a nostalgic attachment to the letter," Endicott continued, "and I promised Mrs. Moriarty wouldn't lose by the switch. Koontz didn't care about that, of course, but he didn't go for the deal."

The banker was caught up in his narrative now. Millie inched towards the shelves with agonizing slowness.

"I suppose Pope didn't actually lose that list?"

He smiled. "I hid it, to buy time to make a deal in case I failed to draw the right disk."

"And I suppose you had a key to the mansion so you could slip out Friday, kill Koontz and get back in."

"Pope's careless with his keys. I made a duplicate for the front door months ago, and one for the keepsakes cabinet after he misplaced them recently—damned bank security gave me no chance before. But I couldn't get hold of a guard's key. I was afraid to try a bribe, because dealing with Felix had taught me I couldn't trust anyone to keep quiet. Anyway, thanks to Fansler's laxness about the door, I didn't even need my house key that night."

Millie's muscles ached with the strain of making tiny, inconspicuous efforts. But finally her heel touched the block. She nudged it, willing it to shift.

"You dropped Hamilton's disk into Miss Peeples's purse at Valley Forge to throw suspicion on her, didn't you?"

"Old bat. One of the worst of an annoying bunch. I enjoyed ridding the world of three Henry descendants, though I did hate killing Ross. He'd have understood my passion for the keepsakes. But I saw he was trouble that first night. He knew as much about antiques as I do, more than Arthur."

The weight on the shelves was fortunately concentrated at the other end. Abruptly, the piece of lumber began to give. It was all Millie could do not to scream her relief.

"But that day when I started hitting Ross, I just lost it, as if he were responsible for all my frustration . . . ."

With each small push, the brace moved a little bit more, the slowness excruciating to her taut nerves.

Get ready to run, hon. The instant that bag hits him.

If it hits him, Millie thought. But even if it didn't, maybe its falling would startle him, let her slip past.

His narrative had become increasingly rambling. " . . . arranged the lottery my way—could always get Pope to follow my 'suggestions' and later believe that my ideas had been his."

A light flashed on in Millie's brain. She knew now which literary characters Pope and Endicott had reminded her of: Mr. and Mrs. Bagnet in Dickens's *Bleak House*. Any friend who came to the Bagnet home seeking the sage housewife's advice had to follow a ritual of putting the question to her husband. He would then turn to his wife and say, "Give him my opinion, my dear."

If only she had recognized earlier how much Pope relied on his colleague in making decisions.

Endicott approached the corner, still talking: "Pope thought I didn't know about his silly plan, getting that slimy antique dealer, Akers, to buy the keepsakes cheaply for him. His downplaying their value that first night was transparent as a veil . . . ."

NOW! Millie shoved hard with her heel, felt the wood slide. The upright dropped, and with it the shelves. The valise tumbled off, striking the banker on the shoulder. He dropped to the floor, the pistol spinning from his hand.

Like a rubber band released, Millie sprang forward and yanked the door open. Flinging it shut behind her, she dashed towards the front stairwell. Her heart beat double-time. If she could get downstairs, out the front door—

Now she knew Pope wasn't the killer or in league with Endicott, she could head for a phone or appeal to the keepsakes guard.

Millie was nearing the front stairs when she heard the door to the luggage room open. Thunk. Thunk. Thunk. Something struck the wall beside her.

Bullets! BULLETS!

The knowledge that Endicott had recovered his weapon added swiftness to her feet. She reached the stairwell and clambered down. Then rounding the second-floor landing, she set a foot wrong. Her ankle twisted. Unable to catch herself, she fell against the wall. Her head hit plaster, right on the earlier bump. She crumpled into a heap, half sick with pain and fear.

A floorboard creaked above her. She staggered up, her weight sending fire through the ankle. Teeth gritted, she hobbled downstairs in a gait reminiscent of when her leg had been asleep. As she reached the bottom, she heard the banker coming down the upper flight, two steps at a time.

Trying to ignore the stabbing pain in her ankle, Millie stumbled through the arch, aware she could not reach the parlor and the guard in time. Endicott was at the second-floor landing now. Any moment, he would get her in his sights and shoot.

Looking back over her shoulder, Millie sobbed, "Help! Someone—help me—"

★ *Chapter Twenty-Four*

Hearing voices, Millie turned her face towards the front door. Three people stood there, one of them Pope.

"Help . . . Endicott . . . gun . . ." She stumbled towards them.

Pope's companions reacted fast.

When the banker ran after her through the arch, pistol in hand, he faced drawn weapons held by Detective Nolen and Special Agent Gathron. Endicott abruptly stopped, a quick succession of emotions playing over his face: shock, then fear, and finally, resignation.

★ ★ ★

Later that afternoon, Millie lay on a couch with an ice pack on her foot, feeling slightly woozy from a painkiller. She had given a statement, and the law enforcement officers had departed with their prisoner. Pope had insisted on accompanying Millie to a nearby clinic, where they learned that her ankle was strained but not broken, the head injury not serious.

"Roomie," Letitia said, her violet eyes large and animated, "how'd you stand it? I'd have died when I saw that gun."

"Mrs. Kirchner—" Pope shook his head— "I can't tell you

how sorry I am. If only I had realized—"

"I knew all along Endicott was too slick to be real," Peeples offered indignantly.

Brad raised an eyebrow. "Sure you did. You were fooled just like the rest of us. I wish I'd been here. I'd have heard you scream and come running up there, Millie."

"You're safe. That's what matters." Scott sat at her side, holding her hand and gazing tenderly at her.

Millie returned his affectionate smile. She felt as if she were floating, and not only from pain medicine. She was alive. Danny still had his mother. Too, she had Scott by her side, looking as fond of her as she had become of him.

"I assume you'll ship us all the real antiques when the police get them from wherever Endicott stashed them?" Brad said.

"Of course," Pope replied. "Though I don't know how long that may be. The wheels of justice turn slowly sometimes." He looked thoughtful a moment, then added, "And it seems only fair that the counterfeit antiques should also belong to whoever will be getting the corresponding keepsakes—that will at least be some compensation for having to wait. They are very good copies, even if Soames's forger did make a mistake or two."

He paused, glanced at Millie, then went on. "I spoke with Mrs. Moriarty, the absent heir whom Soames said he'd drawn the Franklin letter for. He hadn't even called to tell her what he drew in the lottery as he claimed. She's getting on in years and sounds a bit senile—went on and on about her little poodle while I was trying to tell her about the keepsake distribution— so he could probably have gotten away with telling her he drew a dollar sign for her.

"Anyway, Mrs. Kirchner, I know how much you revere Ben Franklin, so it seems fitting you should have his letter. I asked Mrs. Moriarty if she'd be willing to trade it for the candlestand you drew. Of course that's subject to your decision, since I hadn't asked you about a trade before. I told her Mr. Ross's estimates of the value of the two keepsakes and explained that either might actually be worth more than he suggested. But she was very amiable, said whichever item you wanted you could have and she'd be delighted with the other."

Millie glanced from him to Letitia and Brad, whose faces registered surprise, and—perhaps—disappointment. "Of course I'd trade," Millie said. "But would that . . . be fair to the others? Shouldn't everyone have a chance at—"

Scott touched a finger to her lips, stopping her objection. "Sounds like the perfect solution. I agree Millie should have the letter. She'll appreciate it more than anyone else would."

"My thought exactly," Pope said. "Besides, if it hadn't been for Mrs. Kirchner's intelligent sleuthing, at the risk of her own life, Soames's plot might never have been exposed. And then none of the heirs would have gotten the genuine keepsakes."

Letitia and Brad looked at each other and nodded.

"Even Nathan Henry couldn't quibble about that decision, Mr. Pope," Brad said finally.

"I agree that's fair," said a smiling Peeples.

"Thank you," the executor said, glancing at each in turn. "Now that I'm the lone executor, it's about time I make a few decisions—ones that are my own, not ones Soames planted in my mind."

★ ★ ★

Soon the Bennett siblings had to say goodbye.

"Keep in touch, kiddo," Brad said, kissing Millie on the cheek. "Maybe some time I'll give you another chance at me." He shook hands with Peeples and Scott and clapped the executor on the shoulder. "Mr. Pope, this has been a memorable few days."

"For once, my brother understates," Letitia said, with a grin.

She and Millie hugged and exchanged addresses and phone numbers, promising to call or write soon.

Peeples made a reserved but friendly farewell, departing shortly after the Bennetts. Fansler served an early supper of cheesy broccoli soup and salad to Pope, Millie, and Scott, then left the room. Even with the table's middle sections removed, Millie thought the three place settings looked lonely.

"Did I hear you plan to continue your studies, Mr. Wyrick?" Pope asked.

"Sure. I enjoy teaching. And I'm so close to finishing my master's now, it would be a shame not to. I can even afford to go on for my doctorate without waiting, as I'd expected to have to do."

"And your plans, Mrs. Kirchner?"

"I'll concentrate on school, too. I plan to get a double major in history and English."

"So neither of you has grand plans for your new wealth?" Pope teased.

"I'll be doing some traveling." Scott smiled at Millie. "To Dallas, among other spots. And I guess I could use some new clothes. So Letitia informed me."

"I think I'll buy a house." Millie winced as hot soup stung her upper lip, sore from Endicott's slap. "Maybe even have a maid come once a week. Before I got on at the nursing home, I cleaned other people's houses, and that seemed the ultimate luxury then.

"Danny needs a few things, but I don't want to spoil him. And I guess I'll invest some."

"Very practical choices."

"I want to travel, too," she went on. I can't wait to visit other historical sites: Monticello, Mount Vernon, Faneuil Hall in Boston . . . ."

"Now, that's more like it," said the attorney with a smile.

Then he brought the conversation back to Endicott. "I see now that I let Soames manipulate me shamefully. Many of his ideas about how to organize the lottery were really to facilitate his own plans." He shook his head sadly. "I've seen a lot of Soames over the years, and I thought we were friends. I just can't believe he's a murderer—five times over, at that." He gave a shudder.

"Henry's legacy did offer lots of temptation," Scott said.

"I suppose both Soames and I got too caught up in our ties to that remarkable estate. I do understand, though, how he felt about those antiques." Pope flushed. "It was very foolish of me to try to get them cheaply through Mr. Akers.

"Since you overheard my conversation with Fansler, Mrs. Kirchner, I should explain something else. Several years ago, I took a few things from the third-floor storage. They were all of later periods than Nathan Henry's day, and not extremely valuable, but I was short of cash then, desperate to buy that magnificent table in my room that Mr. Ross admired. I was stupid enough to sell those items."

"And the Fanslers found out and used the information to make you do things for their son," Millie said.

"As executor of the estate, I couldn't afford to have even a hint of impropriety come out."

As they rose, Mrs. Fansler came in, limping slightly from her fall that morning. Millie felt they had something else in common now, besides their love of food.

"Excuse me, Mr. Pope," the cook said. "Mrs. Kirchner, here's those recipes you wanted." She smiled shyly. "I hope you'll enjoy making them."

"I'm sure I will. Thank you so much, and thanks again for preparing such delicious meals for us."

Scott seconded the praise.

Mrs. Fansler left just as her husband came in to say that

Millie had a phone call. She hobbled to the office. Philip Judd's voice crackled through the receiver.

"What's the idea of solving the case without me, Millie? I thought we were a team."

"Where were you when I was about to get shot?"

"Glad you survived, love. How's about letting me take you out to celebrate?"

"Thanks, but I have to leave shortly for the airport."

"At least give me some quotes first about your ordeal."

She answered a few questions, then said she had to go. There was a pause at the other end.

"Don't forget me, Millie. I'll sure remember you."

After they hung up, she phoned Danny to say she would be home late the next day.

"Great, Mom! I miss you. Then we'll get our bikes?"

"We will. Absolutely."

She dialed another familiar number. "It's over, Sylva. The murderer's been arrested. I'm coming home."

"Oh, hon, I'm so glad! I'll want all the details, you know, every single one."

"And I'll be—giving notice at the nursing home."

"You're leaving? Oh, of course you are." A tremor entered Sylva's voice. "You quitting me too, Kirchner?"

"An old twinge in the tush like you? Never."

"Okay, then. Hurry back."

"I'm taking a detour first, but I'll see you soon." Millie explained her plan.

★ ★ ★

In their cab to the airport, Millie and Scott held each other close while the outskirts of Philadelphia slipped past the window.

"Nathan Henry has been much maligned lately," Scott said. "And with reason. But I'm grateful to the old boy. You and I might never have met if not for that goofy will of his. You say you're going to visit Alice Ross now?"

"I want to give her my condolences in person and tell her about Hamilton's last days. I hope it'll comfort her a little to know how respected and liked he was here—by most people— and how much he enjoyed the Henry mansion and its antiques. Anyway, she sounds like someone I'd like to know."

"Maybe I'll meet her myself some time."

"Could be. You *are* distant relatives by marriage." Millie stretched luxuriously. "You know, the legacy's finally starting to seem real."

As she snuggled back into his arms, her mind filled with visions of the future: Time for herself, to explore new interests. Studying, whatever she wanted, at her own pace. Giving gifts to those she loved, without tight cost constraints. Simple pleasures, taken for granted by many, but luxuries to her. And travel, of course. To other countries later, but starting with the settings of American history. With Danny.

And maybe, sometimes, with Scott.

THE END

★ Author's Notes

Actual houses and grounds in the Society Hill section of old Philadelphia are smaller and less grand than the Nathan Henry mansion portrayed in the novel. Many features of his residence are taken from the much larger houses in Germantown, several of which offer public tours (including Cliveden, the Deshler-Morris House, Grumblethorpe, Stenton, Upsala, and Wyck). The third-floor room of cast-off luggage, for example, is patterned after a similar room at Grumblethorpe. Germantown is now part of Philadelphia but in the eighteenth century was six miles away, a distance that encouraged many wealthy Philadelphians to build summer homes there, especially as a retreat from frequent yellow-fever epidemics raging through the city at the time. (See *Historical Germantown,* article reprinted from *The Magazine ANTIQUES,* August, 1983, and distributed by Historic Germantown, Inc.) I appreciate the help of various docents at these period homes.

Security at national parks has evolved since the terrorist activities of September 11, 2001, and continues to do so. I chose to set the events of *Deadly Will* earlier, when U. S. citizens and visitors still had easier access to these important sites. As part of security-related changes to Independence National

Historical Park (INHP), a new Visitors Center was built and the state arches described in the novel were moved to another area within the park. The brick enclosures behind the arches were eliminated altogether.

The battle at Olde Fort Mifflin is from my imagination. Although Revolutionary War battles are occasionally staged there, I have not been fortunate enough to witness one.

For technical assistance, I'm indebted to members of various law-enforcement agencies featured in the book, including the Philadelphia Police Department, the Federal Bureau of Investigation, and the National Park Service, as well as personnel at the various historical sites: INHP, Valley Forge National Historical Park, and Olde Fort Mifflin; also at the Free Library of Philadelphia, the Philadelphia Convention and Visitors Bureau, and the Philadelphia Film Office. In particular, I gratefully acknowledge help from Detective Edward Tenuto, formerly of the Public Affairs Office, Philadelphia Police; Robert Davenport, formerly Inspector in Charge, Office of Public Affairs, FBI; and Robert J. Byrne, former Chief Ranger at INHP. Special thanks go to Katherine Korte, former Law Enforcement Specialist at INHP, who generously read the manuscript and assisted with needed changes.

The Henry "keepsakes" presented an unusual challenge. The late Charles Gilpin Dorman, Curator Emeritus, Independence National Historical Park (INHP) helped me choose, describe, and assign values to items that either typified actual artifacts from the Revolutionary-War period, or that plausibly could exist from the time. I was assisted in updating the appraisals after Mr. Dorman's death by his colleague and friend Robert L. Giannini, III, Museum Curator, INHP, and Karie Diethorn, Chief Curator, INHP. I imagined the Betsy Ross quilt with the excellent guidance of Helen Kelley, author of *Dating Quilts from 1600 to the Present* (Watson-Guptill Publications, 1995).

Any errors in accuracy in portraying historical elements or criminal-investigation procedures are my own, not those of any of my sources.

I also thank a host of fellow writers and other friends for their encouragement and critique of the manuscript as it evolved. Thanks, too, to my editor and publisher, Patricia Ricks, whose professional yet compassionate editing improved the book.

And as always, I'm grateful to my husband Elbert for his unfailing and good-humored support.